Contents

SAVAGE KINGDOM BOOK 3

AN ENEMIES TO LOVERS REVERSE HAREM SERIES

JENNILYNN WYER

Copyright

Cover Design and Formatting By: Jennilynn Wyer

Cover Image from Shutterstock, Canva

Copy Editor: Ellie McLove @ My Brother's Editor

Beta Readers: Rita C., Jennifer F., and Jillian B.

Reader's Warning: Savage Kingdom is a dark, enemies to lovers, mafia, why choose (RH) romance and contains scenes that may be triggering to sensitive individuals such as blood, violence, scenes depicting torture, foul language, consensual sexual content, and references to past sexual abuse/trauma. If you are not familiar with why choose (reverse harem) romances, this trope is where the female protagonist has more than one love interest and is in an intimate relationship with more than one man. Savage Kingdom is book 3 and the conclusion to the Savage Kingdom Series. It ends with an HEA. Recommended for mature readers.

Connect with the Author

WEBSITE | EMAIL | FACEBOOK | INSTAGRAM | TIKTOK | TWITTER

GOODREADS | BOOKBUB | AMAZON | NEWSLETTER | VERVE ROMANCE

SUBSCRIBE TO MY NEWSLETTER for news on upcoming releases, cover reveals, sneak peeks, author giveaways, and other fun stuff!

JOIN THE J-CREW: A JENNILYNN WYER ROMANCE READER GROUP
Join link https://www.facebook.com/groups/190212596147435

Synopsis and Reader's Note

Savage Kingdom is the heart-pounding conclusion of the Savage Kingdom Series.

My name is Alexandria Donatella McCarthy, or Andie for short. Former daughter of the don of the Rossi syndicate. Abused. Neglected. Overlooked. After five years in exile, I return home to avenge my brother Kellan's death and to take down my father, Maximillian Rossi, and anyone else who stands in my way. But things don't work out as I planned. Especially when I come face-to-face with four men from my past. Four men who were once my enemies. Four men who are now my destiny.

Keane Agosti, the new head of the Rossi syndicate. The man I love to hate and my future husband.

Jaxson West, his psychotic enforcer with a lust for bloodshed. My Grim Reaper. Pain is our foreplay.

Rafael Ortiz, my ex-boyfriend and youngest son of the head of the Ortiz Cartel. His sadistic older brother, Alejandro, wants me for his own.

And Liam Connelly, the Irish hitman of my family's enemy, Declan Levine. My angel-turned-devil obsessed with making me his.

These four dangerous, brutal, beautiful men call themselves my kings, but it's time for me to become their queen. I must delve into the darkness in order to win the war against Julio and Alejandro Ortiz. And nothing can stop me. Not even them.

Betrayal, lies, and treachery are only the beginning. All the secrets will come to light, and everything will be revealed. Are you ready for the end?

Reader's Note: Savage Kingdom is a dark, enemies to lovers, mafia, why choose (RH) romance and contains scenes that may be triggering to sensitive individuals such as blood, violence, scenes depicting torture, foul language, consensual sexual content, and references to past sexual abuse/trauma. If you are not familiar with why choose (reverse harem) romances, this trope is where the female protagonist has more than one love interest and is in an intimate relationship with more than one man. Savage Kingdom is book 3 and the conclusion to the Savage Kingdom Series. It ends with an HEA. Recommended for mature readers.

Savage Kingdom Series

#1 Savage Princess
#2 Savage Kings
#3 Savage Kingdom

Dedication

To Rita. My friend and the most wonderful kind of crazy a girl could know.

Dear Reader,

Are you ready for their story to end? Thank you so much for reading the Savage Kingdom Series, and loving Andie, Jax, Keane, Rafe, and Liam as much as I do.

I love reverse harems. If you're not familiar with them, it's a story where the heroine has multiple love interests, and she doesn't have to choose only one man to have her HEA; she gets to have *all* of them. I had always planned on writing a reverse harem and am so happy to be able to do that with Savage Princess. Some of my readers already know that my Fallen Brook Series started out as a reverse harem before I changed it so that the female lead, Elizabeth, finally made a choice at the end of which man she wanted to be with. It's also why the book series is about three guys in love with the same woman.

In mid-2021, I decided it was time for me to write my first RH, and Savage Princess was born. I wanted to do something suspenseful, dark, and bloody, with a kick-ass, strong heroine who took no shit from anyone. As an avid reader of all romance genres, especially reverse harems, I got tired of all the stories where the woman was weak and allowed the men in her life to control her. I didn't want that for my female lead. So I created Andie and had her come storming right out of the gate, strong and fierce and stubborn.

And speaking of going dark, I do with this series, so please be mindful of the triggers if you are sensitive to such topics such as: blood play, violence, references to past sexual abuse, gun violence, foul language, multiple sexual partners, marijuana use, and scenes depicting torture.

Savage Princess (book 1) laid the groundwork for the story's plotline. Savage Kings (book 2) amps up the action and chaos, and the trilogy ends with Savage Kingdom (book 3). Books 1 and 2 end with cliffhangers and Book 3 gives Andie the HEA she deserves. *(Oh, if you've read my other books, be sure to watch out for those little Easter eggs I love dropping into the story.)*

So, get comfy in your favorite reading spot with a cozy blanket and a warm drink, and enjoy the ride. I hope you enjoy Andie and her savage men as much as I enjoyed writing them.

P.S. At the end of the book, I include the first two chapters of my next RH Series, Beautiful Sin and a sneak peek at Forever His, Julien and Elijah's story.

Jennilynn Wyer

Five years ago

LIAM

The lights to the bedroom flicker on, and the gorgeous raven-haired beauty falters on her high heels when she sees me sitting in the corner, a glass of scotch in my hand that I've been nursing slowly in the dark for the past few hours.

Sophie's ethereal corn-blue eyes flutter when she sees me. "Liam? You scared me," she says, touching a delicate hand to the pearls around her feminine neck.

Her hips sway seductively as she walks over to the dresser, taking off her jewelry, piece by piece, and placing them in the velvet-lined box her mother gave her for her sixteenth birthday. She reaches a hand under her long, waterfall of hair and shakes it out, moaning softly as she does, and my cock twitches.

My eyes leisurely trail over her body from head to toe and back again. Sophie is wearing a body-hugging black silk wrap dress that vees down the front, showing off the creamy half-globes of her breasts. Her nipples are puckered underneath, and I can see the outline of each one through the thin, gossamer fabric. More pearls adorn her ears and a finger.

"We missed you at dinner," she says conversationally, bending slightly to slide her feet out of her heels, one at a time. "I brought back a take-out box for you. It's in the fridge if you're hungry." Her voice is husky and smooth like a fine-aged bourbon.

Everything about Sophie is beautiful. Her red-stained lips I've kissed a million times. The black kohl liner she uses to make her eyes look like a cat's. The floral perfume she wears that follows me everywhere. Her long, milky thighs that I've spent hours between. She's every man's wet dream wrapped in a package of a fucking goddess. I should be down on my knees worshipping her every damn day. Grateful that she chose me out of all the other men she could have had.

But there was always something there, beneath the surface. Something that nipped and nibbled away at my subconscious. Something that never allowed me to love her. Never allowed me to fully give her my heart.

And now I know why.

Slowly standing up, I put my drink down on the side table next to the chair and walk up behind her. She arches back into me, her breaths panting out between those scarlet lips when I curve my hands around her waist, gliding them up her torso. I dip one hand inside the opening of her dress to cup a heaving breast. So fucking soft. Sophie purrs, her eyes glazing over as my lips brush up the side of her neck, her tuberose perfume instantly enveloping me.

"I love when you touch me," she moans, pressing her spine into my chest, the back of her head tucking in at the dip of my shoulder, her eyes closed now.

When my lips get to her ear, I nuzzle behind it with my nose, squeezing her breast a little harder at the same time my left hand comes up.

"You've been a bad girl, Sophie," I tell her, my voice low like a hum, and the pliant woman in my arms goes ram-rod rigid.

She knows my words are not foreplay. There will be no bending her over the dresser and fucking her like I normally would have done. There is no pleasure in my touch anymore as my left hand circles her neck, my grip crushing as I start to choke her.

Sophie knows she's about to die.

"Liam, I love you. Does that count for nothing?" she rasps, the small tremor in her voice the only evidence of her fear.

"Not in this life," I reply, and push the knife into her back.

Chapter 1

KEANE

Molding her naked body flush with mine, I bury my face in her fragrant hair, soaking in the delicate way she smells like ambrosia and the softness of her skin. I never thought I'd ever get the chance to hold Andie like this. Be with her like this. That she'd want me just as much as I've always wanted her. I honestly couldn't give a shit that I just shared her with two other men. One, my best friend. The other, my enemy. Jax was right. If I want to keep her, I have to accept all the baggage that comes with her. That baggage being Jax; Liam Connelly, Declan's top enforcer; and Rafe, my other best friend who betrayed me and switched sides.

We all love her. There is no budge to that. No give. No compromise. Andie has made it perfectly clear where she stands and what she wants.

The entire situation is a fucking mess.

Andie and I are like rotating magnets. The forces between us repelling and attracting. We fight and argue. Bicker and butt heads. But that's who we are and what has made this thing between us electric and all-consuming. We are two powder kegs on short wicks, ready to explode. That spark finally flared to life tonight when Andie asked us to help rid her of the demons from her past, and after a decade of denying myself, I gave in. To her. It was inevitable anyway. From the moment I laid eyes on Alexandria, she owned me. Didn't matter that we were kids at the time. Didn't matter how many other women I screwed to fill the empty void as the years went by. Andie is my beginning and my end.

Cupping her breast, I brush my thumb over her nipple until it peaks. Her sharp intake of breath is music to my ears.

"Keane," she moans huskily, her body arching back into me.

Jax and Liam just left the room. Jax to get us some food and coffee, and Liam to make a phone call.

"Shh, baby. I just want to touch you," I whisper into her ear, kissing her temple and feathering my fingers up and down her side, over her hip, and back again. She hums in pleasure, her body relaxing into my arms.

I'm surprised we didn't break her after four hours of hard, hedonistic fucking. But my girl has always been strong.

Andie rolls over to face me, those gorgeous violet eyes looking at me in a way I had only dreamed about. She wraps a long, toned leg over my thigh and scoots closer to press tender kisses to my lips. My fingers thread through her silky hair, holding her in place. I could stare into her eyes forever. The unique color of them has always fascinated me. No matter how many photographs I take, I can never capture anything as beautiful as the woman lying next to me. Photography is a way for me to escape; to try and find beauty in the ugly world I live in.

When Andie snuck into my room at Kellan's cabin, she saw the framed photographs I had taken over the years. My favorite one was an image I secretly took of her when she and Kellan were out for one of their walks around the Rossi property. A spear of sunlight had broken through the clouds, and Andie, so young at the time, reached her hand out, trying to grab onto the ray's warmth as if it were a physical thing.

Andie's touch grounds me back into the present. "Does your offer still stand?" she asks, moving to kiss down my jaw and neck.

Her question takes me by surprise. "What offer?"

Her plump, kiss-swollen lips roam for a minute, tasting me with little flicks of her tongue. She pulls back and cups my face between her palms. "To marry you."

I go silent, my mouth slightly parted as I stare at her in bewilderment. She can't mean... "What?"

Those beautiful pale indigo eyes roll in playful exasperation. "You said to think about it. I have. My answer is still yes. I already said yes, if you recall."

She's referring to my proposal of marriage. The one I suggested because it was the only solution I could come up with to stop Max from handing her over to Ortiz.

But that deal's off the table. She's under the protection of Declan Levine now. Her real father. She doesn't need me or Jax to save her anymore. My heart starts thumping wildly the more I process her words. She wants to be my wife. Not because she's being forced to, but because she wants to.

The only time I have ever felt any semblance of happiness in my life was when I was in her orbit. Didn't matter if we were fighting or playing that stupid hand slap game. Just being in her presence was enough. But right now, the surge of absolute joy that's rushing through my bloodstream and invading the beating organ I thought had died when she left five years ago is almost painful with its intensity.

Rolling on top of her, I force her back onto the bed and settle between her thighs. My cock is rock-hard and aching to sink into her. My mouth presses a path of soft kisses along her chest and neck, her moans getting louder when I pull a puckered, rosy nipple into my mouth.

I release her tiny bud and blow a caressing breath over it, watching how the color darkens from pink to red.

"You're safe now with Declan. You're not being forced to marry Alejandro anymore," I murmur into her neck as she writhes under me, trying to get the friction she needs on her clit. Greedy girl. You'd think after all the orgasms we gave her that she'd be satisfied.

"And?" Her breath stutters when I nibble her earlobe.

My skin tingles and erupts into goose flesh when her hands glide up my arms and shoulders, stopping to explore every bump of muscle.

I need to make sure that I'm not just reading into her question what I want to hear. "And you don't have to go through with my stupid idea anymore."

When my lips reach hers, and I dip my tongue inside her mouth, she abruptly pulls back, eyes raging at me with a mixture of desire and anger.

"Keane, I know I don't have to. And my answer is still yes."

Those are the words I needed to hear. I had to be sure.

Without taking my eyes off her, I stretch an arm out to pull on the drawer of the bedside nightstand and take out the small black jewelry box I'd put in there. She looks at me in shock as I carefully place it in the valley between her breasts. Her wide eyes move from the box to me, waiting. I didn't think my heartbeat could hammer any faster, but the tempo increases as I rest my weight on an elbow and open the ring box for her. Inside are a delicate, yellow princess-cut diamond engagement ring nestled next to a matching eternity wedding band.

"These were my mother's," I tell her, and her eyes gloss over.

"Jesus." Her hand goes to her lips, her chest rising and falling fast, with only silence engulfing the room.

Steeling my emotions, I tell her, "She would be honored for you to wear them."

Andie's breath exhales like I just knocked the oxygen right out of her lungs. "The honor would be mine," she says breathlessly, and my heart clenches.

Not able to speak through the sudden lump in my throat, I grip her neck and jerk her to me, kissing her like the world will end. I slide both rings onto the fourth finger of her left hand. But it's not enough. I may have just claimed her as my future wife, but my body needs to claim her as my woman. Her pussy is soaking already, her sweet nectar dripping down my cock that has been pulsating at her entrance, ready to take her. In one smooth thrust, I'm seated fully inside her, and we both vocalize at how good it fucking feels.

"Andie Agosti. Has a nice ring to it," I say, pulling out ever so slowly before sliding back in.

On the next thrust, she bursts out laughing. "Oh, hell no."

I grip her thighs, spreading her legs wider to better take me, and deep-tongue her smiling mouth, our kiss becoming as slow and sensuous as the way I'm making love to her.

"Hell no, what?" Jax asks, walking over to the bed, seeming to *forget he's holding four mugs of coffee by the handles between his fingers of both hands. He watches with heated interest as I fuck our girl. My future queen. My Andie.*

Panting out her words when I pick up the pace, Andie moans, "Looks like... there's going to be... a wedding." Her inner walls convulse, choking the life out of my cock, as she loses herself to her impending orgasm, head thrown back, neck exposed for the taking, my name erupting from her lips like a benediction. So damn gorgeous.

"Over my dead fucking body," Liam growls at the doorway.

I rouse with a loud groan at the sound of hushed voices. Sitting up stiffly, I crick my neck from side-to-side, having fallen asleep in the chair, body bent over the side of Rafe's bed, my head tucked under an arm.

"Next time I fall asleep like that, drag my ass to the floor or something," I grumble and rub the nape of my neck.

I look over at Rafe and relief hits me in a torrent. I may still be pissed at him for what he did, but he will never stop being my brother or my friend. My love for Jax and Rafe go bone-deep. Ride or die to the end.

He'd been out for days after being shot in the chest by one of Alejandro's men. The doctors Declan has on his payroll kept Rafe sedated, wanting to give his body the time it needed to start healing without him fucking it all up by trying to move around. Stupid asshole already tried to get out of bed earlier and wound up bleeding all over me and his bedsheets.

Rafe gives me a pained look of regret, then turns his head toward Jax and asks, "Where's Andie? Is she okay?"

Silence. Nothing but dead silence. Andie and Rafe still love each other. It's plain as day, even though Andie pretends to hate him.

"That's what we're trying to find out," Jax replies, but his tone of voice is off, and Rafe picks up on it immediately. As soon as he hears about what happened to Andie, he's going to lose his shit.

Not knowing how to break the news to him, I say, "She and Liam were in a car accident." Not the whole truth, but whatever.

He demands, "When? How fucking long have I been out?"

Jax reluctantly looks away from his screen and glowers at me. "Just tell him, already. He'll find out eventually."

"Tell me what?"

The door bursts open, light flooding into the room. Liam points at Jax. "Tessa wants you."

Jax runs out of the room like his pants are on fire with Liam hot on his footsteps right behind him. Did Tessa find where Andie is being held?

I stand abruptly, about to follow them, when Rafe calls out, "You're going to tell me right the fuck now what the hell's going on."

My blood turns to stone as rage rises. I give him a brief glance over my shoulder. "Your fucking brother is what's going on," I inform him and walk out just as Pearson walks in.

I hear Tessa before I see her.

"What the ever-living *fuck*?" Tessa shouts at her laptop. "You've got to be kidding me. *Shit! Goddamnit! Motherfucker!* Why isn't this stupid algorithm working? Jax!"

Jax comes up behind her on the sofa and bends over her shoulder. He's been working in tandem with Tessa to locate where Alejandro took Andie. Leaving them to figure out the high-tech shit, Liam and I pace the room like caged animals, while Declan sits stoically in the leather armchair, taking slow sips of what I assume is whiskey from a tumbler.

We got back from New York six hours ago, having dealt with Ricci and Barone and slaughtering every man in their organizations. They're the ones who sent men to capture Andie, wanting to honor the agreement Max made with Julio Ortiz to give Andie to his sadistic son, Alejandro—Rafe's brother—in order to cement a deal between the Rossis and the Ortiz Cartel.

It's been days. *Days.* And not a single clue as to Andie's whereabouts. I'm about to lose my mind. Thoughts of Alejandro touching her. Hurting her. My eyes squeeze shut to stop the unwanted images from forming.

Tessa briefly glances to her right. "Rafe, what do you think you're doing?"

Rafe is leaning heavily on Pearson, who's basically holding him up. I know not to open my mouth to tell him to get his ass back to bed. The stubborn fucker would just give me the finger and ignore me.

"Consider me Inigo Montoya," Rafe says, and we all stare at him like he's high. Which is probably a given considering the amount of drugs the doctors have given him.

Tessa laughs loud and long, apparently understanding his gibberish, while the rest of us stand around in confusion.

"More like Westley when he confronts Prince Humperdinck," she replies, and rolls her eyes at us when we remain clueless. "Seriously? Forget it," she huffs. "I suppose you don't happen to have a direct way of communicating with Voldemort, or some floo powder that will take us right to him?" she says to Rafe.

What in the hell is she going on about?

"What if I said I might?" Rafe finally replies.

Turning back to her laptop, she waves him over. "Then you, Rafael, just became my best-*est* friend."

"Did any of you understand that?" Declan asks us, and we shrug.

Jax moves out of the way when Pearson helps Rafe over to the couch where Tessa is sitting.

With a grunt, Rafe picks up a cell phone that's on the coffee table next to Tessa's laptop. "Can this be traced?"

It must be her phone because she answers, "If it can, they'll think the phone is calling out from Jakarta." She takes it from him, unlocks it, and hands it back.

Rafe dials a number. There's a beat of silence, then Rafe turns his back to us when someone answers on the other end.

I snap my fingers at Jax and mouth the words, "Can you trace it?"

He immediately picks up Tessa's laptop and sits down with it on the sofa, his fingers flying across the keyboard.

A big part of me wants to rush over and strangle Rafe with my bare hands. He's known how to contact his father this entire time and never told us?

Rafe mumbles into the phone in Spanish, words that I can't make out because Liam's loud-ass voice bellows, "What?" into his phone when it rings.

His eyes fly to me, but his words are to Declan. "Andie. She's here."

Declan is already up and running to the elevators.

Chapter 2

ANDIE

As soon as I hit the dusky cream marble floor of the lobby of Falcon Tower, I stumble over my feet and fall to the floor on my hands and knees, my body finally giving out. Six men are on me, guns trained, shouting at me not to move. Not a problem. I don't think I could even lift my head at this point.

My mind blurs in a haze, shutting down. I'm caked in dried blood, my face once again swollen and bruised. A look that I seem to be wearing a lot since I returned to the States. When I crashed through the lobby doors of Falcon Tower, the adrenaline that had been fueling me to fight and to escape runs out. I'm exhausted and just need a moment to catch my breath.

"Andie!"

I can't even muster the strength to acknowledge his voice. Lying down, I curl in on myself on the hard foyer marble floor. Hands grab at me and lift me up, and I whine in pain at being jostled.

"We've got you, *bella*. Hold on," Liam says.

"Where the fuck did she come from? How did she get here?" Keane barks, pressing in.

I blink tear-glassed eyes up at him, and his face darkens when he takes in the abused, bloody, and beaten sight of me.

Jax appears to my other side, and I can tell that he wants to rip me out of Liam's arms and into his own by how his hands keep outstretching then ebbing, reaching toward me then away, uncertainty plaguing him on what to do.

The elevator doors open and Declan rushes forward, a mixture of fear and relief in his violet-colored eyes when he sees me.

"Get her upstairs to her room, right fecking now," he tells Liam. He turns to one of his men. "Tell Mike if he isn't here in five minutes, he won't live to see the sun come up in the morning."

My mind blocks out the cacophony around me and becomes numb, not able to handle anything more, as I'm carried into the elevator. I just need to sleep.

Someone slaps gently at my face. "Stay awake, princess." Of course, Keane would be the asshole who won't let me even close my damn eyes for two seconds. "You gotta stay with us until the doctor checks you out."

I know I have a concussion. Multiple actually. But the need to sleep is overpowering. That feeling quickly and painfully dissipates when I'm placed in a bed. God, every-fucking-thing hurts so much.

"Keane, I'm so sorry," I rasp out.

"Tinker Bell, there isn't a damn thing for you to apologize for," he tells me, bending over the side of the bed and caressing a hand down my matted, tangled hair.

I try to shake my head, but it hurts too much. He doesn't get it. "Alejandro took them. The rings."

Keane releases a string of very vocal curse words when he looks down at my left hand and sees where Alejandro broke my finger.

I meet the green eyes of my Reaper. "Jax, my knife. Keep it safe for me," I tell him, my vision wavering. "Rita is dead. He killed her."

"Good," Keane growls. "Saves me a bullet."

I must've blacked out for a second because I suddenly come to when someone shouts, "When is the doctor getting here?"

I'm in a bed, in a room I don't recognize.

"Pearson, can you handle things for now?" Declan implores.

"Out," a thick Russian accent says, and I assume the person speaking is the mysterious Pearson I haven't met yet.

"Not fucking happening," four angry male voices say at the same time, and for some bizarre reason, I want to laugh because it's the first time that Keane, Jax, and Liam have all agreed on anything.

But it's the fourth voice that catches me by surprise. The one I thought I may never hear again.

The mattress dips and Rafe whispers, "Shh, baby. It's okay."

I burst into tears, so freaking happy that he's here and alive. And so fucking sad that he's absolutely wrong.

Because what he just said is a lie. It's not going to be okay.

My senses awaken with the smell of spice and sandalwood, and I open my eyes to see gorgeous blue ones watching me. I know better than to try and move, because if I do, the killer migraine I'm sporting will only intensify. My head is nestled into the soft goose down pillow, the silk pillowcase smooth against my swollen cheek where Alejandro punched me. Rafe is facing me, his head resting on the same pillow as mine, my right hand and his left one joined together and lying between us.

"Hey," he whispers.

"Hey," I whisper back.

Somehow, I'm dressed in clean clothes—an oversized tee and loose sweatpants—all remnants of the blood now gone from my hands and arms. My hair is pulled back in a ponytail. Someone must have cleaned me up and dressed me when I was out cold. Whoever it was, deserves a huge thank you.

I let go of Rafe's hand to reach up and stroke his face. The short, dark beard he's grown since the last time I saw him looks really good. I trace my thumb over his cheek and chin and back again.

"I like this." My fingertips play with his short stubble.

Rafe winces when he moves closer to touch our foreheads

together, and I'm immediately concerned because he's still recovering from his injury.

"Do you need anything? Are you in pain?" I ask him.

He should be in his own bed, taking it easy, but I'm selfish and will refuse to let him leave if he tries to go.

"Shouldn't I be asking you that?"

My heart soars with his small grin.

"Where is everybody?"

Instead of answering, his thumb touches my sore lip. "Andie, I'm so sorry. I tried so hard to protect you from my family, but—"

I stop him immediately by covering his mouth with my hand. When he ceases trying to talk, I remove it and replace my hand with my lips, kissing him softly. He sighs, and the tension in his body relaxes. He takes over and kisses me deeper. I refuse to allow the sting of my cut lip to prevent me from living in the moment with him.

"No apologies. Ever. You don't control what your brother or father do," I tell him, smiling when I remember something. There is so little right now to smile about.

"What?" he asks, confused at what I'm finding humorous about the current topic of conversation.

"Just a promise I made myself," I reply, but don't go into any detail about the promise to lock us into a room and fuck his brains out the next time I saw him.

We're both not in any condition to pursue that little fantasy. I also need to tell him what happened between me, Keane, Jax, and Liam. It wouldn't be fair to assume he would be on board with me sleeping with all three men. However, as much as I want him and still love him, I'm also in love with *them*. The reality of that hits me like a freaking sledgehammer because it shouldn't be possible. And yet, it is.

"By the way, you've earned my trust back," I tell him and giggle when he sends me the most boyish, lopsided smile I've ever seen. This is the Rafe I fell for when I was a teenager.

"I want to take you out on a date," he blurts, the sentiment completely out of the blue.

"You do?"

He pecks the tip of my nose. "Oh yeah. I never got the chance to do that for you. Like a proper date where we hold hands and flirt. Fancy attire, music, candlelight, expensive food, dancing—the works. I would tell you how pretty you look and open doors for you like a gentleman. All in the hopes of getting in your pants later, of course." He winks at me, his grin showing the dimple on his left cheek that would always make me swoon.

This man. The shit he's been through that should've erased any boyish charm left in him. Yet, here he is, teasing and flirting with me as if we were teenagers again with hearts in our eyes. If we weren't both so injured right now, I'd be crawling all over his dick.

"I'd rather lie under the maple tree and count the stars at our place in the park."

He lightly kisses me again. "I can do that. Andie, there's something—"

"Safe to enter?"

I'm lying on my side facing the door, so I see when it cracks open and Tessa pokes her head inside, a hand covering her eyes.

"Put your damn hand down, drama queen."

"I never know with you," she comments, and Rafe's eyebrows raise to his hairline.

There's a lot I need to tell him, but not right now.

She walks over and slides into bed with us, snuggling on the other side of me, and I'm grateful I'm in a California King or else it would get very uncomfortable with the three of us smooshed together.

"So this is what it's like," she chirps. "Except there'd be two guys. Sorry, babe. You're badass sexy and all, but…"

Even though she can't see my face, I roll my eyes.

"Seeing as Rafe hasn't answered me, where are the guys?" I ask her.

"Ummm… Liam is outside with Declan."

"It's nothing for you to worry about right now," Rafe intercedes. "The important thing is for you to rest. All that other shit will still be there when you're healed and stronger."

The lighthearted banter from minutes ago dissipates quickly into the ether as reality comes tumbling back. I don't need to rest or heal. I don't need coddling or protecting. I need vengeance.

"How long was I out?"

Tessa rests her hand on my hip. "About three hours."

Oh, thank fuck. Only a few hours.

"Would you mind giving us a moment?" Declan says, entering the bedroom.

I have a feeling that my room is going to be a revolving door of people for the unforeseeable future.

"Pearson wants to check your bandage," he says to Rafe. Tessa gets up and offers her arm to help him get out of bed.

"Want some homemade biscuits and molasses to eat?" Rafe asks me.

"Hell, yes." My smile is genuine.

"Oh, dear God," Tessa bemoans.

"Hey, you said you liked it now," I remind her.

She purses her lips together. "I lied. It was the only way to get you to shut up about it."

I decide the pain of throwing my pillow at her is worth it.

When they're finally gone, Declan stands just inside the room, his reading glasses hanging from his shirt, his hands tucked into the pockets of his trousers. It's a stance he often takes, and I find that I like it. He looks very fatherly.

"How are you feeling?"

I force myself to sit up. "Better."

He moves over to the side of the bed and rearranges the pillows around me. I recline back in a more comfortable position against the headboard.

"You look tired." There are purple smudges under his eyes the same color as our unique irises.

Chair legs scrape across the floor, and he sits down, then reaches across the bed to take my right hand.

"I never thought I'd ever have kids of my own. Didn't want them, to be honest," he confesses. "The type of life I live isn't one to subject an innocent child to. But I'm so damn glad that you're my daughter, Andie."

Tears I seldom shed immediately gather in my eyes and spill over.

Declan squeezes my hand, a look of love, regret, and remorse marring his face. "I love you. You will always come first. I will gladly sacrifice anything for you."

His words rip me open, but they also heal a deeply buried part of me. The part that is the little girl who grew up yearning for a father to love her, not to abuse and hurt her. But Maximillian Rossi isn't my real father. Declan is.

"I love you, too," I whisper, and he smiles wistfully. Like what I said is the most wonderful, beautiful thing he has ever heard.

Bending over me on the bed, he presses a kiss to my forehead, and I soak it up, so starved for the tenderness of a parent. "Get some rest. I need you ready."

A mask falls over his face when our eyes meet. It's a mask I'm all too familiar with after growing up as a child in the mafia. The man before me is no longer my father.

"Ready for what?" I ask. But I already know.

"War."

Chapter 3

JAX

I'm so fucking pissed right now that I'm more than likely going to murder everyone in this goddamn nightclub. I don't give a shit that most of the people here are innocent and had no clue Alejandro had my woman somewhere in this building, torturing her for days.

The strobing lights pulse to the beat of the music, illuminating faces as I push through the mass of bodies dancing, drinking, and dry humping without a care in the world. My damn glasses keep fogging up from all the body heat being given off from the patrons drenched in sweat as they carelessly writhe to whatever the DJ is playing. In my peripheral, Keane is talking to the bartender, slipping him a few Benjamins for his troubles and to pump him for information.

Andie was here all along, right under our noses. Just blocks from Falcon Tower. My Angel. So close. And I failed her. I'm supposed to be the smart one. The guy who can find anyone, anywhere with a quick keystroke. I can erase you from existence like you were never born. Yet, I couldn't find my woman, who was less than ten minutes away from me.

A guy backs into me as he dances, and my hand automatically goes to my knife. The one with the red handle I gave Andie that she asked me to keep safe for her. The knife I used to slit my father from groin to neck. The one Andie used to kill Max. And the same one I'm going to enjoy using on Alejandro. Slowly. Just the thought of it has my eyes about to roll into the back of my head and my cock getting hard. Images of Alejandro strung up —pieces of his flesh carved out and sliced off, my body covered in his blood while I fuck Andie in front of him—send waves of wicked pleasure through me.

A firm hand grips my wrist, stilling me from taking out my weapon. Keane's voice speaks into my ear over the loud music. "Upstairs."

I nod to let him know I heard him and follow him off the dance floor. I've already messed with the security cameras in the building, putting the feed on a loop to hide that we were ever here.

Adjacent to the bar is a set of stairs that leads up to the VIP section of the club. At the back of the dark hallway is a red door. The grunts and moans of people having sex are heard from behind closed doors to a few of the private rooms we pass. Two guys are openly fucking against the wall of the hallway, not a care in the world that Keane and I are there. There's an open door to the right where two men are doing lines of coke off a woman's naked body while she finger-fucks herself.

As soon as we reach the red door, Keane pulls out a gun. In a lowered voice full of repressed violence, he says, "Bartender said the owner arrived a little while ago."

With a swift heel kick from his shit-kicker boots, the door flies open, and we step inside.

"What the fuck!" a guy shouts, abruptly standing up from the chair he was sitting in behind the desk and knocking over the woman who had been sucking him off. She scrambles to her feet and ducks behind him. Like that'll save her.

I quietly close the door and lean back against it. Keane approaches the man, gun steady and aimed at his head. This is his show now. I'll be a quiet spectator until it's time for me to join the party.

"Get the fuck out of my office!" the man yells, tucking himself back into his trousers and zipping up his fly.

The man has a slick look that you'd expect from a nightclub owner. Blond hair greased back off his forehead. Expensive silk shirt with the top four buttons undone to show off an expanse of chest hair. Gold chains around his neck and a couple of large, gaudy gold rings on his fingers. Stupid wannabe fucker is also wearing a thick gold chain bracelet around his right wrist and a solid gold Rolex on his left. Couldn't get more clichéd if he tried.

I've already snapped a picture of him and sent it to Tessa to run a facial recognition with her software. In a matter of minutes, I'll know everything about him from his time of birth to what he eats for breakfast.

Keane looks the man over as he stalks toward him. "You get one chance to tell me what I want to know," he says, and I know he's telling the truth. Keane won't hesitate to kill him if the guy tries to spew bullshit to save his own skin.

The dark-haired woman whimpers as she clutches the back of the man's black dress shirt and peeks around him at us with mascara-streaked brown eyes.

Keane cocks his head at her. "I suggest you sit the fuck down right now and shut the hell up," he warns her. We have an unspoken rule about not killing women. Doesn't mean that we haven't in the past if they deserved it.

Absolutely terrified, she does what he says and immediately sits down in the chair next to her.

"Now," Keane says, his demeanor black with rage, directing his gaze back at the man. "Alejandro Ortiz was holding a woman here."

The guy swallows thickly. "I don't know—"

He never gets a chance to finish his sentence. Keane smashes the butt of his gun against his head, and the guy falls to the floor, crying out in pain.

"Get up," Keane states coldly.

Staggering back to his feet, the man shakes as he wipes blood away from his temple. The click of the safety disengaging on the gun Keane is holding has the man wide-eyed with fear. If he didn't understand before that Keane's threat was serious, he does now.

"Not going to repeat myself."

Licking his thick lips, the guy says, "I don't know their names."

My phone vibrates and I smile.

"We know yours, Michael Elliot Donahue of 1431 Grand Parkway. Age twenty-seven. Graduated from Highland High School with a two-point-three GPA. College drop-out. Three speeding tickets. Never married. No kids. One brother, age eighteen and a senior in high school. Two sisters. One's a housewife with one kid. The other, a veterinarian, recently graduated from NC State. Mother's name, Barbara Michelle Garrett Donahue. Father deceased. Died in a car accident last year. Shall I go on?" I ask him.

Michael's face blanches of all color. "How did you... Jesus, fuck."

Jesus, fuck indeed.

"I swear, they never told me their names." He looks pleadingly at Keane, who is still holding a gun at his head.

"Describe them," Keane clips out, close to losing whatever patience he has left.

Michael scrapes trembling hands over his face. "Some scary dude. Hispanic. Had tattoos all over his head and face."

Alejandro. As Michael talks, I type everything he says into my phone so I can send it to Tessa.

"What about the other man? Older. Dark hair and eyes. Hispanic like the first guy. There was security footage of him here with a woman in the back alley."

Keane and I know about that now. This club, Spanks, is one of the businesses under the "protection" of the Rossi syndicate. Dom managed this part of the city for Max. That's how Rita knew about it, and why she was here meeting with Julio in the back alley. And I never put two and two together. Andie suffered because of my careless mistake. I'm still berating myself over the fact that I wasn't the one who discovered that Rita had been meeting with Julio right under our noses in our fucking city. Betraying our family. Keane killed his own father because of a similar situation. We don't tolerate snitches in *la famiglia*.

Tears pool in Michael's eyes when Keane steps closer until the muzzle of his gun touches the middle of Michael's forehead.

"Older guy was more polished. Wore an expensive suit. Didn't talk to me. Only the young guy did. That's all I know. I swear on my life."

I follow Keane's gaze when he looks down at the dark, wet patch that quickly spreads out and soaks the man's trousers at the crotch. He literally pissed himself. What a pussy.

The woman hasn't made a peep, continuing to obey Keane's command to remain quiet.

"What did the two men want with you?" Keane asks him.

"Use of the private rooms downstairs. I needed the money. I'm late on a payment."

Satisfied that he's gotten all the answers he can from Michael, Keane jerks his chin at me, giving me the signal that it's my turn to play. A smile creases my cheeks.

"What's your social security number, sweetheart?" I direct at the woman.

She quickly rambles it off, knowing better than to ask why or what for.

Sliding my phone into my back pocket, I tell her, "You're now the proud owner of Spanks. The deed of ownership for the building and all licenses have been transferred over to your name, along with one million dollars in a secured offshore account."

"What are you talking about?" she asks with confusion, her body quaking so badly, the chair she's sitting in moves jerkily across the floor.

"A man named Garrett will contact you tomorrow. I suggest you pick up when he calls." She nods yes. "You never saw us. Understood?"

"I understand," she says, on the verge of hyperventilating. I know she won't talk about what she saw tonight. And if she does —

"Good. Now watch closely," I tell her, grabbing the stapler off Michael's messy desk. I want her to see every second of what I do next.

Chapter 4

KEANE

"Mind sharing that?"

My attention travels in Liam's direction, and I hand him my joint. He takes a long pull and closes his eyes, then blows the smoke out slowly. The wispy tendrils float around his head before disappearing completely.

"Thanks."

"No problem," I reply, taking it back.

I didn't know if Declan had a policy about smoking of any kind inside the building like Max did at the house, so as soon as we returned from Spanks, I came out to the back alley of Falcon Tower. Jax and I aren't in a good head space right now, and we both needed some downtime after what happened at the club. Amazing the damage a stapler can do in Jax's skillful hands. Andie's been through enough and doesn't need to deal with knowing that shit right now.

"Rafe tell you yet who he called?"

I offer him a negative shake of the head just to get him off my case. Jax wasn't able to trace the call, so we don't know who was on the other end. The only information Rafe let slip was to inform us that Julio is back in Mexico, sans his oldest offspring. And that makes me very curious as to why. It also makes him even more dangerous to Andie. Without Julio to pull his leash and keep him in check, Alejandro has become a wild card capable of anything. The guy is a full-blown psycho.

A ruckus of noise echoes down the alley just as a group of

women drunkenly stumbles past, giggling and clinging to one another. There's a bar a block away and a couple of luxury hotels, which creates a steady flow of foot traffic along the sidewalk that passes by the alley. Liam and I quietly watch the women, oblivious to the two killers in the midst.

I finish my smoke and toss it into a murky puddle next to the dumpster. "You need something, or you just enjoy my company all of a sudden?"

It's no secret that Liam and I don't like one another very much. He's an unexpected problem that got thrown in my path that I have no fucking clue how to handle. To be honest, I'm kind of struggling with everything at the moment. For fuck's sake, I'm the new don of the Rossi syndicate, and I'm only twenty-five years old. How is that possible? Then there's what to do about the Riccis and Barones after we cleaned house in New York. Should I let those houses die? Make Dante and Enzo capos and rebuild? Or just walk away from it all and follow Rafe's dream of living a normal life with a wife and kids.

Blowing out a ragged breath, I muss my hands through my sweat-slicked hair. I need a shower.

Liam leans back against the wall, kicking at a piece of plastic trash that tumbles over his Doc Martens. "I wanted to talk to you about Andie."

Immediately, my hackles, along with my distrust, rise. Who Liam Connelly is to Andie is a complex puzzle I'm trying to figure out. Like, how did he and Andie really meet? Because I know damn well it wasn't by accident. Nothing this man does is happenstance. His reputation in the business is what it is for a reason. He's also obsessed with Andie, and I don't like it one damn bit. Then again, I have no leg to stand on in that area. Jax, Rafe, and I have pretty much been obsessed with her as well since we were kids.

Liam rolls his head my way, his eyes shining like silver under the yellow and red exit lights above the door next to him.

"The stuff that went down at the house last week. What happened to her there?"

He doesn't have to explain what stuff. He saw what was in the room downstairs and her reaction to all of it. Andie practically destroyed the house. Then the fuck-fest. She had two decades' worth of demons to exorcise.

"She hasn't told you?"

He shakes his head.

I haven't slept well since the night Andie took the jaws of life to her chest, ripped it wide open, and confessed to me, Jax, and Rafe what Max did to her. All the years he raped her, beat her. Locked her in the cage in the basement we used for torturing people. The baby of Max's she lost when she was only thirteen fucking years old. And none of us, other than Kellan, knew. That night I learned to hate my dead best friend. Kellan should have done something. He should have told us. Fuck that. *I* should have known. *I* should have seen what was happening right in front of me.

"If Andie wants to tell you, that's up to her. But I think you can put two and two together and figure it out on your own."

Liam clenches the back of his neck.

"Alejandro locked her in a fucking cage."

Liam breathes out a quiet, "Fuck."

Out of every possible punishment Alejandro could have given her, he chose the one that had the greatest potential of breaking her. But it didn't. Because Alexandria Donatella McCarthy is the fiercest, strongest, most resilient woman I have ever known.

"I can't get that cage at the house out of my head. And knowing Alejandro put her in one—" He stops talking and thunks his head back against the concrete.

Jax and I have reserved a special place in hell for the oldest son of Julio Ortiz. His day of reckoning can't come soon enough.

After our little visit with Michael, Jax and I went downstairs to where he said the private rooms were located. The room Andie was held in was hard to take in. The smell alone, blood and death, was overwhelming. We didn't find any bodies, so Michael must have disposed of Rita before we got there. There were other bloodstains on the floor near the stairs belonging to who the hell knows.

Fierce pride fills me, knowing my woman escaped. She held her own against Alejandro and didn't let him break her. Andie had already told us he had killed Rita, and I meant what I said. Good fucking riddance. But it was seeing the cage that almost undid me. It was too similar to the one Max would lock Andie in when she was a kid. Near the broken cage, there were also chains on the floor and a big hole in the ceiling above it. After a meticulous search of the rest of the private rooms, we came up empty. Alejandro was long gone, and there was no sign of Julio.

"Do you think he ra—"

I grip his collar and violently slam him against the wall. "Shut the fuck up," I snarl.

I can't even go there. Not after finding out what Max did to her. And if Alejandro hurt her the same way—my stomach lurches, and I hold back the vomit that wants to come.

"What do you really want with her?"

Liam's spine stiffens, his face full of righteous indignation. "Not a damn thing."

"Bullshit."

He shoves me away and jabs a finger in my face. "I'm not the one forcing her to marry me just so I can play king to a crumbling dynasty."

"That's not what—"

He cuts me off, and we round on each other. Two apex predators ready to battle it out, and Andie is the prize.

"Save your breath. If you truly cared about her, you, Jax, and Rafael would leave her the hell alone. Let her be happy. Give her a chance to know her father. She belongs here with Declan."

My laugh is unrepentant. "And with you?"

He shrugs. "If that's what she wants."

Unbelievable. This narcissistic bastard.

Never one to back down, I push into his space. "Not fucking happening."

The muscle in his jaw tics, and I know he's just dying to get a punch in. Bring it, asshole.

Liam will have to put a bullet in my head before I'll give Andie up. Not now. Not after I finally got to taste her sweet lips, and my cock got a taste of her sweeter pussy. Not after wanting her for more years than I can remember. That woman is the air I breathe.

I take a step back. I came out here to get a minute of peace and quiet, and Liam fucking Connelly had to ruin it.

Of course, my damn phone starts ringing, adding to my irritation. It's Dante. I left him in charge while Jax and I handled business here.

Answering his call, I snap, "Let me call you back."

Liam scowls at me. "This conversation isn't over, Agosti." He says my last name like a curse.

Tempering my anger because Andie is my first priority—and she would probably stab both of us if we were to get into a fight right now—I reply, "Have a good fucking evening."

Shoving past him, I fling the door open and walk inside. Taking the stairs, I hit the button on my phone to call Dante back.

Liam is right about one thing. It's not over.

Chapter 5

ANDIE

The door to my room cracks open then closes. It's almost four in the morning. I know this because I've been lying in the dark, staring at pictures of Kellan on my phone, not able to relax enough to fall asleep. Every time my eyes close, I see the metal bars of the cage. Max's. Alejandro's. Doesn't matter which one. They both swirl together into one giant nightmare. My body also aches. Everywhere. And I gave up getting comfortable hours ago. Maybe I should've taken the painkillers Pearson tried to thrust upon me earlier. At least then, I would be unconscious in la-la land right now.

Footsteps come closer, and I hear the sound of clothing being shed and falling to the floor with a soft rustle. The bed dips when Jax slides in next to me. I knew it was him. I can sense each of the guys without looking. The way my body reacts and comes alive when they look at me. Their palpable presence whenever they walk into a room. The scent of their cologne or body wash. The aura of power and attitude they carry. Each man unique.

Scooting over, I make room for his six-foot-plus frame. "Hey."

"Hey," he says back. He smells like Ivory soap, and his hair is still damp from the shower he must've taken. "You good?"

My lips bend in a small smile. "Better now that you're here."

Jax hooks an arm under my back and repositions me so that my head is tucked beneath his chin and my body is plastered to his side. He lifts my leg and drapes it over his crotch. I can feel how hard he is, and every part of me responds immediately—nipples tightening to hard peaks, breaths becoming shallower, and a slick of wetness that soaks my underwear. If I wasn't so beat up, sore, and exhausted, I'd climb on top of him and make good use of the massive erection he's sporting.

"What're you looking at?"

The soft glow of the phone's screen casts ghostly shadows over our faces as I hold it with my uninjured hand and use my thumb to swipe right. I'd been slowly flipping through the photos, one by one, wanting to remember the good times with Kellan and not the lies and the secrets he hid from me.

"Memories," I reply.

I stop on one—a selfie of me and the guys. Kellan and I are sticking our tongues out. Keane is scowling, per usual. Rafe is crossing his eyes and making a goofy face. And Jax is standing a little behind us and to the side, staring right at me with such longing, I can actually feel it. Funny how when we're younger, we don't see the same things we do as adults. It's like our younger selves wear differently tinted glasses that blur the edges of the reality we live in.

The photo was taken on the day I turned fourteen. Max and Cecelia were gone. Max to a meeting with the New York families, and Mom to wherever the hell she went when he was out of town. Kellan and I had the house to ourselves, if you didn't count all the armed guards and the other men there who worked for Max. My birthday was never celebrated, but Kellan always tried to make it special. He invited the guys over and we gorged on cupcakes, ran around the backyard with sparklers, and stayed up watching slasher movies. It was one of the rare times in my life when I was almost happy.

I turn off the phone and slide it under my pillow, then roll over, taking care not to knock my left hand. Pearson did a makeshift splint on my finger using a tongue depressor and medical tape from a first aid kit. Not perfect, but good enough.

Jax removes his glasses and places them on the nightstand nearest him, then rubs his eyes with the heels of his palms. Behind the tired veneer is something deeper. Darker. Something similar to the night he sought me out after he tortured and killed a man, and I was the only person who could save him from himself. But he saved me as well.

With a fingertip, I trace the words "My Reaper" on his chest, just like I did in my blood that night we first hooked up.

"Going to tell me where you and Keane got off to?"

They disappeared soon after I literally passed out, but when I woke up, looking into Rafe's sky-blue eyes and asking about them, he and Tessa wouldn't tell me where they went or why. I'm pretty sure I know.

"Tomorrow."

I bite into his pectoral. "It's already tomorrow."

He pinches my boy-short-covered ass in retaliation. "Then the day after tomorrow," he says, flattening his hand to soothe the area he pinched.

My legs scissor underneath the covers, trying to ease the instant ache in my core that his touch manifests. I may be injured, but I'm not dead.

"You don't have to hide that stuff from me, you know."

Jax snakes his way down my torso and uses my boobs as a pillow. "Shh. Just want to sleep listening to my Angel's heartbeat," he says, and I swoon hard.

Running my fingers through his still slightly damp hair, I hum a nonsensical tune that I make up on the fly. Jax has suffered from insomnia most of his life, and it does something to me knowing I can offer him a safe place where he can close his eyes and let himself go.

"Hey, Jax?"

"Hmm?" His reply is scarcely a rumble as sleep finally claims him.

"I love you."

"I love you too, Angel."

Chapter 6

KEANE

The car pulls up in the circle drive of the Rossi mansion, and two men come around, opening the back doors to let me and Jax out.

"Good morning, sir," John greets me with respect, and I glance over the top of the sedan at Jax, catching his smirk.

After Jax and I cleaned house, we're down about fifteen men. Men who infiltrated our organization and were loyal to Declan Levine. Water under the bridge now, seeing as we've been practically living in the man's skyscraper the past several days.

"I still say we should douse the place in gasoline and hand Andie a match," Jax says as he stares up at the massive house.

I'm not going to tell him that I'm starting to come around to his way of thinking. I can't bring Andie back here once we're married. And I fucking refuse to live at Falcon Tower. We need a fresh start. Something we build together that's our own.

"We should take Andie to Ireland sometime soon to see Sarah."

"Andie would love that," Jax agrees, a sinister grin forming. "We can take her to Blarney Castle. I'll add fucking her up against the Blarney Stone on my bucket list."

"What the fuck are you talking about?"

Jax's grin spreads to the point it takes up his entire face.

Giving up, I turn to John and tell him, "Come find me in an hour." He knows I expect a full report of everything since the last time we spoke.

"Yes, sir."

I bump Jax's shoulder when he snorts out a laugh. I don't think I'll ever get used to grown men calling me sir.

"Let's get this over with," Jax says, and I know the feeling.

I don't like being away from Andie any more than he does. Liam has proven that he can't protect her like we can. He should have seen the car coming from a mile away before it ever got a chance to run them off the road.

Jax and I climb the steps to the house, and the double doors automatically open to the foyer.

"Nice to see you up and around," I tell Enzo.

"Bed rest is for pussies," he replies, leaning heavily on a walking cane.

"Don't overdo it. I need you ready," I tell him.

After thinking it over, I've decided to send him and Dante up to New York to head the restructuring of the Ricci and Barone organizations. Then, they'll take over as capos, answering only to me.

"Dante around?" I ask him.

"Finishing up with some business downstairs."

The "business" is what he called me about earlier when I was ready to go to blows with Liam in the alleyway.

"You up for another interrogation?"

Jax's eyes shutter, and I hate it. I hate taking away the contentment he's had since waking up with Andie between us this morning. He's a completely different person with her. Happier. Not drowning in the demons that he's lived with most of his life. Jax never smiled or laughed until she came back.

As I follow him to the secret door that leads down to the torture room, I'm surprised by how different the house looks. The foyer is completely devoid of anything Max. The ugly portrait of himself that he hung on the wall. The expensive artwork and priceless sculptures. Andie smashed all of them to dust.

Jax enters the code on the panel, and as soon as the door unlocks, I know we're both thinking the same thing. The ghosts of Andie's childhood smash into us, and we both hesitate on the first step. With a deep exhale, I wall up that part of me, sealing it tight. There's no place for emotions where we're headed.

Fluorescent lights flicker on as we descend the staircase. I don't look behind me at Jax when I hear the metallic snick of the new knife he now carries. I leave the Grim Reaper alone. He has a job to do.

Ignoring the familiar stench of blood and piss that never goes away no matter how much bleach is used to clean the room, I walk over to the back wall and lean a casual shoulder on it.

"Who do we have here?"

Dante already told me, but my question is for Jax's benefit. As soon as he learns who the man chained to the floor is, he's going to lose his shit, and I'm smart enough to know to stand back and keep out of his way.

Dante rubs his bloody knuckles on his pants. From the man's face, Dante hasn't been at it for long.

"Well, seeing as he refuses to tell me his real name, I'm going with the only thing he has said. Keane Agosti, meet Fuck You." Dante switches his attention to Jax and takes a few steps back. Like me, he knows to stay out of the way. "Julio's man who shot you and Enzo."

Jax is on him before I can turn around and head back upstairs; Fuck you's screams only cutting off when I shut and seal the door. Hopefully, Jax will get the information we need before he carves the man into unrecognizable pieces.

"I'll be in the office," I tell Enzo as I head to the second floor. There are a few phone calls I need to make before John interrupts me.

Once I enter Max's old office, I go over to the wet bar and pour a full glass of whiskey, needing more than a finger's worth to help mellow me out.

My phone vibrates.

Jax: FuckU bashed his head into the wall and killed himself. Never saw someone do that before. Didn't get much out of him.

Is he serious? What the fuck?

Me: Throw the body in the furnace and get cleaned up.

Alejandro will mess up at some point. And when he does...

The scratch marks on the desk catch my eye, and I smile at what Andie carved into the wood. KARMA IS A BITCH NAMED ANDIE. God, I love that woman. And soon, she'll be my wife.

Sitting down in the leather executive chair, I stare out the window while sipping my drink. Karma is definitely a bitch. And it's coming for you, Alejandro.

Chapter 7

ANDIE

At some point during the night, Keane managed to sneak into my room while Jax and I were asleep. I came to realize this when I woke up to one dick poking my ass while another prodded my stomach. Not complaining one damn bit.

When I blinked my sleep-crusted eyes open, I was met with a soulful hazel assessment.

Keane's fist was propped against his temple, elbow bent. He hadn't shaved in a few days, and I couldn't resist running my fingers all over his short dark beard.

"Bad dreams?" His morning voice was a deep husk, devoid of the usual assholery and snark I'm used to.

Even with Keane and Jax sleeping beside me, the nightmares refused to abate.

My response was to snuggle into my pillow as our gazes remained connected.

Keane rubbed his thumb across my lower lip. When my tongue slipped out to taste it, the pupils housed in his sleepy hazel eyes instantly blew wide with desire.

"I'll be right back," the doctor, who goes only by Mike, says, knocking me out of my daydream about this morning.

I only remember a few lucid seconds of him attending to me last night. Mike doesn't look like your typical doctor with his disheveled brown hair and shaggy beard, wearing a blue button-down and jeans. He more closely resembles a lumberjack recluse, who lives in a log cabin on the side of a mountain.

During our small talk as he poked and prodded me, I found

out he was a special forces medic who served two tours before an IED took half his leg and ended his military career. Helping people had always been his passion, so instead of letting depression over his circumstances sink him under, he went to medical school. I'm dying to ask him how he wound up being the personal physician for a mafia boss but decide to keep that curiosity to myself.

Declan and Liam ambushed me this morning as soon as I walked into the kitchen to get coffee. Keane and Jax had already left to go back to the Rossi estate, with a promise they would see me later tonight. However, I refused to go anywhere until I checked on Rafe. He was still asleep, and I didn't have the heart to wake him. So, I stood in the doorway and looked my fill. The sheet had slipped down, exposing an inked, tanned chest with a happy trail of black hair disappearing into his sweatpants. His face was softer in slumber. Jet black lashes fanned over his cheekbones, his hair a soft mess on the pillow, one muscled arm thrown back over his head. Rafe was gorgeous before, but as a man, he's mouth-watering. And nothing like his psycho older brother.

"Am I done? We can leave?"

It's been fourteen hours since I escaped from Alejandro, but in that short time, I've been pampered, coddled, babied, and driven out of my ever-loving mind by overbearing, obstinate men who mean well. And now, I'm about to leave a private practice clinic that I was dragged to before I had my requisite two cups of coffee, so Mike could examine me from head to toe and take X-rays of my hand to show what was already glaringly apparent. I have a broken finger, a mild concussion, and several new contusions.

"Looks that way," Declan says, his hands shoved deep inside the pockets of his black trousers.

Liam startles me when he softly kisses my lips. "I'll get the car and pick you up outside," he says.

My eyes dart to Liam as he pulls the door open to walk out, then they return to Declan. I think I blush a thousand shades of red as Declan gives me a knowing look about what he just witnessed. It's only a matter of time before he knows that I'm with all four guys. But that's a conversation to have at a much, much later time, not at the doctor's office. It's also a conversation I really don't want to be present for when it happens. Yeah, we can skip the whole "I'm fucking four men, one of whom is your enforcer" conversation altogether.

Needing to change the subject, I happily announce, while raising my splinted and wrapped finger high in the air to make my case, "I told you I was okay."

Okay isn't exactly one-hundred-percent true. I'm still healing from all the other bruises and injuries I've incurred over the past few weeks, along with the newer ones from the car accident and Alejandro's fist. I look like a walking Rorschach image.

Declan just arches a blond eyebrow at me, not dissuaded in the least. "I think we should talk about that."

"Let's not."

His lips twitch under his short beard. "I know I'm new at the fathering thing, and Liam is one of three people I trust completely, but—"

"Please don't finish that sentence," I hastily interject.

Holy hell, I didn't think my cheeks could get any pinker. I'm almost twenty-one fucking years old, not ten. The days are long gone where I need the awkward birds and bees lecture. But it's cute that Declan feels the need to try. We both missed out on so much together.

Thankfully, Mike comes back in, and I hop off the examination table, eager to get going.

He hands me a stapled printout with aftercare instructions. "Thank you," I tell him, rolling the papers into a cylinder.

Mike gives Declan a white bottle containing painkillers that I'm supposed to take but most definitely won't, and leaves after quickly going over the aftercare instructions with me.

Before I can take a step toward the door, Declan is at my side. He cradles the elbow of my right arm and guides me out of the white-walled room that smells like rubbing alcohol and disinfectant. I don't protest the help, even though I don't need it. His overcompensation is coming from a good place. I can only imagine what he went through while Alejandro had me. To finally find your daughter, who had been kept secret from you, only to almost lose her again.

"How about an early lunch?" I guide us to the exit for the stairs, not wanting to be stuck in an elevator again. I get enough of that confined hell at Falcon Tower. My unease about small elevators is getting better, especially when the guys are riding with me, but if I can avoid getting into one in the first place, I will.

"I can ask Pearson to prepare something."

Upon meeting Pearson for the first time last night, he was not at all what I was expecting. The man is massive, as in total brickhouse huge. The side of his face is scarred from what looks like a nasty knife wound that didn't heal properly, and he has more ink on him than Jax, which shouldn't be possible.

"It would be nice to get some fresh air. We can grab some food from a street vendor and find a bench at Greenway Park," I suggest.

There's a nearby city park with a small koi pond just a few blocks from here. After Alejandro had me locked in a cage, then strung me up like a pig carcass in that small room, I need the space of the open outdoors right now.

We push through the clinic doors and step out onto the sidewalk. Most people are at work now, so the street and sidewalks are pretty much empty, with the exception of a few pedestrians, a jogger, and a metro bus that passes by.

Shielding my eyes from the intensity of the late morning sun, I peer down the street and see the black Range Rover coming out of the parking garage exit and heading our way.

"Liam's here." I turn and look up at Declan. He hasn't given me a yes or a no about lunch in the park. "Pretty please?"

I know he's about to give in when he smiles down at me. But that smile never completely forms.

Because in the blink of an eye, several things happen at once.

The squeal of tires. Declan shoving me behind him. The staccato of gunfire. The rev of an engine. The smell of burning rubber. My screams.

And the wet, warm feeling of blood as Declan collapses on top of me. My brain short circuits for a second before I understand what just happened.

Declan's heavy body crushes me with dead weight.

"Declan?"

He doesn't respond.

"Declan?"

Tears stream from my eyes like rivers. Please, no. Don't do this to me. I just found him. We just found each other. It's like the night Rafe was shot.

OhGodOhGod.

It takes effort to roll us over. So much red, everywhere. I cradle the back of Declan's head, pushing my face to his ear.

"Open your eyes. Please open your eyes." I can't go through this again. I can't lose another person I love. "Kellan! Help! Don't let them take him!" I scream.

Shouts erupt all around me, but all I can do is stare at the man lying beneath me, motionless, on the sidewalk.

My father.

"Jesus fuck, Andie!" Liam shouts, jumping out of the SUV he drove onto the sidewalk.

I look up at him with bleak, beggar's eyes. "Liam, do something."

Suddenly, Mike is on his knees beside Declan, pushing me away to get to him. Without thought, I lunge at the doctor, but Liam grabs me and pins me in his arms.

"*Bella*, stop," he grunts as I go feral—kicking and screaming and clawing at his arms to let me go.

Chaos explodes all around me. The lingering smell of sulfurous cordite fills my nose as my ears fill with the sirens of police cars and an approaching ambulance. But my gaze never leaves the man who, within a handful of days, gave me more love than anyone else in my entire miserable life. I finally got to experience what it was like to have a real father.

"Dad," I whimper, going limp against Liam.

Drip. Drip. Drip.

It's a sound I'm used to. But instead of water, the drip is from my heart which is steadily leaking out of my chest the longer I sit in this goddamn uncomfortable chair in the waiting room at St. Mercy Hospital.

I need to itch the tickle on my cheek, but I don't remove my hand from Liam's strong grasp. He hasn't left my side. Or maybe he has, and I didn't notice. I've been zoning in and out like I did at the cabin after I killed Max. The ghost-white wall across from me serves as the movie screen for the horrific replay of today.

The police were here with their annoying questions that I refused to answer, but thankfully they didn't ask too many once Declan's lawyers got involved. And the mayor and the district attorney and the captain of the PD. Seems like Mike, the doctor, isn't the only person in this city who's on Declan's payroll.

"Out," a Russian accent barks, and several men scramble out of the waiting room. The voice is Pearson's. "How is she?"

A rough hand cups my cheek, applying gentle pressure to turn my face. "*Bella*, look at me. Come back to me," Liam says, brushing away the tears I didn't know were still falling with swipes of his calloused thumbs. I'm shaking so badly, the chair rattles. Not from fear, but from rage.

Alejandro did this. The bullets were meant for me, but Declan shoved me out of the way and stepped in front of me. He saved me by sacrificing himself.

Lips kiss the corner of my mouth. "Alexandria."

"Don't call me that." How many times do I have to tell them not to call me by that fucking name?

The buzzing in my ears lessens, and my eyes focus on the room and the two men next to me.

"There she is," Liam says softly.

"Any news?" I ask Pearson.

"Still in surgery. Go home." Pearson, I'm finding out, is a man of few words.

I glare at the scary Russian. "No."

"It wasn't a yes or no question."

"I've got her." Liam lifts me in his arms and cradles me to him like a coveted possession. Like he's daring anyone to try and take me away from him.

"I don't want to leave him," I protest. My voice is so raw and hoarse, it sounds like I'm choking out shards of glass.

Liam's arms tighten around me, but I'm too numb and too spent to put up much of a fight. I think I'm going into shock. Everything is shutting down. I wish I could just crawl into the tub and feel my insides liquefy down the drain.

Pearson stands in front of us. This up close, he's even scarier. Not because of his scars or his bald head covered in tattoos, but because of the intensity in his eyes. Black, fathomless eyes that could suck your soul right out of your body.

"Go home and get some rest."

"I don't want to leave him!" I shout in his face.

Declan was shot just like Rafe. Just like Kellan.

I live in limbo every day with Kellan's ghost. What if I don't get a chance to say goodbye to Declan like I never got to say goodbye to Kellan? Those thoughts circle around me like a vulture waiting to pick the bones of my devastated heart.

"Declan is going to pull through," Pearson promises me. I want to believe him. So badly. "Repeat it, word for word. Say it back to me," Pearson insists, waiting for me to comply.

I shake my head no. I've been lied to my entire life by everyone. I'm not going to add myself to that long list.

"Liam is going to take you back home. If anything changes, you'll be the first call I make."

I flinch when his hand comes to my face, hovering briefly before he runs a finger down my cheek. "Declan would not want your tears. Never show your weakness, *Andie Levine*."

The way he emphasizes my name, Andie Levine. I *am* the

daughter of Declan Levine. The king of an empire. Ruthless. Strong. Cunning. But also a man who could love. He loved me. *Never show weakness*. But God help me, I *am* weak.

Pearson sees my struggle to control my emotions as the tears keep falling. "You will survive this, *little flame*," he says in Russian.

Chapter 8

KEANE

Something happened between the time Jax and I left this morning to go back to the Rossi estate to now, and if this motherfucker doesn't lower his gun, I'm going to break his hand. As soon as Jax and I entered Falcon Tower, we were swarmed by eight of Declan's men and had our weapons taken. Jax lost it when one of the guards tried to take his knife. Let's just say that there are now four men lying bloodied and unconscious on the floor, with three more sitting on top of an enraged Jax.

Jax is still lost in his blood rage from earlier, and these stupid assholes are making it worse.

"Stand down," Liam barks to the men as he hits the lobby and takes in the scene before him.

The guard next to me relaxes his stance and lowers his weapon.

"Jesus, feck, get the hell off him," Liam tells the other three men piled on top of Jax. He must be pissed because I've never heard his Irish accent so thick before.

Jax holds grudges, so as soon as he's able to stand, he punches one guy in the face, knees the other in the balls, and kicks the third.

A shrill whistle rings out. "Jax! Don't make me tase your ass. Both of you, come with me," Liam tells us, already walking off and returning to the bay of elevators.

As soon as the doors close, I tell him, "We found one of Julio's men."

"Fill me in later," Liam curtly replies.

The quiet dinging indicating each floor as we rise seems to get louder and louder in the silence of the lift. Thank God there isn't any crappy elevator music pumping out.

"Why were we greeted with guns in our faces? If Declan thinks he can back out of our agreement—"

"Declan was shot."

How can three words make this day go from bad to even worse?

"What happened? Why didn't anyone call us?"

A migraine starts throbbing like a jackhammer behind my eyes from the stress. I think Rafe had the right idea. This shit just isn't worth it anymore. Not if it means Andie will constantly be in harm's way. We've been lucky so far in this dangerous life that we lead, but luck only holds out for so long.

Jax shoves Liam back against the lift wall before I can do it myself, his face full of worry and anger. "Where's Andie?"

Liam doesn't put up a fight or try to push Jax away from him. "She's safe. But she's hurting. She's locked herself in her room and won't let us in."

"Then pick her damn lock," I shout at him. Stupid jackass.

Liam's eyes slice to me. "The drive-by was meant for her. Declan took the hit instead. He's still in surgery, and Andie went ballistic when Pearson made her leave the hospital and come back here."

It feels like he just tossed a grenade into my chest. Alejandro came after my woman. Again.

Jax explodes. "That motherfucker!" He punches the elevator wall, denting the panel in with each hit.

"Jax, calm the hell down. Focus on Andie. She needs you."

His fist stops mid-flight, and his chest rises and falls with effort as he tries to rein himself in.

Liam and I exchange looks. "What do you need us to do?" I ask him.

"Save our girl. She's hurting," he says as the doors open to Andie's floor.

I shove his shoulder to stop him from exiting. "We've got this."

I expect him to argue and am shocked when he doesn't.

Liam speaks to a few of the guards, letting them know to give me and Jax access to any floor, room, or whatever the hell else we want.

Jax immediately takes off down the hallway to Andie's room. If there's anyone that can help her, it's him. The two of them share a soul-deep connection that I hope one day I'll have with her. I'm not jealous of what Jax has with her. We each carry something in ourselves that fills a void in Andie. And as much as I dislike even thinking it, I can't ignore Liam's place in all of it. We're like Aristotle's four elements: earth, air, fire, and water. Or perhaps, we're more like the Four Horsemen of the Apocalypse, and Andie is the goddess who controls us. Whatever. I'm not making any sense. I need a drink.

Tessa is curled up on the sofa, quietly crying. She looks like shit.

"You okay?"

Sniffling, she wipes her nose on her shoulder. "No."

Tessa is such a tiny thing, physically, but her inner strength and her heart are fucking huge. As well as her big brain. The girl is smart like Jax.

"How do you do it? How do you keep your humanity, your soul... your morality?"

With sadness, I curl my thumbs around the belt loops of my trousers and try to let her down gently. "You don't."

She bites on her bottom lip, mulling that over. "If that were true, then you wouldn't be able to love her like you do. None of you would."

I consider the truth of that. See, like I said. Smart girl.

"If you're wondering how I know, it's clear as day." She pauses for a beat, nibbling her lip again. "Please don't hurt her."

That's a promise I can keep. "I won't. Not in the way you mean."

Because Andie and I will always fight. We'll argue. We'll

disagree on just about everything. We'll want to strangle one another on a daily basis. It's who we are. But we'll love each other just as fiercely. Just as passionately.

Liam drops down next to Tessa, and she takes the opportunity to dig her feet under his spread thighs.

"Your feet are fucking frigid."

She smiles at him, still sniffling. "Deal with it."

"Pearson will let us know when Declan is out of surgery or if anything changes." Liam tilts his head toward the hallway, his silent way of telling me to get my ass back there to Andie. But he doesn't need to say anything because I'm already walking away.

"Angel, open the damn door," Jax shouts, pounding on it with a fist.

"Anything?" I ask him.

"No. Stubborn fucking woman."

Andie should know better. Not even locked doors will keep us from getting to her.

"Step back and plant your ass here until I say otherwise," I tell him, right before I kick the door in.

Chapter 9

ANDIE

It's the constant chattering of my teeth that has me slowly coming back from wherever my fractured mind has taken me. No wonder I'm freezing, I think, as ice-cold water pelts me from the showerhead. How long have I been in here? My blue-tipped, pruned fingers and toes indicate that I must have been in here for a while.

You will survive this, little flame.

Will I, though?

My body is suddenly shocked with a scorching heat, the jarring sensation like thousands of sharp needles embedding into my skin. As I blink away the cloudy haze from my vision, bright hazel eyes come into focus.

"Keane?"

"I've got you, princess," he says softly, vigorously rubbing my arms and back with a thick towel, taking great care not to touch any injury or jostle my left hand.

He perches me atop the bathroom vanity counter. I'm shivering like mad as all my senses click back on, one by one. My first thought is that I feel like a human popsicle. My second thought is...

"How did you get in?"

A small smirk appears on his face. "Kicked your door in."

Typical.

Keane drapes a second towel over my shoulders, then begins rubbing my thighs and legs. Warmth spreads along my extremities as he switches back and forth from thighs to legs to arms to torso.

Once my trembling abates, he steps between my legs, gathers me in his arms, and holds me. It feels so good being in his arms. His lips nuzzle my wet hair, my neck, the sensitive patch of skin behind my ear. Everywhere he touches feels like I'm being electro-shocked back to life.

"I can't lose you." His voice cracks slightly, showing me a glimpse into the vulnerable part of him he never allows anyone to see. But I see it because he lets me.

Keane cradles my face, our cheeks brushing in a soft caress, like a kiss. Then our lips meet and linger, barely touching.

"Keane, I—"

His warm breath fans over my face when he hushes me. "Not yet," he says, the pads of his fingers beginning to roam, the blunt edges of his nails dragging tenderly down my spine. He splays his large hands across my shoulders and dips his head to lick a trail of open-mouthed kisses along my clavicle and between my breasts. My nipples instantly bead into hard points when he nuzzles each breast, and the valley between my legs slickens with instant arousal.

A moan catches in my throat when he takes a taut bud into his mouth, laving it with soft sucks and pulls with his tongue. He switches to the other breast and gives it the same attention.

Desire replaces the dark misery that had taken up residence inside me.

The next time Keane's lips reach mine, I open for him, the kiss he gives me, slow and deep and perfect. My uninjured hand grips the nape of his neck, keeping him close.

He pulls back slightly. A long, masculine finger tucks a few loose strands of my wet hair behind my ear, and then Keane pecks the tip of my nose. "Don't move."

Bending down, he reaches under the vanity and pulls out a hair dryer, plugging it into a nearby socket. Then, to my utter astonishment, Keane turns it on and begins to dry my hair. I swear, if I hadn't already acknowledged to myself that I was in love with him, this right here would have tipped the scales. I'm in love with four dangerous, ruthless men. Men who challenge me, but who also show me tenderness and seem to always know how to glue my fragmented pieces back together whenever I break apart.

My lashes flutter close when Keane tilts my head and runs his fingers through the damp mass, lifting it up to dry it better. After several minutes pass, he turns the dryer off and places it on the counter next to me.

"Thank you," I tell him.

"Anytime." He holds up a lock of my hair, bunching the ends between his thumb and middle finger. "Your hair is so soft," he says.

"I thought you said you hated it." At Kellan's cabin after they rescued me from the warehouse, Keane had commented that he disliked the new light brown color.

"I'm a lying asshole," he replies, and a small chuckle escapes me. "You'll always be beautiful to me, Andie."

Air rushes out of my lungs, and I drop my forehead to his chest.

Beautiful, even when broken. Isn't that what Jax said to me?

Keane bundles me in his arms, towels and all, and carries me out of the bathroom and over to the bed.

"Where is everyone?" I ask when he yanks back the goose down comforter and lays me on top of the satiny sheets.

"Waiting for you." He pauses and fans my hair out on the pillow. "Whenever you're ready. No rush."

"Has Pearson or the hospital called?"

He indicates no with the shake of his head.

In the darkened room, I watch as he sheds his clothes, revealing gorgeously inked arms and chest, and solid, muscled legs, until all that remains are a pair of black briefs that outline his thick erection. Keane climbs into the bed behind me, manipulating me like warmed clay until we're spooned together so tightly, not a millimeter of space remains. His strong arms lock around me, his head finding a home nestled in the crook of my shoulder, our bodies fitting perfectly together. Then we both sigh as the weight of the day begins to ease.

"I always feel safe with you," I whisper into the silence of the room.

The hard thump of his heartbeat pounds against my back. "I haven't done a good job of keeping you safe."

I reach around with my right hand and twine our fingers together. Keane throws a leg over me, anchoring me to him and the bed. Tears that I thought I couldn't cry anymore, raced down my cheeks. Oh God. I feel like I'm dying.

"Declan... he..."

You will survive this, little flame.

Keane kisses my neck, biting down on it. The brief pain stops me from freefalling back into that dark place of self-loathing and regret.

"Declan will pull through. You hear me?" He pinches my chin and angles my face toward him. "You asked me recently if I was ready to set the world on fire with you."

I nod.

"Then that's exactly what we're going to do. Do you trust me?"

I twist around in his firm embrace. His eyes are like twin green-brown infernos, hotter than the image he just painted with his words. Eyes that hold the truth to his statement, and for the first time since watching Declan being placed in the ambulance, hope surges through me.

"Yes," I answer because I do trust him. It's a hard concept for me—to trust anyone—after everything I've been through. But Keane has it. They all do. Even Rafe. "But I guess the more important question is: Do you trust *me*?"

"A hundred fucking percent," he replies. "Now, get some sleep. I promise to wake you if word comes in about Declan," Keane says, reverting back to his bossy ways. He kisses me lightly on the lips.

"Okay."

He's right. I'm no good to anyone as exhausted and heartsick as I am now. Declan needs me to be strong, and I need him to live.

Everything else will just have to fucking wait in the back of the line.

Just as I settle my head on Keane's chest and close my eyes, I feel Rafe's bracelet come undone and fall off my wrist. My injured hand hurts like a son of a bitch in the splint and wrappings Mike put on me.

"What are you doing?"

Keane slides his ring off his middle finger—the silver one with the snake design and small round rubies for eyes.

"Until we get yours back," he says, slipping the ring onto the bracelet, then reclasping it around my wrist.

I stare at the heavy ring dangling between the bead charms that spell out **Rafael + Alexandria**.

"I tried to stop him from taking them. I fought with everything I had. But it wasn't enough."

Keane kisses the bracelet, then kisses me. "You're so wrong, princess. You are more than enough. And the rings don't matter. They're just pieces of metal and stone."

"But they were your mother's." I cradle his cheek in my hand, my sorrow over not protecting something that was so important to him evident.

He kisses me again. "They don't matter. You do."

God, this man.

Snuggling into him, I force my tight muscles to relax.

"I want one," I tell him, my good hand smoothing over the tattoo on his back of the fire phoenix rising from the pits of hell.

"One what?" he asks when my forefinger traces the letters of the words Rafe designed, even though I can't see them.

"Your mark. The one you, Jax, and Rafe have," I reply.

Death is only the beginning.

"My savage little princess," he says against my hair, and I finally succumb to a restless sleep.

Chapter 10

ANDIE

Nearby voices filter through the sleep fog clouding my brain, but that's not what wakes me up. It's the orgasm I'm about to have, caused by the tongue stud flicking rapidly over my clit.

Like getting twelve shots of espresso mainlined into my bloodstream, I jerk wide awake just when Jax's teeth bite down on my swollen nub, and I come. And *holy shit*, do I come. With thighs clamped tightly around his head and my loud, guttural moans filling the room, I detonate like a fucking supernova.

Before I can catch my breath, Jax crawls up my body and slides his steel-hard cock inside me; the stretch of his sudden invasion wipes away any lingering drowsiness I had.

"I missed you," I tell him, happiness to see my Grim Reaper making me lightheaded.

Jax stills, hovering over me, his sea-green eyes glossy with tears behind his glasses. "Please don't ever leave me again."

Worried, I trace his full, gorgeous lips. The raw emotions spewing out of him are like a punch to the stomach.

"Never," I promise him, wanting to remove the haunted, lost look on his face.

Out of the four of them, Jax may be the crazy one with a lust for blood, but he's also the one who wears his feelings for me like an open wound. I used to be scared of him, never able to get a read on him with his unemotive gaze, passive, stony façade, and wicked intelligence that could see right through me. But I haven't felt that way since the second day at Kellan's cabin after we had that fight in the kitchen when I leaped over the counter island and started choking him. Pain has always been our foreplay.

Jax scans my bruised face until finally landing on my splinted left hand resting on the pillow at my head.

I pull his mouth down so I can kiss him, craving the taste of me on his lips, but Jax resists, and I growl. His cock is pulsating inside me, driving me out of my freaking mind, and I need to come again. So fucking badly. Having him on top of me, inside me, and not moving a muscle is torture.

My legs wrap around his lean waist, my feet pressed flat to the back of his thighs, trying to pull him closer. Still, he resists.

"Are you going to fuck me?"

His lopsided, boyish smile steals the air from my lungs.

"Eventually."

The voices I had heard earlier have stopped.

"Told you he wouldn't be able to resist dicking her while she was unconscious," Liam quips. "Pay up."

"Jax, you fucking reprobate, you just cost me a hundred dollars," Keane grouses, and I can't hold back my giggle any longer.

It feels weird to be laughing right now, with all the horrible shit going on.

Liam walks over and goes down to his haunches at the side of the bed next to me. "How are you feeling, *bella*?" he asks, like Jax isn't there on top of me, his bare ass up in the air, and his dick shoved up my pussy.

"Hungry," is the first thing that pops out of my mouth.

Liam grins when Jax dips down and sucks on my neck, and I gasp.

"I bet," Liam insinuates and kisses me lightly on the lips. "Be right back."

My hand snatches his wrist. "Any news?"

"No, baby. But it's only been a couple of hours." He kisses the underside of my wrist, then walks out, closing the broken door—that Keane kicked in—behind him as best as he can.

Keane makes a home on the other side of me and Jax, stretching out his long legs and getting comfortable. "She come yet?"

"*She's* right here," I tell him.

"Once," Jax replies and finally starts to move—carefully, gently, taking care not to aggravate my injuries.

It's not going to take long for me to fall into the bliss of a second orgasm, especially with Keane watching.

Keane strokes my hair. "I think she's ready for a second." He shifts down on the mattress until he's lying on his side, his breath in my ear. "Fucking magnificent. I love watching you come undone on Jax's cock." His dirty words have me practically panting.

Keane's hand heats my skin as it snakes down my stomach. His thumb reaches my already sensitive clit. He gathers the wetness from where Jax and I are connected, not fazing Jax in the least that he's touching his dick in the process.

As he swirls small circles over my clit, every ache and pain I'd been feeling melts away until there is nothing left but Keane and Jax and the pleasure they're giving me. My head lolls to the side to meet Keane's kiss, and he swallows the tiny mewl I emit when Jax's mouth suckles my breast. His tongue-ring rasps my nipple and sends little electric shocks straight to my pussy. *So good. So damn good.*

This time when I come, it's not in an explosion, but in gentle waves like the rolling surface of the ocean on a calm day. I'm floating, existing in an out-of-body experience of absolute heaven.

Jax pulls out and cuddles behind me while Keane continues to capture my sated sighs with his tongue. It's then I realize that Jax didn't come inside me, his cock still hard against my ass as he spoons me.

Keane must sense my frown. "Did we hurt you?" he asks, worry filling his scruffy, handsome face.

"No, but Jax didn't—"

"Not about me, Angel," Jax says, his lips on my neck. "Just

wanted to make you feel good."

Well, damn. I think my heart actually flipped a somersault at that.

Liam walks back in carrying a tray loaded with food and four coffees. Seeing four mugs and not five has me inquiring, "Where's Rafe?"

Placing the tray down on the bench next to the foot of the bed, Liam waits while Jax and Keane help me get upright into a sitting position, albeit with difficulty because my muscles have taken a double-orgasm vacation.

Jax gets off the bed and grabs his sweatpants from the floor, shucking them on, but it does nothing to hide the giant bulge he's still sporting. The memes about guys and gray sweatpants are spot on. It's absurd how fucking sexy they are.

"Knocked out and fast asleep in the room next to us. His wound started bleeding again, so Pearson dosed him good to ensure he wouldn't try and get out of bed again to get to you," Liam replies, handing me the steaming coffee, his gaze traveling down from my face to my naked tits. He licks his lips. "Tessa was about to barge in, and I told her you were... occupied at the moment." His cocky smirk has me rolling my eyes.

Sipping from my mug, I relish the burn of the scalding liquid on my tongue. No doubt I'm going to get an earful from her later. The guys gather around me on the bed and dig into the sandwiches Liam made. I get offered bites of different sandwiches between my sips of coffee. Watching these men pander to my well-being is ridiculously endearing. However, I soon become weary of how they're blatantly ignoring the giant-sized elephant in the room.

"I want to go back to the hospital."

I want to be there when Declan comes out of surgery. I want to be the first person he sees when he opens his eyes. I want to tell him how proud I am that he's my dad. I want to tell him so many things I regret not saying sooner. Like, how in just a few days with him felt like a lifetime of love. Something I never had with Max or Cecelia, but something Declan gave to me so freely, along with his acceptance and understanding.

Liam is quick with a "No."

"It's not your damn decision, Liam! Shit!" I shout, hot coffee spilling over onto the sheet across my waist. Keane takes the mug out of my hand and away from my reach.

"It's not yours either, *bella*. It's Pearson's."

My mouth clamps shut as anger mixes with my grief. "Then tell him—"

Liam cuts me off. "No."

Jax lifts me into his lap and wraps me in his arms. "We'll make sure you get to say goodbye if it comes to that."

That's what he assumes my outburst is about. Not being able to say goodbye. Max wouldn't let me attend Kellan's funeral. I never got closure over my brother's death. I never got to say goodbye. Maybe that's why my brother's ghost still haunts me.

Declan would be ashamed of me right now. Hiding in my bedroom, crying and worrying. That's what the old Alexandria would do. She was weak. Powerless. Pathetic. Useless. I swore to myself that I would never be her again.

Declan doesn't need old Alexandria. He needs Andie. He needs payback. And I'm going to be the daughter to give it to him.

I had once made the metaphor about my plan for revenge being a game of chess. Each player crucial, and each move carefully planned. Fuck that shit. This is no longer a game being played with Alejandro and Julio. It's no longer a war. It's time to bring forth fucking Armageddon.

Getting out of bed, I walk over to the adjoining bathroom. "Give me ten. I need to get cleaned up."

I don't wait for a reply or an acknowledgment. I go inside the bathroom and shut the door.

Chapter 11

ANDIE

With my right hand, I smear a clear path through the condensation of the bathroom mirror and stare at my blurry reflection. Even though I told the guys to give me a few minutes, they still hovered. I could hear their voices through the bathroom door. I know their concern comes from a good place, but it's not what I need right now. I don't need coddling or sweet words said to make me feel better. I don't need to lose myself in the euphoria of hot, wild, toe-curling sex. What I need to do is get my shit together. I will not shed another damn tear, so help me God. I will not allow my fears to stop me from doing what needs to be done. My smile will be wicked and fierce when I bathe in the blood of Alejandro and Julio. It's time to release my chaos and end this. But not as Alexandria McCarthy.

"I'm Andie Donatella *motherfucking* Levine," I declare in the mirror.

I rip off the water-logged wrapping and splint from my broken finger and toss them into the nearby trash bin. The swelling has gone down some, leaving behind ugly black and purple bruising. It's difficult bending the digit, and I hiss as pain explodes and travels up from my fingertip to my wrist. Fuck it. I'll just have to ignore the throbbing agony and hope that I don't irreparably damage my finger to the point where a good hand surgeon can't fix it. A fighter needs both fists to break their opponent.

Ignoring the other bruises, both old ones and new ones that litter my pale skin from head to toe, I get to work. Time to put on my war paint. Grabbing the makeup kit Tessa got for me, I slather on face lotion and eye cream, followed by foundation and under-eye concealer, making sure to pay special attention to where the bruises and cuts are. I can't do much about the swollen cheek or lip.

Next, I line my eyes with black kohl and add dark eye shadow, enhancing the violet color of my irises, making them pop. Black mascara coats each eyelash, and a rose blush sweeps up both cheeks. I leave my lips for last and turn them a dark scarlet red with my favorite Pretty Poison lipstick.

Picking up the blow dryer Keane left out on the counter, I artfully dry my hair, leaving it down and flowing around my shoulders in its natural waves. Satisfied with my appearance, I walk into the bedroom and into the closet. My fingers flick through the clothes Pearson procured for me and stop on a body-hugging deep red corset top and black leather pants that are soft and flexible. I study the selection of shoes before choosing a low-heeled black ankle boot. With care because I still hurt every-fucking-where, I finish getting dressed, shove Jax's knife into my ankle holster, and make sure Rafe's bracelet with Keane's ring is secured to my wrist.

Time to get to work.

Stepping out into the hallway, I hesitate for a second outside the door to the room next to mine, wondering if Rafe is awake. Deciding not to disturb him, I walk down the hallway toward the living area. I can already hear Liam and Keane arguing, and smile. Nothing with these guys will ever be easy, but I wouldn't want it any other way. Only things worth having are worth fighting for.

As soon as I enter the room, conversation stops, and all heads turn my way.

"Fuck me," Liam, Keane, and Jax say at the same time when they see me—and sweet Jesus, the hungry eye-fucking I'm getting from all three guys sends a wild shudder through me.

Tessa's whistle is loud and shrill. "*Damn*, girl."

But I ignore them because my sights lock on the enormous

Russian standing across the room.

"Why aren't you at the hospital?" He was supposed to call me when Declan came out of surgery.

His eyes drop briefly before he raises them again, and it feels like he just shoved his hand inside my chest and fisted my heart.

Be strong. No matter what he says.

Switching to Russian, I implore, "Tell me."

"He made it out of surgery, but there were complications."

My world crashes in around me just as profound relief hits me. Declan's alive.

"What complications?"

"When the fuck did you learn how to speak Russian?" Keane says from his corner of the couch.

"Whatever it is they're talking about, stay out of it," Liam warns him.

"He took four bullets. One lodged in his left lung. Two went through muscle tissue. But a fourth nicked a major artery. He coded during surgery. The doctors were able to bring him back. He's in ICU now." Pearson rattles off the information robotically, but it's his eyes that give him away. So much emotion, pain... and love. It should shock me, but it doesn't.

"How long have you been in love with him?"

Pearson doesn't even hesitate. "Declan and I have been lovers for a while. Twenty years."

"That's how old I am," I mumble to myself.

It helps bring me some peace to know that Declan got to experience real love, something that is so rare to have and so difficult to keep in this violent, fucked-up life we're forced to live in.

I close the distance to Pearson. Jax is silently watching us in his usual calculating, stony way, but I see the tension coiled in his body. If he thinks Pearson is a potential threat to me, he'll kill him without a second's thought.

"I'm happy he had you all these years. That he wasn't alone."

Pearson's midnight black gaze holds me prisoner. I'm standing only a foot from him now. This close, I can see every scar, cut, and tattoo on his face and bald head. This man has lived a very hard, painful life, yet still has gentleness inside of him. I recall all the meals he cooked for me and Declan, but ones he never ate with us; the clothes he picked out for me to have after I arrived here. Pearson was always behind the scenes, taking care of Declan. And me.

He reaches up, his gargantuan hand grazing the side of my face, and I stop myself from flinching when he caresses where Alejandro punched me.

"Don't fucking touch her," Jax seethes, rushing forward, but is blocked by Liam.

"I'm okay, Jax," I assure him.

"You look so much like him," Pearson murmurs in his thick accent.

The compliment settles deep in my chest.

"I'm so sorry," I tell him, still speaking in his native language. "Everything that has happened is because of me."

His hand drops away. "You do not need to apologize, nor do you need to feel any guilt about what happened. You're his daughter. His flesh and blood. He loves you deeply and would sacrifice anything to keep you safe."

"I don't deserve it." My chin dips to my chest in shame, but Pearson lifts it back up with his finger.

"You are his, Andie, deserving of everything he could give you. He'll pull through and come back to us." Pearson reaches down and lifts my right hand. "There was a minute after he came out of surgery when he was cogent. He wanted me to give you something." Pearson places a heavy men's ring in my hand.

"Pearson, what are you doing?" Liam demands, clearly not happy.

I look at the piece of jewelry in confusion. It's Declan's, the one he wore on his forefinger to show his affiliation. My fingers curl around the unusual ring. Something with intricate symbols carved into the metal surrounding a blood-red ruby, much like the smaller rubies in the ring Keane put on my bracelet.

"We're clearly missing something, so why don't you fill us in?"

Keane demands, but Liam is too busy cursing a blue streak.

"Are you out of your fecking mind? She's not ready!" Liam shouts at Pearson.

"Declan thought otherwise," Pearson replies in English.

"Declan isn't thinking properly. He just had major surgery!"

I round on Liam. "Why are you freaking out?"

"What the hell is all the shouting about? Quiet the fuck down," Rafe grouches as he hobbles into the room.

He looks awful. Hair a mess, purple bruises under his eyes, and he's swaying slightly, more likely from the cocktail of painkillers they've been feeding him.

I immediately go to his side and wrap my arm around his waist, encouraging him to lean on me.

"You shouldn't be out of bed."

Rafe's hand goes to my hair, and he fists it. "I'm never leaving your side again," he declares and pulls my head back, kissing the daylights out of me.

Any coherent thought I had flies right out of my brain. I've missed this man's kisses. How they make me melt while also sending me on a high at the same time.

"And you look fuck-hot," he adds, giving me one last, lingering kiss. I tamp down the lust suddenly flowing through my veins because now is not the time.

An arm wraps around me from behind and pulls me away from Rafe. "Sit your ass down before you pass out," Jax says, gripping a possessive hand on my hip.

Rafe looks down at Jax's hand and back up to me, a question in the way his eyebrow jacks up. *Shit.* I haven't had time to talk to him yet about what happened at the house with Keane, Jax, and Liam because he's been doped up and sleeping the majority of the time. I don't even know if Rafe has figured out that Jax and I had already slept together the night I found out who Sarah was.

Arguments erupt around me, coming from my four men. Tessa looks on with her mouth gaping open, and Pearson stands silently waiting.

I yell, "Will everyone shut the hell up?"

Turning to Rafe, I point at the couch. "Sit. You and I will talk later. I promise I'll explain everything." I turn around and face Jax, cradling his face in my palms, hoping my touch will help calm whatever darkness is lurking inside him. "Yours," I remind him, readjusting his glasses, and he releases a pent-up breath.

Next, I meet Keane's scowl, and our stare-off quickly ends when he gives me a small chin lift and sits down. Lastly, I face Liam.

"What am I not ready for?"

"That ring and all it entails," he says, his face turning as hard as the timbre of his voice.

"Explain."

Pearson motions for me to sit, and I take the seat next to Tessa.

She leans over and whispers, "This feels like some heavy *Lord of the Rings* shit. If you start calling that thing 'my precious,' I'm out of here."

I try not to laugh, but she makes it difficult.

Pearson shoves Liam into the armchair and keeps a hand on his shoulder to hold him in place. "That ring which is now yours is the Levin crest. It signifies your position as the head of the family."

Declan explained how Levin became Levine due to a clerk error when his grandfather immigrated from Ireland.

"I can't take Declan's place," I reply incredulously with a huge amount of 'holy shit' infused as well.

"With Declan out of commission for the foreseeable future, the business doesn't stop and needs someone at the helm. The men are at your command. You are now the queen of an empire," he states bluntly, and fuck me, I was not expecting this.

To say everyone else in the room, except for Liam, are stunned silent would be an understatement. Declan wants me to take over his organization? Pearson or Liam would be better suited. My heart starts hammering as what Pearson says sinks in. Holy fucking shit.

"Why can't you handle things?" I ask Pearson, desperate for

him to throw me a lifeline.

"You're his daughter. The rightful heir."

I close my eyes, my father's ring burning my hand as I hold it in a death grip. I don't want this kind of power. I've seen firsthand how power corrupts and warps. How someone can use it to do horrific things. But I've also seen how someone can use it for good. Declan may have been a killer, but he was fair in the punishment he dealt to those who deserved it. He was the opposite of Max.

Keane is like Declan. Circumstances put him at the head of the Rossi syndicate, but he wields his newfound power with diplomacy and fairness. Can I do that? Or will my quest for vengeance turn me into someone Declan would be ashamed of? How am I even worthy of this responsibility?

"I... I don't... can I have a minute?" I finally get out, feeling the weight of the world suddenly fall upon my shoulders.

Tessa goes to help Rafe stand up, but I still her hand. "I'd like Keane, Jax, and Rafe to stay."

The hurt on Liam's face when I don't include him squeezes my rapidly beating heart.

Pearson waits for Liam and Tessa to leave before he says to me, "When you're ready, we'll meet with the men. They are expecting blood for what happened. I know you won't disappoint them, *little flame*."

Curious, I inquire, "Why do you call me that?"

A smile breaks through the crevices of his face and stretches the raised scar that runs down his cheek to his jaw. "'*The phoenix hope, can wing her way through the desert skies, and still defying fortune's spite; revive from ashes and rise.*' Miguel de Cervantes."

"That's very poetic."

"It's also very true," he replies.

Okay. I can do this. Declan wants me to do this.

"Are you going to stop me from going to see him at the hospital?"

"No."

"I want men stationed outside his room, and only doctors and nurses we vet are allowed to treat him. No one gets in to see him without our approval."

"Already took care of that."

Of course he did. Pearson knows how to handle this type of situation. I'm going to need to rely on his guidance to help me navigate my way through this new reality.

"One last thing, Pearson. I want as many men as we can spare scouring the city for Alejandro and the person or persons who shot my father. Scorched earth style."

Pearson gives me an approving nod.

"What the fuck was that all about?" Keane asks as soon as he hears the elevator doors close, signaling Pearson's departure. The guys don't know what was said because Pearson and I conversed in Russian the entire time. They only saw Liam's reaction to Pearson giving me the ring.

Guessing correctly, Rafe solemnly explains, anguish coating his words. "That was Pearson handing over the throne to the Levine empire to Andie. She's now in charge."

Keane and Jax get deadly quiet, and Jax's handsome face falls. It breaks my heart.

"Andie, for fuck's sake, no," Keane implores and grabs me in his arms, pulling me to him and holding me tight.

I hold him just as fiercely. This is a gamechanger. A new, unexpected twist in this fucked-up dance we're toeing. And I will not lose. Declan chose me for a reason. I owe him. And I will not fail him.

Against the muscled column of Keane's neck, I breathe him in and gather my resolve. "I need you with me on this. I don't want to do this alone."

Keane grips the sides of my face and roughly attacks my mouth with a soul-curling, panty-soaking kiss that has me clinging to his arms as my knees go weak.

"We're not going any-fucking-where."

I want them with me, by my side, every step of the way. But that may not be possible.

With Keane now in control of the Rossis, Riccis, and Barones, his plate is full. He and Jax shouldn't even be here with me. They need to start restructuring, solidifying alliances and weeding out weak links. One thing that's a constant in this life is that there will always be someone in the shadows wanting to take what's yours. Keane will have to deal with a lot of blowback for what he did. You can't just take out a don of a family, put yourself in that position, and not expect retaliation.

"As much as I want you and Jax here twenty-four-seven, you also have other responsibilities that need your attention. You can't look weak or uninvested. Keane, you of all people should know how precarious a time it is when there's a power restructure. You saw it happen when we were kids and Max pushed my grandfather out and took over."

Grandfather slips out before I can stop myself. It's been difficult to remember that the people I grew up with are not my real family.

"Dante has it covered."

Why does he have to be such a stubborn ass all the time?

"Dante isn't the Rossi don. *You* are."

"Jax and I are exactly where we need to be, princess." He stops my further protests by kissing me.

Rafe makes an angry growl. "I think it's time for someone to explain why everyone has been shoving their tongues down my woman's throat," he coldly states, grunting with effort as he leans forward, elbows to knees, with fists clenched in front of him.

"She's not your woman." Jax sends Rafe a deadly smirk, flipping his knife over and under his fingers. "She's ours."

Chapter 12

RAFE

She's ours?

I knew it. I fucking knew he and Keane wanted her. That's why I claimed her first. Kissed her first. Made love to her first. Then that night with Max happened, and she was taken from me. Because I wasn't strong enough to protect her. I'm still not. I've got a bullet wound in my chest that proves it.

I can't help the upwelling of anger at my two best friends that suddenly erupts like a firestorm.

"You've got to be fucking kidding me."

"Hey, watch your mouth," Keane says, which is seriously asinine since every third word that comes out of his mouth is fuck.

I helplessly watch him turn Andie around until she and I are facing one another, and I want so badly to throat punch him when he curls his hand around her hip and pulls her back to his chest, kissing her neck as a direct challenge to me. My jaw locks, teeth clenched, when her violet eyes cloud with arousal. My dick wars with my emotions, clearly on board with what I'm witnessing since it hardens against my permission. Seeing Andie in another man's arms, albeit one of my blood brothers, shouldn't turn me on, but fuck me if it doesn't.

"Keane, not now," Andie tells him, but she doesn't pull away.

Jax moves in front of her and to the side, giving me a clear view of his hand sliding under the waistband of her tight leather pants. That outfit she's wearing is lethal. Tight leather that hugs every toned, muscled, and curvaceous inch of her bottom half. A sexy red halter encasing her gorgeous tits. The sight of her draped between my two friends, ruby-stained mouth parted as Keane delivers another nip to her neck. Her hair a sexed-up mess. All of it will live in my spank bank for the rest of my life.

"I think now is the perfect time," Jax replies.

I know the moment he slides a finger inside her because her head falls back onto Keane's shoulder, a delicious moan coming out of her mouth in the form of Jax's name. My cock jerks eagerly behind my sweatpants.

Those moans used to belong to only me.

Her breath hitches, and she sighs when Keane bites behind her ear.

"Rafe deserves to know where we stand," she weakly protests.

"Princess," he whispers across the soft skin of her shoulder as we glare at each other, "he knows."

I helplessly watch Jax's hand move behind the tight leather of Andie's trousers, and her soft, breathy pants increase. Her hips raise, seeking more of what his fingers are giving, and a noticeable tremor shakes her body.

"Like I said—she's ours," he says, slowly removing his hand.

Andie makes a disappointed whimper, but then moans loudly when he sticks his fingers in her mouth and commands her to suck them clean.

It's clear as fucking day that the three of them have been together, and I rack my brain to figure out when. How did I miss the signs?

Jax removes his fingers from her mouth, then licks a path up the curve of her throat. Andie smiles at him, brushing fingertips over his lips and cheek. *Jesus.* How can I be so angry and so turned on at the same time?

"You're going to finish what you started, Reaper," Andie tells him, and he smiles devilishly at her. Jax never smiles. When the hell did he start smiling?

"Always, Angel." He wrenches her from Keane and sits with her in his lap on the armchair across from me.

Her face flushes, and she can't meet my intense stare when his possessive hands splay around her middle; one resting across her stomach and the other on her thigh.

"Andie, look at me." She eventually does, and the pleading for understanding coming from her is palpable.

But it's the vulnerable expression on her face that gives her away. It's a mien I know all too well because it's how she used to look at me when I made love to her. Shit, this is really happening. She's in love with them. I can see it with my own damn eyes. I've lost her. She's not mine anymore. *It's your own fucking fault.*

"Andie wants to talk, so let's talk," Keane says, sitting down next to me on the couch.

I thrust shaky hands through my hair, giving the strands a good pull in frustration. "Someone get me a drink first. Preferably vodka. The entire bottle," I say.

Huffing like a diva, Keane reluctantly gets up and goes into the adjoining kitchen. I have a feeling that I'm going to need it to get me through the conversation we're about to have.

Wanting something else to distract me from the visage of Jax holding Andie and the heart-breaking revelation I just came to, my attention bounces around the room. This is all Andie's now. The entire building, actually, and all the men in it. The helicopter. The private jets. The palatial homes scattered across the globe. The money. The control. The power. She's now become the most dangerous woman in the world. She kind of already was, if I'm to be honest. The girl I'll never stop loving changed over the five years we were apart.

How could so much have happened in such a short amount of time? Lies, betrayal, blood, death. I'd wanted out of this miserable life so badly. Take Andie with me and run away somewhere to a place Max and my father could never find us. Be happy for once in my fucking life with the woman who has owned me completely since the moment I saw her. But bad shit keeps happening and people keep erecting roadblocks in that path. And now this. There's no way I can compete with *this*, I helplessly surmise, finishing my perusal of the room and the men in it. Men who are my brothers.

A half-empty bottle of Irish vodka drops in my lap when Keane comes back. I'm tempted to ask Jax for one of the joints I know he always carries, but don't when an image of my mother's frothing mouth and limp, emaciated body pops in my head. Technically, I know I'm being hypocritical because alcohol is a drug, but it's the only one I'm comfortable with. Alcohol didn't kill my mother.

Removing the cap, I take two large swallows and shudder as the burn races down my throat and settles warmth in my belly.

"You sharing that?" Keane asks, and I give him a deadly look.

"I think we're *sharing* quite a lot, don't you?" I take another swallow, refusing to pass him the bottle.

"You're such a bratty shit sometimes," he replies.

"I was planning to tell you." Andie's hands fidget in her lap, but it's what Jax is doing that pisses me off.

"I swear to God, if you don't stop molesting her in front of me, I'm going to shank you up the ass with this bottle."

"Sounds fun," he quips and cups Andie between her thighs.

"Jax, stop trying to rile him up," Andie huffs, full of annoyance. But then again, she doesn't do anything to remove his hand from her crotch.

He rolls his damn eyes, and it's so similar to what Andie does. Another small smile slips free when he kisses the side of her head and relents. "Fine."

What the hell alternate reality have I woken up to? Jax smiling and being playful. Keane and Andie in the same room without trying to kill one another.

Deciding that vodka isn't going to help after all, I shove it at Keane. "I guess this is it."

Andie leans forward on Jax's lap, her now golden-brown hair falling forward over her shoulders. I do miss her natural blonde, but only because it reminded me of sunshine whenever I looked at her. But the darker color looks good on her too and makes her light purple eyes stand out. Those eyes of hers are unique, remarkable, and rare, just like she is.

"What is?" she asks.

"Us."

She did warn me. Said she actually hated me and didn't trust me. What were her words? *I don't fuck guys I don't trust.* I don't blame her for any of what happened between us. The destruction of what we had is all on me because of the choices I was forced to make.

It's as if someone hooked a defibrillator to me and amped up the power to max when she replies, "It doesn't have to be."

"I can't share you, *rosa*." The words tumble out of my mouth before I can stop them, caused by a knee-jerk, jealous reaction.

I jump at Keane's loud bark of laughter. "That's what Liam said at first."

Perhaps the vodka is working after all because the room goes topsy-turvy for a second. "You're fucking Liam?" I shout at her.

Her pale skin flushes red, but her chin juts stubbornly. "Liam and I met in Switzerland over a year ago. Years after we ended. You don't get an opinion about that."

And the plot thickens. I had no clue the two of them already knew one another. Liam has a damn good poker face for me not to pick up on it. I'm usually able to read people better.

"And you're both okay with it?" I ask Keane and Jax in utter disbelief.

Jax's arms tighten around Andie's waist like he's trying to shield her from the hurt of my question.

"I wasn't, until I was," Keane states cryptically. "In the end, it was an easy choice to make." Keane looks directly at Andie with such visceral want and desire, I'm surprised the room doesn't spontaneously combust into a ball of fire.

"I can't do this right now." Struggling, I lift myself off the couch, weaving a bit when I stand.

"Can't or won't?" Keane says.

"Keane, it's okay. Let him go," Andie tells him.

"Fuck that noise," he declares, standing up as well. He throws his arms wide. "You run away from every goddamn thing," he says in disgust. "Fight for what you want for once in your life!

You love her. You've always loved her."

"So have you! So has Jax!" I spit the hard truth back at him. Besides, it doesn't matter anymore if I love her. She chose them. Not me.

Andie sucks in a breath when Keane doesn't deny my accusation.

Great. Me and my big mouth. I can't listen anymore. It hurts too much.

I'm walking away when Andie quietly says, "You know damn well how I feel about you."

I turn my head and glare at her, my heart ripping open at seeing her in Jax's arms. "Yeah, I do. You said you hated my guts."

"You're a stupid, jealous man, Rafael Ortiz. There has never been a day since I was thirteen years old that I haven't loved you."

My feet refuse to move and stop me in my tracks. "What did you say?"

"You heard me," she sasses with her fuck-me lips I want desperately to kiss. "I'm not going to hide how I feel anymore." She takes a deep breath. "I lied."

"You lied?"

"Yes, I lied."

I suppress a grin when she throws eat-shit vibes at me and cross my arms over my chest like I have all day.

"About what?"

I need to hear her say it again. I need to be sure.

Growling, she replies, "I still love you. I never stopped."

"I—"

"I'm not finished," she says. Her hand tightens on Jax's arm. "I also love them."

The silence that hits the room is short-lived when Jax bites her on the neck like a rabid animal. "I want to fuck you so bad right now."

Andie's breath hitches when Jax turns her lips his way and devours her. His eyes remain open, and I can see the challenge in them. The dare he throws at me. And fuck me if I'm not hard as galvanized steel right now.

Keane tries to step around me to get to her, but I shove him back. "Don't."

I won't stand on the sidelines and watch my two best friends kiss and touch my woman. Be forced to watch as their hands cup her breasts. Their tongues delve into her mouth. Their fingers stroke her pussy through those skin-tight pants she's wearing. Marking her as theirs as her moans fill the room.

Something dark and primal inside me takes over. A gut-wrenching need to punish her for hurting me and punish them for touching what's mine. But underneath all the hurt is the desire to have her kiss me the way she's kissing Jax. Moaning for me like she used to as I fucked her under the stars at our favorite spot in the park.

"You still love me? Prove it."

Andie abruptly ends her kiss with Jax and gets up from his lap, flinging attitude at my ultimatum. They may say she's theirs, and she may say she loves them, but I *own* every part of her. Lips, pussy, and heart.

"On your knees, *rosa*."

Chapter 13

ANDIE

Jealous motherfucker.

I know exactly what he's doing, and the point he's trying to make. And as much as I want to drop-kick him where he stands, this messed-up tangle of a relationship between the five of us isn't going to work without compromise and reassurance. Each of my guys needs different things from me. Jax needs my reassurance and closeness, Keane my stubborn strength. Liam needs my attention and understanding. And Rafe? Right now, he needs me on my knees in supplication to prove to him that I'm still his. And he needs Keane and Jax to witness it. I get it. Doesn't mean I have to make it easy for him.

"Make me."

Those sky-blue eyes behind dark lashes turn black as his pupils expand, like an eclipse blotting out the midday sky.

Rafe takes a step toward me but stops, and I quirk a dark-blonde eyebrow at him. He matches it with one of his own, and I suppress the stupid grin from curving my lips. A small part of me is mad at him for all the shit he's pulled since I came back, but the bigger part—the part that still loves him and wants him—wins out over the hurt. Life is too short not to go after what I want. And I want them.

He glances at Keane, then at Jax, a silent message passing between the three of them. Keane's face hardens, but he stays back and folds his arms over his thick chest.

"Turn around," Rafe says, and I do, which puts me face-to-face with Jax.

He's white-knuckling the arms of the chair, and I can only assume it's because Rafe has taken control and he's being forced to watch.

Fingertips touch my back, stroking up the dip at my lumbar where the halter top doesn't cover. An explosion of tingles cascades over my flushed skin like popping embers. Rafe's hand moves to the back zipper of my pants. The click of the zipper teeth as he pulls the slider down has heat quickly building between my legs. Soft lips meet the nape of my neck, and my eyes briefly close at the contact as memories of the other times Rafe kissed me there come flooding back.

"Be careful with her left hand," Keane says.

Rafe glides his fingers over my shoulder and down my left arm, carefully lifting my hand. "Does it hurt?" he asks me with concern. He examines his bracelet with Keane's ring now dangling from it.

"Your fucking brother snapped her finger in four places. Of course it fucking hurts," Jax spits out.

Rafe pulls in a painful breath of air, gently pressing my injured hand to his cheek. I can tell the exact moment he changes his mind about what we're about to do and tries to step away from me.

Twisting around, I grab his forearm. "Don't." When his glassy eyes raise to search my face, I step closer. "Don't let him win. Alejandro has no place here."

Rafe rubs over the bruise on my face. "He hurt you. I should have been there to stop him."

Tapping a light finger above where he was shot, I say, "He hurt you too. He doesn't get to win. He doesn't get to have this," I emphasize, bringing his hand to splay over my heart.

With as much grace as I can, I peel the leather pants down my legs and kick them away, leaving my ass and pussy bare because I wasn't wearing any underwear. Then I shimmy out of my halter until I'm standing before him completely naked. Keane makes an appreciative noise at the sight of me, and it helps bolster my courage.

"I decide who to give my heart to," I tell Rafe and drop to my knees, pulling his sweatpants down as I go.

At the sight of his hard cock, my core throbs with eagerness. I remember every time Rafe and I were together. Every thrust of his narrow hips. Every orgasm he gifted me. I want to feel that again.

But instead of taking what I want, I sit back on my heels and wait. These men are the only ones I'll allow to see this side of me. Being on my knees for them isn't a sign of weakness. The opposite in fact. I may be giving him my submission, but that doesn't mean I've given up my power.

I tip my head up to see his hungry blue gaze devouring every inch of me. Whatever brief internal war he was having with himself, dies a sudden death as I kneel at his feet.

"You are such a damn gorgeous sight. *Te amo muchísimo, mi dolce rosa.*" He gathers my hair in his fist. "I don't deserve your heart. But I won't give it back."

"I don't want you to."

The air conditioning kicks in, causing my skin to gooseflesh and my nipples to harden. Anyone could step off the elevator now, walk around the corner, and see us. I couldn't care less.

I can see the second he finally makes a decision and fully gives in.

A cocky smirk appears. "Show them who you belong to."

Licking my lips, I curve my good hand around the base of his thick cock and give him one long lick from root to tip along the underside vein. Rafe moans, his girth thickening in my hand, so I do it again. I remember all his pleasure points, and I'm going to hit each one until he's begging for me to let him come.

"Again," he rasps, tightening his hold in my hair.

My hand starts to roam through his soft, curly pubic hair before I'm helpless to stop myself from nuzzling there with my nose and breathing in his masculine scent. I cup his balls, massaging them before moving to stroke my thumb over his slit. Precum seeps out, and I hum when I lap up his musky taste. I've missed him so much. I've missed this. The intimacy between us that used to be so easy. I want that back.

Opening to suck him deep, I do it slowly, torturing him and loving every curse word, grunt, and whisper of adoration he emits as I take him to the back of my throat and swallow, letting the muscles close around him like a vice.

"God, fuck, baby. So good."

I hum again so that he can feel the vibrations. I bob a few times to slick his shaft to make it easier for my tongue to glide over him. His hips jerk, wanting to fuck my mouth, but he's holding back because he thinks he's going to hurt me.

I release him with a pop, then nip along his inner thigh, nibbling across his tanned flesh. He has new tattoos I haven't seen before. Beautiful, thorned vines of red roses that wrap around his leg, the words, *Forever My Rose*, written around the petals of the largest flower. He did that for me. Just like Keane has the Tinker Bell tattoo on his lower calf. Jax also has a tattoo he got to represent me, one of an angel. I discovered it that night when he, Keane, and Liam purged my demons, making love to me all night long until no memory of Max remained.

Tracing the roses with my finger, I kiss the design, my hand snaking around to palm his ass. "I love this," I tell him. "I love *you*, Rafael. No more fighting or denying how I feel. Now please stop holding back and fuck me."

My teeth graze the tip of his dick, and he succumbs to the fire between us. In one second flat, he rips his T-shirt over his head, steps out of his sweats that have pooled at his feet, and I'm suddenly lifted off the floor and into his arms.

"Rafe, stop. Your bandage," I try to protest because he could tear his stitches again.

My concerns are silenced by his mouth that crushes mine in a brutal, tongue-lashing kiss that steals all my thoughts and has my clit pulsing in expectation of what's to come. Being back in his arms feels overwhelming, and I hold on for dear life as he carries me across the room.

All too soon, my feet hit the cold wood floor, and I gasp when

I'm pushed up against the wall of windows that overlooks the city. The chilled glass shocks my overheated skin, my breasts flattening on the smooth surface, and circles of condensation form from my ragged breaths.

"I want everyone to see that you're mine," Rafe growls at my back, roughly palming my ass as his front collides into me. Those clever hands mold to my curves, one reaching under to slide a finger through the wetness trickling down my thighs. His finger enters me, and my hips buck backward, needing more. Craving his touch.

"Has Keane touched you here?" he croons, adding a second finger.

"Y-yes."

Rafe drags his thumb over my swollen, needy clit and taps it brusquely. I feel it like a drumbeat reverberating throughout my entire body.

"Has Jax fucked you with his tongue, tasting how sweet you are?" he says, licking up my spine, his cock prodding between my legs which are now shaking and are barely holding me upright.

My thighs clench together. An image of Jax waking me up earlier with his head buried between my legs has me moaning out a yes. Rafe slaps my pussy in punishment, but all it does is make me wetter and hungrier for him.

Rafe sucks on the sensitive skin at my shoulder right above where Jax bit me, marking me with a bruise I know I'll see later. Dragging his hand up along the curve of my hip, he circles around to play with the thin chains of my belly button ring, before dropping lower to roughly thrust his fingers inside me once again. But this time, he doesn't stop as he brutally invades my tight channel, three fingers deep. My hands slap on the glass to hold me in place as his hand pummels me to a quick, screaming orgasm.

Just as I'm about to explode into a thousand, glorious pieces, Rafe pulls out and thrusts his cock into me. And I fucking shatter.

"Rafe, fuck!" The sudden intrusion and stretch mixes pleasure with pain, an aphrodisiac that I can't deny I'm now addicted to. Jax was the first to show me how enticing pain can be with sex when it comes from a place of love, not cruelty.

"I'm never letting you go again. Never," he declares, fisting my hair and wrenching my head back.

Our kiss is desperate and sloppy as the force of his thrusts knock my feet off the floor. One of his hands grips my hip to hold me steady, while the other wedges between my breast and the window, pinching my nipple. I want to turn around so I can touch him, my fingers longing to reacquaint themselves with every smooth, defined ripple of muscle of his chest and abs. His breathing becomes shallow and harsh, and I know it must be taking every bit of strength he has to fuck me right now. He's still weak and recovering from his injury.

"Baby, I can't hold off. I want you to come again," he grunts out.

"I'm close."

"Not close enough." And then he surprises the hell out of me when he calls for Jax and Keane.

Words are not spoken as I'm pulled away from the window. Jax positions himself underneath me and Rafe, sliding his tall, lithe form between our legs. Keane stands in front of me, his sinful smirk irresistible. I grab him and pull him to me, our tongues tangling wildly. Keane fondles and manipulates my breasts, catching the keening cry I make when Jax's mouth latches on my clit and sucks hard.

"*Fuckfuckfuck*," Rafe shouts, his cock swelling and pulsing, stretching me even more.

Keane breaks our kiss. "Scream his name, princess." His lips move down my chest and take a nipple, flicking it over and over. Jax's tongue stud batters me like a hammer, and it's all too much.

"Rafe!" I shout, every muscle locking and trembling at the same time.

My orgasm triggers his, and he releases everything in me as he comes. All I can think, as my sated body collapses forward into Keane's awaiting arms, is that the final, missing piece to what was once my empty, broken heart—the last piece that belonged to Rafe—has found its way back and snapped into place.

Jax stands up and licks his lips clean, grinning like an idiot. "Never tried it like that before."

Red, hot envy overcomes me at the reminder that he, Keane, and Rafe have fucked other women. Shared other women. The blonde from the bar comes to mind; the one Rafe disappeared with into the back hall the night I saw the guys again for the first time in five years. I recall the moony way Meribella looked at him. And as much as I want to ask Rafe if he ever fucked Rita, I'm not going to. That's something I'll be happy never knowing. Ignorance is bliss. And it's not like I was celibate during those five years. While at school, I had a few casual hookups with nameless men. And I had one glorious, passion-filled night with Liam in Geneva.

Rafe stumbles away from me and drops on his ass, his back hitting the floor and his chest heaving in air.

"You okay?" Keane asks him as he holds me steady.

"Fucking bullet wound and the meds," he replies. "Just give me a sec."

Shrugging out of Keane's arms, I hastily pick up my clothes off the floor. Rafe's cum is sliding down my legs, but I don't give a shit. I need some time to process and get my thoughts under control.

I'm stopped by a hand on my hip just as a wet paper towel swipes up my inner thigh.

"Thanks," I tell Jax as he gently cleans me.

The grin he was wearing falls when he catches the look on my face. He could always see right through me. It's one of the reasons why I was so wary of him.

"They never mattered," he says quietly.

I pull my halter down over my breasts. "I know that," I snip, then blow out a sigh.

Because I do know it. Deep down I do. Just as I know what we have together is so much more, even if it is unconventional. But it doesn't stop the pesky questions from forming in my mind.

What if I'm not enough? What if they meet someone else and want them more than they want me? Am I just being completely delusional thinking I can keep four men all to myself?

Or am I just setting myself up again for more heartbreak? Destined to live in a world where I don't belong. Alone, like I've always been.

Chapter 14

ANDIE

After asking Tessa to pull up the live camera feed, I finally locate Liam in the gym on the floor two levels below mine. I'm going to have to get Pearson to give me a crash course on the layout of Falcon Tower, all exits and entryways, what each floor is used for, and what's behind every door. There's so much I have to learn—real quick. Why Declan thought I was ready for this...

As soon as I step out of the elevator, I hear Liam's loud grunts. I find him punching the shit out of a heavy bag hanging from the ceiling. He's shirtless, sweat dripping off curled strands of his dark brown hair. His muscles bulge and flex with each forward punch and uppercut of his arms and every shift of his legs as he switches positions. I've had four orgasms so far since waking up today, but fuck me if my clit isn't pulsing like the greedy whore it is as my eyes trail over Liam's gorgeous, glistening body.

Toeing my ankle boots off, I silently pad barefoot over to him, the sounds of my footsteps dampened by the foam board floor. The gym, open and airy, takes up the entire space on this level. Every piece of workout equipment imaginable is in here, including a massive functional training system that looks more like a jungle gym on steroids. Near the back is a full-sized boxing square like the one the guys were using at Kellan's cabin. And everything is matte black, red, or gray in color, even the flooring and walls. It's like the room has been color-coordinated where the color of the wall matches the color of the equipment and weights next to it.

Carefully approaching Liam so I don't startle him by my sudden presence, I take a stance behind the heavy bag and hold it steady for him as he delivers two hard jabs with his right fist. I have to plant my feet at the impact to hold myself in place against the raw power of his hits, and even then, the force of them manages to slide me backward a few inches.

Liam suddenly stops when he notices me, his unwrapped, red hands falling to his sides. He really is absolutely beautiful. All masculine power in a ripped body with the face of an angel. My angel-turned-devil.

"Hey. I've been trying to find you," I tell him, raising my hand to touch him.

He steps back out of my reach when his stormy gray gaze immediately goes to the bite marks on my neck. He growls at them before turning on his heel and stalking away.

I guess we're doing this the hard way.

"Liam, stop."

Whirling a one-eighty, he demands, "Why?"

I come around the bag, propping my hands on my hips. My broken finger protests but I ignore the pain. "Because I want to talk to you."

Clearly angry, he replies, "You didn't want to talk to me earlier. I was asked to kindly fuck off and leave." His focus returns to the bite marks on my neck. "Are you that desperate for dick? I don't want their sloppy seconds."

As low blows go, that one hits its target straight into my heart. Part of me wants to lash back out at him. Flay him with cruel words that I don't mean. But I refuse to go there. I knew when I made my decision that choosing to be in a relationship with four different men would have its problems, fights, arguments, and misunderstandings. Our road is not going to be an easy one to traverse. I accept that. I want it. Nothing good in life is worth having if you don't have to fight hard to obtain it or to keep it. Liam is lashing out because he's jealous. He feels like I chose them over him, when clearly that isn't the case. If only he'd give me a fucking minute to explain.

Getting an idea, I walk over to the center of the room. When my feet hit the spongy mat, I turn around.

"What are you doing?" Liam's voice doesn't sound as angry anymore.

Standing barefoot, I curl my index finger at him, telling him to come here. Of course, he doesn't. The stubborn bastard.

I challenge him with the hard set of my stare. "You want to punch something? Fight? Get whatever it is off your chest so we can talk without you trying to bite my head off? Come on then. Because you don't get to walk away from me."

I bend at the waist to stretch out my back and legs, my hands gripping my ankles as I do a slow count of five before straightening back up.

Liam hasn't stormed off again, but he's tracking every move I make. "I'm not fighting you."

I arch to the side and reach an arm over my head, then switch to the other side. Straightening up, I go through some warm-up practice punches while bouncing and shuffling on the balls of my feet.

He scans me from head to toe, the movement of his eyes like a physical caress across my skin. My nipples tighten painfully behind the stretchy fabric of my halter, and I have an urge to pinch them just to get some relief.

When Liam still doesn't make a move to join me, I bring my left leg fully up into a ballerina's high hold, thankful the leather of my pants is pliable.

His breathing becomes labored and his fists clench into tight balls as we stare at one another.

"I'm waiting."

Like he has no control over his body, he takes two menacing steps toward me, then abruptly jerks to a standstill.

I tense in place, ready for whatever is coming. But nothing happens. Because he turns around and walks away from me, spitting out a "Fuck this."

"Damn it, Liam. You difficult asshole," I mutter under my breath.

I sprint across the room and tackle him from behind. It's like running headfirst into a brick wall. We tumble together to the floor like a felled sequoia, but Liam somehow manages to twist midair and cradle me protectively in his arms right before we meet the ground. His back hits the mat with a hard thud. I allow myself a nanosecond to relish being pressed against his sweaty, hard chest, wanting more than anything to lick up each ridge of muscle from his abs to his neck. Unfortunately, that'll have to wait.

Taking advantage of our positions, I immediately break from his grasp, shoving on his shoulders and pinning them down, then anchoring myself to his broad chest with the grip of my thighs. Pleased with this outcome, I blow out a breath to get my loose hair out of my eyes when it cascades over my shoulder and circles his stunned face like a waterfall.

"Now are you ready to talk?"

His moonlight eyes eclipse with dark determination. I yelp when he rolls us over and pins me beneath him. But I was expecting it. In a single, lithe move, I bring my knee up between us and push against his chest while rolling out from under him. We both pop up onto our feet at the same time, facing off like two pit bulls.

Liam slowly circles me. "I don't want to do this with you right now, Andie."

Andie, not *bella*.

"Too fucking bad." Lunging, I drop low, sweeping a leg out to knock him off his feet, but he's quick to react and evades it.

I go through the motions of a few punch combos, ones he easily blocks. It's all for show. I'm not trying to hurt him. What I am trying to do is break down those fucking walls he put up.

"Andie, stop it."

I fake an uppercut and step to the side, hooking my foot behind his left leg. His thigh muscles lock, and he grabs my arm, flipping me over with a twist of his wrist. I gracefully roll across the floor and come up in a kneeling position. Unfortunately, I push down with my left hand, and the pain from my finger has me cursing.

Liam is on the floor in front of me in an instant, worry and regret that he hurt me drawing his mouth down in a frown.

"Fuck, *bella*. Let me take a look at it."

He palms my hand within his, delicately lifting it to his lips, and the pain gradually ebbs away with each butterfly kiss he presses to my finger. This man is always taking care of me, even when he's mad as hell at me.

When his face lifts, those long lashes shuttering his slate-gray eyes, I slide myself into his lap and snuggle into him, my head finding the perfect resting place on his shoulder. Liam breathes in deeply and wraps an arm around me, pulling me in closer.

"I love you, Liam." My confession is like a whisper of the wind against his neck, but I know he hears it by the rapid thud of his heart and the tightening of his arm. "But I love them, too." I lean back and brush my fingers over the rough stubble of his jaw. "The part of my heart that I gave to you, they will never own. It's yours forever. If you want me, I'm yours. But I'll also be theirs. I'll never choose between you and them because there is no choice to make."

I don't demand he say he loves me back. He could never utter those words for the rest of our lives, but I would know the truth. And that's all that matters. Words are meaningless without the actions to back them up, and Liam has proven his loyalty, obsession, and love for me a thousand times over.

But love can also be a shackle. You can come to regret loving someone if it binds you to a life you don't want. Look at how many relationships are destroyed when one person loves another to the point where they give up their dreams. When they give up who they are just to conform to what the other person wants. That's not true love. True love is selfless. It's both wonderful and painful. It makes you feel alive and gives you strength. It allows you to forgive, but also be forgiven.

Like it's the last time I'll ever kiss him, I cover his luscious mouth with my own, slipping my tongue inside to stroke and taste him, crushing my body to his until we become one. And as much as I'd love to rip the remainder of our clothes off and fuck him until we can no longer move and pass out, I know there are cameras on us and eyes other than my men's watching. I'm honestly surprised that Keane and Jax haven't barged in yet. Surely, Tessa would have gleefully informed them by now about me and Liam sparring.

Liam grips the back of my head and pulls me in to deepen our kiss. I swear, I absolutely melt into it.

When we eventually pull apart, I place a sweet peck to his nose, and I'm rewarded with double winks of his dimples when he grins.

"There's nothing that makes me hotter than when we argue and fight, but this right here—" I trace his full lips. "These moments are the ones I love the most."

The tip of his finger glides under the strap of my halter, and he traces a lazy, sensuous line back and forth. His eyes dip, locating every bite mark and hickey blemishing my pale skin.

"May I?" he asks, and I nod yes, tilting my head to the side to give him better access.

He pulls my shirt down and chooses the area right above my heart, sucking on the skin in hard pulls and then giving me a quick nip with his teeth. He smiles broadly as he examines his handiwork.

"Are we good?" I ask him, curling my hands around his neck, my thumbs caressing the underside of his jaw and behind his ears.

He sighs, kissing my lips. "I've never wanted a woman as much as I want you. I don't know how to do this with them."

"Neither do I," I reply. "And it's not like I planned it. It just happened." When our eyes align, I chuckle lightly. "To be honest, I came home prepared to kill them if it came down to it. Attempted to do just that a couple of times when they pissed me the fuck off."

Liam's low rumble of laughter joins my own. He threads his fingers through my hair, playing with the silky ends, then tucks the strands behind my ear. "Wish I could've seen that."

My smile grows. "You'll probably get a lot more opportunities to in the future. Especially between me and Keane."

Liam brings our foreheads together. "Aye."

"I love it when you go all Irish on me," I comment. "Can you do dirty talk in Gaelic?"

He shifts me in his lap, and I hum when his hardness presses against my center. "Maybe."

"Can we talk now?"

"Hmm," he murmurs, nuzzling the hair at my temple.

"I know you're not happy about Declan putting me in charge. It should be you or Pearson."

His lips freeze their journey.

"Andie, I'm not mad because he didn't choose me. I'm upset because it puts you in even more danger. Declan has a lot of enemies. So do I. And those enemies will become yours once they find out who you are."

"Your enemies?" I'm not stupid enough to think that Declan hasn't amassed a list of people who would love nothing more than to take him out, but who's after Liam?

"I told you I wasn't a good man."

"And I remember telling you I only care about the man you are with me now, not who you once were. Do you blame me for the things I did in my past?"

"No. But if you knew about the awful shit I've done, you'd think otherwise."

Chapter 15

ANDIE

If you knew about the awful shit I've done, you'd think otherwise.

I force his gaze to mine, needing to see his eyes. The truth always shows in the eyes. The way someone looks up or whether or not the pupils dilate. Watching someone's eyes is as good as hooking them up to a lie detector.

"No, I wouldn't."

His mouth shuts, the muscle in his jaw distending.

I lock my ankles around him just in case he tries to get up and leave. His face hardens, and creases appear between his brow.

"Christ, Andie. The night we spent together in Geneva, I'd tortured and killed a man in a back storage closet of the club right before I approached you on the dance floor."

"Why?" I know it's morally fucked up to not feel horrified by that. But I also know Liam, and he wouldn't have done it unless he had good reason. Again, fucked up to think that way, but that's the world he and I live in. Blurred lines and blood. There is no black and white. Not in the mob.

"He had been following you. Rossi sent him."

I had always thought Max had eyes on me while I was in Switzerland, even though, to find out, he also planted a tracker on me.

Needing to get through to him, I say, "We've all done things we regret. Things we had to do to survive." I lift my hands between us, spreading my fingers, then curling them into fists. "We've all got blood on our hands."

I've racked up my own body count in the last week, and that number will continue to grow once I wipe Alejandro and Julio off the face of the earth.

Like he did before, Liam grips my hands and kisses each finger. "Some of us more so than others."

I twine my fingers with his until we're holding hands. "Tell me."

It takes a few minutes, and I wait patiently for him to find the words.

"Her name was Sophia—Sophie. We were engaged to be married."

Jealousy at this unknown woman digs sharp barbs into my heart. Did he love her? He must have if he proposed.

"She was Cillian's sister's oldest daughter. His niece."

"My cousin, Cillian?" I ask.

Cillian is a McCarthy from my mother's side of the family. He's the one I reached out to after Kellan's funeral. Keane and Jax had asked me where I learned how to fight. The simple answer is Cillian.

"Aye."

"What happened? Did you call off the engagement?"

He takes a slow breath and exhales it. "No. I killed her. She betrayed me. Betrayed the family. She was feeding information to one of our rivals, the McMurphys. A lot of our men had died because of her. Come to find out, she was also fucking their eldest son." Liam's eyes glaze over as he gets lost in the memory.

Am I shocked by his confession? A little. But overriding that is the compulsion to comfort him.

"Liam," I whisper, kissing him chastely. "I'm so sorry. Do we need to worry about the McMurphys or Cillian?" Are they the enemies he was referring to? I could reach out to Cillian. See if there's a way we could cancel any blood debt owed.

He shakes his head. "Cillian was the one who ordered her death. The McMurphy son, Niall, didn't give a shit about Sophie. Why go to war over a woman who meant nothing other than a few good fucks?"

His question slaps me in the face. Sophie was like me. A woman in a male-dominated world, whose only value was found between her legs.

Not wanting to know the answer, but asking anyway, I inquire as casually as I can, "Did you love Sophie?"

He doesn't even hesitate. "Not like I should have, considering she was to be my wife. I guess Rafael and I have that in common. Being forced to marry someone for the good of the family business."

I couldn't stand the thought of Rafe marrying Rita—good fucking riddance to that duplicitous bitch. And Liam is right. Their situations are eerily comparable.

"I don't deserve your love, *bella*. Not after the things I've done. How could you want to be with someone who murdered his own fiancée?"

He makes a valid point, except it's one I disagree with wholeheartedly. I'm already in too deep with these four men.

"I gave you my love, Liam. You can't give it back. The return policy expired the night you fucked me in Geneva."

Liam discharges a huff and buries his face in my chest.

"I have one more question," I say.

He grazes a knuckle over my nipple, making it peak into a hard nub beneath my top. He switches to the other breast, and sparks light me up from inside, making me hungry for more.

"Does it feel like I'm cheating on you?"

Sophie was sleeping with another man. One that was his enemy. I can't blame Liam for being angry with me that I'm doing something similar, regardless of the fact that I've been completely honest with each of them on where I stand. I won't be made to choose.

"I guess it should. But the honest answer would be no."

My confusion must show.

"Sophie didn't go through the horrific things you've had to endure, *bella*. Her life was easy. The shit you've lived through... the fact that you trust me, trust them, with this—"

He lays a fingertip to my breastbone where my heart beats,

then slides his hand over my shoulder, down my arm, and across my stomach.

"—Is a fucking miracle. And I'll protect and love any part of you that you'll give me."

"I do love you." These men may be broken. Damaged. Their pieces jagged and sharp. But that's what makes them perfect.

He smiles as he kisses me, and my stomach flutters with what feels like intense happiness, an emotion that is still so foreign to me.

"Then that's all I need."

I look down at the large ring I'm now wearing on my right hand, glimmering in the overhead lights of the gym. Declan's family crest. *My* family.

"I'm sorry if you thought I was excluding you earlier. There were some things that needed explaining to Rafe."

Another sigh. "I'm sorry for overreacting."

I pull his lower lip with my teeth and then soothe the bite with several tiny flicks of my tongue. "You're forgiven."

He tugs my hair, wanting more, and that little bite turns into a frantic kiss laced with need. He holds me to him, a comforting embrace that I appreciate more than he'll ever know.

"Baby, I'm so fecking sorry about everything," he says, his accent thick with emotion.

He stands up with me still wrapped around him. The amount of strength that must take... *damn*. Gripping my ass, he walks with me to the back of the room where the lights are dimmer.

"I'm going to take great pleasure in ripping Alejandro apart with my bare hands. I swear to you, *bella*, I won't fail you again."

"You've never failed me," I assure him, bracing his shoulders as he carries me.

With determined eyes full of love and the promise of the vengeance he plans to reap on our enemies, he rasps against my lips, "Before we head back, I need to fuck you first."

My pussy flutters in response, craving the feel of his Jacob's ladder inside her.

"Do you have your phone on you?"

Stopping, he pulls it out of the side pocket of his sweats, unlocks it, and hands it to me.

"Thank you."

I type out a quick text.

Me: Hey, GirlDownLow. I'm on Liam's phone. Can you shut off the cameras in the gym please?

Tessa: Seriously? Damn you and your golden vagina. I'd be crazy jealous if I didn't love you so much.

When I burst out laughing, Liam gives me a questioning look.

Me: Just do it.

Tessa: Done. You owe me.

Me: Thank you. Tell the guys I'll be back in a few minutes.

Tessa: On it.

Seeing what I typed, Liam remarks, "A few minutes?" He takes his phone back and tosses it onto the floor.

"Yep."

"I think I can make you come at least five times by then."

"I sure as fuck hope so," I tell him as my back impacts with the wall, and Liam crushes his body to mine.

He pulls the edge of my halter down and immediately attacks my nipple with his talented tongue. I expect him to dive right in and pound me into the wall, but when he doesn't, I meet his steadfast, slate-gray gaze.

He runs a thumb across my clavicle, tracing the curved bone there. "I never did answer you."

My brows knit together. He answered the two questions I'd asked. He opened up to me and shared a fragile part of himself. The guilt about how he sees himself as too damaged and not good enough for me, and the insecurities he has that I want Keane, Jax, and Rafe more than him.

"Thank you for trusting me enough to tell me about Sophia."

"Not what I'm referring to, *bella*."

I'm at a loss, then. I don't remember asking him anything else.

"You told me that you loved me."

"I do," I immediately reply.

Those three words don't come easily for me. Not after

everything I've lived through. But I will make damn sure the guys hear them often.

"I love you, too," he quietly declares, setting me down and dropping to his knees. "You might want to hold on to something. I promised you five orgasms."

Chapter 16

ANDIE

"Hey. I was about to make a midnight snack. Grilled cheese. You in?" Tessa says, walking into my bedroom. I must have forgotten to close the door.

I've been staring out the wall of windows for the past half hour, my eyes scanning over the city lit up like Christmas in the dark of night. Things look so *normal* from up here. The night sky with its twinkling stars. The gibbous moon glowing brightly despite the light pollution trying to obscure it. The silhouettes framed in the windows of the adjacent building. Lovers. Families. Friends. So many of them oblivious to the dangers surrounding them. The evil that lurks just beneath the concrete and steel façade and polished glass. Do they know about the corruption that manipulates their lives every day? The gangs, the guns, the drugs. The killers who walk among them. The woman who now controls a majority of it and all of them.

I spent most of the day at the hospital. It was rough. Some shit went down that required me to make snap decisions. I'm still second-guessing myself over them. Only time will tell if I did the right thing.

Tessa slides her arms around me and leans into my side. "Beautiful, isn't it?" she asks, taking in the view.

I nestle my head on the top of her blonde head. "Yeah, it is."

We stand in peaceful silence together for a minute.

"How were things while I was gone?"

"Oh, the usual fisticuffs when you get four very territorial and possessive men into one room."

I pinch the bridge of my nose and sigh. "Do I even want to know?"

"Probably not. Jax handled it."

"Where was Rafe?"

She sucks in air through her teeth. "You probably don't want to know about that either."

I tip back my head and groan at the ceiling. The animosity between Keane and Liam is something that I'll need to deal with soon.

Tessa plops down onto my bed and bounces a few times, then falls onto the bedcovers dramatically. "I'm bored and too wired to sleep. Want to play *Never Have I Ever*?" She wiggles her eyebrows.

"Without the Jägermeister."

"*Aww*," Tessa whines.

Me, Tessa, *Never Have I Ever*, and hard liquor make for trouble, and I have enough trouble going on right now.

"I'll go first." I wasn't going to say anything to her about what I saw tonight when I came in, but decide, fuck it, and dive right in. "Never have I ever been accepted to MIT."

Her shoulders slump. "Well, shit. How did you find out?"

"You left your laptop open on the kitchen island."

I saw the tail end of the DMs between her and her mother; the last one from Tessa telling her mom that she was going to inform the admissions committee that she'd changed her mind and wouldn't be accepting their offer to attend. Which means Tessa had been accepted to MIT before we graduated over a year ago, applied for a gap year, and MIT granted her a deferral. It doesn't take a genius to figure out why she did that or what she's been doing this past year. Or the guilt I feel knowing she's giving up her dreams because of me.

"You're going," I tell her.

Tessa sits up. "Not your decision. Besides, I'm gainfully employed. I don't need MIT." She tries to make light of it, adding in a soft chuckle, but I'm not buying it.

All Tessa ever talked about the entire time we knew each other at school was going to university. How excited she was about it. She didn't care where she ended up, just as long as she got to experience it. I won't let my fucked-up life mess up hers.

"Too bad."

I can literally see the hairs on her arms raise, and it reminds me of a hissing kitten. I know better than to tell her that, though.

"First thing in the morning, I'm going to get Jax to wire them your first year's tuition. MIT doesn't give refunds," I quip and watch as her mouth falls open. "Let me do this for you, Tessa. I *need* to do this for you," I implore.

Those big doe eyes of hers blink up at me and for the first time in her life, she's speechless. I know she won't give up the argument that easily. She'll try a million different ways to convince me to let her stay here, all because of some fucking ideology she has about friendship and loyalty. She can try, but her stubborn ass is still going to college. And I'm not done with my demands.

"I need you to promise me something. It concerns Sarah," I say.

Her head tilts to the side just as her eyes widen when she picks up on the gravity of what that is.

This life isn't guaranteed. If Declan hadn't stepped in front of me, I would be dead right now. And there are certain things I want put into place, just in case. The first being Sarah. The second is something I need to talk to the guys about.

"Don't you dare—" she begins before I cut her off.

"Sarah needs a woman in her life. To be there for her. Someone who can help her navigate things as she grows up. The guys love her and will give her the world, but—"

"Good thing she'll have you then," she says sternly, her body starting to shake as her anger rises.

Pearson called me an hour ago. Something went down at the hospital that I need to deal with. I've been waiting for Jax to get back because I'm going to need his help. Looking out at the city as I waited got me thinking about the fleetingness of life. Deep, philosophical shit, I know. But if something happens to me, I want Sarah to have Tessa—a strong, smart, sassy woman—to be her role model.

My hands lift in front of me before I drop them. "You know damn well what I'm trying to say."

"Yes, I do! And it's utter bullshit! You don't get to martyr yourself, Alex. You don't get to be selfish like that!" she shouts. "Sarah doesn't need me. She needs *you*. The guys need you. *I* need you. So don't you fucking dare insinuate that something is going to happen to you."

Her shoulder-length hair swishes wildly as she shakes her head in denial. After a year of working for Declan, she should know by now the consequences of this job. Not everyone comes home.

Tessa glares at me, her bottom lip trembling as we stand off, neither of us willing to budge or cede the argument. Jax appears in the doorway, an eyebrow quirked at the scene in front of him.

Tessa notices my attention is no longer on her and glances over at him. "Maybe you can talk some sense into her," she tells him before saying to me, "And the answer is yes." With that, she turns on her heel and walks out.

"What's her problem?" Jax asks as he watches a very pissed-off Tessa stalk past him.

"Girl stuff," I reply.

He doesn't believe me, but he also doesn't call me on it.

Jax approaches slowly, those green eyes behind black-rimmed glasses, scrutinizing me. Just having him near is instantly calming. As soon as our bodies touch, he takes my face between his inked hands, angling it up to his.

Jax is so breathtakingly handsome. Dark blond hair. Penetrating moss-green eyes. Full Cupid bow lips on a clean-shaven jaw. Gorgeous ink coloring his skin in reds, blacks, and grays. However, I can't help but look at him and still see the lost boy I knew long ago. The quiet boy who was forced to become a remorseless killer. The man with hidden demons who now holds a huge part of my heart.

The tips of my fingers run over his shoulder to where the bandage covers his bullet graze, and I trace the edges of the medical tape securing the gauze square. Right now, Jax, Rafe, and I are the walking wounded. But we're all stubborn as hell and refuse to let our injuries hinder us.

Jax lets go of my face to grip the back of my neck with both hands. "I brought you something."

He gives me a quick kiss and walks over to the bedroom door, bending down to get something from the floor in the hallway. My heels lift up as I try to peek around him to see what he's doing. When he turns around, holding a familiar glass Mason jar filled with fairy lights, my heart tries to soar right out of my chest.

"Is that what I think it is?" I reach for it when he brings it to me.

"Kept it safe for you in a box under my bed at the house."

I can't believe Jax kept the jar he would fill with fireflies for me. So many nights, I would sleep with this jar clutched tightly to my body. I used to hide it under the corner of my mattress. We had maids to clean the house, but they would never clean my room. Max had decreed it off limits for obvious reasons.

Coming around to my back, Jax drapes his arms around me and brings his face flush with mine. "I'm sorry I couldn't give you the real thing. Not the season for them."

Holding the jar up, I marvel at the tiny, white, battery-operated fairy lights twinkling inside.

"It's perfect," I tell him and tip my face back to meet his lips, needing him to kiss me more than I need my next breath. This beautifully damaged man who loves me.

Placing the jar down on the bed next to us, I turn in his arms. "Why do you call me Angel?"

Jax's hand trails down my back and settles at the dip of my spine right above my ass. Applying pressure, he pulls me in until we are meshed together, my cheek lying flat on the hard plain of his chest, our bodies swaying slightly from side-to-side. It's like we're slow dancing.

"Because that's who you are to me," he murmurs, his lips nuzzling at my temple. "The sweet little angel with the amethyst eyes. The girl who held a murderer in her arms and begged him never to leave her. You saved me that night."

Without having to say which night, memories from my childhood come flooding back.

I'd been hiding in Kellan's closet like I often did, even though I knew Max would eventually search for me when he came to my room that night and saw that I wasn't there. I could've found another hiding place, someplace that would make it harder for Max to find me. But I'd always chosen Kellan's closet. Perhaps it was because being surrounded by his things brought me a semblance of comfort.

I'd been used to the boys sleeping over or staying in Kellan's room. They'd done it for years. But that particular night when Jax walked into Kellan's bedroom, covered in blood, would be forever imprinted in my mind. I remembered cringing in my hiding place when I heard another raised male voice. My breaths became labored and harsh, knowing what would happen to me once Max found me and dragged me out of Kellan's closet. But Max never came that night. The voice belonged to Kellan. He was yelling.

Peeking through the slit underneath the door where it didn't quite touch the wood floor, I watched my brother shove a blood-soaked Jax into the open doorway of the adjoining bathroom. I didn't know what had happened to Jax, why he was covered in blood, or why Kellan was so mad. Had Jax hurt himself? Is that why Kellan was yelling?

As soon as the water in the shower turned on, Kellan left the room. My back and legs had begun to cramp, and the right side of my cheek went numb where it was pressed to the floor, but I stayed in that position, wanting to see what happened next. Minutes later, Kellan came back with a plate of food, a bottle of water, and a large, black trash bag. He rifled through his chest of drawers before taking out a clean T-shirt and a pair of gray sweatpants.

I remember holding my breath when Jax came out of the shower, the scent of soap and tendrils of steam wafting around him as he stood in front of the closet, blocking my line of sight into the room. I couldn't hear everything Kellan told him—just snippets of phrases like "Dad is sending men to handle it," "burn the evidence," "keep your mouth shut," and "you'll live with us now." Soon after, the sound of the bedroom door closing pricked my ears. Then, complete darkness as the bedroom light turned off.

I quietly opened the closet door when I heard whimpers, like someone was crying. Jax was sitting in the dark at the end of the bed, head bowed and shoulders shaking, his sad tears squeezing my tiny heart. A sliver of moonlight hit him from the window, reflecting off a piece of metal he held in his hand. A knife with a red handle. He was shakingly holding the blade to the underside of his left wrist. Without thought, I walked over to him and wrapped my arms tightly around his lean frame. Even though I was young, I'd already seen and experienced too much of the horrors of the world. I understood what Jax was about to do with his knife, and I couldn't stand by and let it happen.

"It's going to be okay, Jax. I'll protect you from the demons. Stay with me. Don't go. Please don't go."

I found out a couple of years later from Kellan what had happened that brought Jax to live with us. He had murdered his father after witnessing him rape, then beat his mother to death. Max took care of everything just as Kellan promised. Then Max used it to force Jax into the business. To remain a killer for the rest of his life. To become a man who enjoyed hurting and torturing others. Sometimes, I wonder if I did the right thing that night. Instead of begging Jax to stay, I should have begged him to run away and never look back.

"Why did you ignore me and pretend I didn't exist all those years?" I ask him.

Jax never spoke to me again until the day the guys rescued me from the warehouse. Until a few weeks ago, whenever he looked at me, it was with cold, lifeless, disinterested eyes. He became the bogeyman, haunting the Rossi hallways at night when insomnia and the nightmares chasing him refused to let him rest.

"I didn't deserve your light. I still don't," he says into my hair.

Lifting my head away from his chest, I pin him with the truth. "You're right. You deserve so much more. I love you, Jaxson West. My Reaper."

A startled sound escapes my lips when he lifts me in his arms, his mouth crushing mine, tongue probing deep. An explosion of heat erupts between us like it always does when we're together. Passion and pain. And so damn good.

Then my fucking phone chimes with an incoming call, and the screen lights up the room.

"Ignore it." Jax drops me on the bed and falls on top of me, opening my legs wide. Rough hands knead my thighs and curl under my ass. With a hard jerk, I'm pulled to the end of the bed, and Jax forces my legs wider when he steps between them.

My phone sounds again.

"Jax, I need to see if—"

The rest of my sentence gets stuck in my throat when he bunches up my top and greedily sucks my nipple into his mouth.

My phone starts ringing, and Jax and I both groan at the interruption.

"Jax, I really need to get this."

Jax swirls his tongue around my navel, then reluctantly eases off me so I can roll over and grab my phone where it got pushed off the bed and onto the floor.

"Can't believe I'm being fucking cockblocked by a fucking phone."

"I didn't say stop," I tell him, folding almost in half off the bed to reach the phone.

"Good point." Jax takes advantage of my awkward position, giving me two hard spanks on the ass.

I swipe to answer, already knowing it's Pearson when I see Unknown glowing green on the screen.

"He's gone, *little flame*."

He's gone.

I tap Jax's shoulder for him to move. Getting up, I walk to the bedroom door and shut it. Jax leans back on his elbows on the bed, his interest piqued when I start conversing in Russian. Turning my back to him, I pace over to the window, leaning my forehead against the cool glass. A circle of condensation magically forms at the area of contact. My hand shakes as I listen to Pearson, and I will the trembling to stop.

He's gone.

Jax comes up behind me and takes my waist. His chin comes to rest on my shoulder.

"Angel, what's going on?" he asks when my arm drops to my side as soon as the call ends.

There's a turning point in everyone's life. A metaphorical fork in the road and point of no return. A path to choose and a choice to make. You know your life is about to change when you come to that point. For most people, it's when they hit rock bottom. When things get so bad, they either give up or fight like hell to claw their way back up. For a chosen few, like me, it's when your fated destiny comes calling, whether you're ready for it or not.

"The phoenix hope, can wing her way through the desert skies, and still defying fortune's spite; revive from ashes and rise."

"Pearson wants me to meet him somewhere, and I need your help."

He grips my shoulders with his warm hands. Hands that are roughened and scarred, a killer's hands. But hands that are gentle and tender when they touch me.

My open palms glide across his shirt, taking my time to smooth out wrinkles that aren't there. Jax stills my ministrations and lifts my right hand, kissing the Levin crest of the ring on my finger. It's like he already knows.

I meet Jax's steadfast, green gaze. I'm about to ask him to do something I'll regret for the rest of my life. I'm about to ask him to become the thing he hates most in order to strike down my enemies. Worst of all, I'll willingly fall off that cliff with him.

"What do you need, Angel?"

"I need the Reaper."

Chapter 17

ANDIE

The gravel of the lot crunches under the vehicle's tires as we slowly approach the dilapidated warehouse. The rusting corrugated sheet metal façade shows the structure's age and state of disrepair. Jax and I were able to leave Falcon Tower without bumping into the other guys. Part of me wishes they were here with us. But I know how they'd react. Especially Keane. He would try hard to stop me from what I'm about to do.

Jax gets out of the passenger side and comes around to open my door for me. The car ride here was made in silence, but I know he must have questions. Surely, he recognizes this place.

My legs unfold, and I take the hand Jax offers. Once I'm standing, I scan my surroundings. It's so quiet. And dark. I can't even hear the cacophonic noise from the interstate highway located a mile to the west. The warehouse is situated in the northern outskirts of the city in an abandoned industrial district where the old paper mill used to be. Most of the area is now an EPA Superfund site due to all the hazardous material and pollution the mill created and recklessly dumped into the surrounding environment during its period of operation. In ninth-grade science class, I had to do a report on it. I can still smell the chemicals and rot in the air; or maybe that's just me being psychosomatic.

"It looks different from how I remember it," I tell him.

Jax's hand goes to his Glock as he steps in front of me. He's in enforcer mode, making sure I'm protected.

"How do you know about this place?"

This is the warehouse Kellan unknowingly brought me to the night I hid in the trunk of his Mustang. It's the night I saw who and what the guys were for the first time when they beat and tortured a man. It's the night Max took what was left of Kellan's soul, forcing him to shoot a man point-blank in the head. How many times have I relived it in my nightmares?

"I was curious, so I stowed away in the trunk of Kellan's car one night," I reply.

Jax's mouth is thinned in a grim line when he turns slightly to look back at me. "What did you see?"

"Everything."

His eyes fall shut, his lungs sucking in a deep, dejected inhale of regret.

Keane and Rafe have said more than once that they never wanted *this* for me—this life and the horrors it entails. But what they fail to realize is that I've always been a part of it. I know who these men are and what they've done. And I love them regardless.

A shadow passes over the side window of the SUV—a reflection of a face in the glass. A familiar face with soft brown eyes framed by dark brown hair. *Kellan.* It's brief and fleeting and disappears almost as soon as I see it.

Kellan's ghost has haunted me less and less lately. I'm still angry with him for keeping secrets, but I also miss him. It doesn't hurt to think about him as much as it used to. Maybe that's why I don't see his ghost as often anymore. Maybe the broken parts of me are finally healing.

"Pearson should already be inside," I tell Jax.

As we approach the building, the humidity infusing the night air causes lines of sweat to drip down my spine and neck. Even my arms feel like they're already coated in a thin film of liquid salt. A light fog billows around our feet as we walk around the side building, searching for the door. The last time I was here, I climbed through a broken window in the back.

Just like in B-movie horror flicks, a black cat jumps out of its hiding place behind a loose drainage pipe, scaring the shit out of me, before hissing and dashing away.

"Fucking cats," Jax mumbles. He's allergic to them and thinks they're the tiny spawns of Satan.

Finally finding a door, I give it a good tug. It opens with a loud creak, like nails on a chalkboard. The stench of piss and feces hits me right away. Not surprising. The north part of the city is known for its drugs, and abandoned places like this building are hotbeds for buying, selling, or shooting up. Or killing someone.

Jax pulls me to his side as we enter the empty warehouse. It's hard to make out anything in the pitch black of the expansive building. My right foot catches on something, and I stop to get out my phone so I can use it as a light. The screen glows a faint blue for a few seconds, illuminating the floor and the used, shriveled-up condom and broken syringe I crushed with my shoe. Oh, gross. I'm going to need a scalding shower and several rounds of vaccinations and antibiotics when I'm done here.

The warehouse must be infested with rodents because I can hear their tiny squeaks and the pitter-patter of their feet scurrying around. A spear of moonlight beams down from an opening in the roof, and like a spotlight from the heavens, I see the woman bound and gagged on the floor right in the middle of it.

My footsteps are now sure and with purpose, bringing me closer to the woman who'll soon regret she was ever born. The woman jerks and thrashes when she sees me. Her brown, terrified eyes and strangled whimpers beg me to help her.

"Where's the man?" I ask Pearson as he slowly materializes behind her the more my vision becomes accustomed to the darkness.

He looks down at his feet to a large male body lying on the floor, his wrists duct-taped behind his back, and his leg bent at an odd angle. The way the man is positioned reminds me of a contortionist I once saw during a street performance.

"Is he alive?"

"Yes," Pearson replies in English.

"Good. Thank you, Pearson. Jax and I can handle it from here."

Pearson disappears back into the shadowy darkness. There's a loud groan of hinges and a clank as a door opens and closes. I assume he'll stick close by to make sure no wayward trespasser wanting to find a place to sleep for the night or get high will interrupt us.

Squatting down in front of the woman, I gently help her to sit up—which is difficult the way Pearson has trussed her like a turkey—and look her over. Up close, she has chestnut brown hair streaked with a darker auburn red. Brown eyes the color of smoky quartz. A heart-shaped face and a button nose. Small diamond studs adorn her ears. Her whimpers get choppier, and her crying gets louder when I brush her sweaty hair from her face.

"Shhh," I whisper, peeling off the black duct tape covering her mouth and pulling out the wad of newspaper that was used to gag her. "What's your name?"

Her throat works as she swallows. "St-Stacy."

"Last name?"

"*Please* don't hurt me. *Please*. I'll do whatever you want."

My fingernail taps against my thigh, and I look up to Jax for guidance. But it's not Jax standing there. My Grim Reaper has arrived.

"Ask her again," he says.

I don't have to. She takes one look at Jax, and terror fills her eyes. She senses what he is. The Angel of Death.

"Mar-Martinez."

"Jax, meet Stacy Martinez. Stacy Martinez, meet Jaxson West."

"Your knife, Angel," Jax says, and I follow his lead.

This is why I need the Reaper. I've never tortured anyone before. I need his guidance. I need to draw from his experience and his madness and his bloodlust. Only the savage will win this war against the Ortiz cartel and the two men who run it.

I take my time, slowly sliding Jax's red-handled knife out of my ankle holster, twisting the blade so that it catches the moonlight. Stacy goes into full panic mode. I wouldn't be surprised if she hyperventilated herself into a passed-out blob on the floor. Can't have that happening.

She cries out when I smack her across the face. I ignore the pain it causes in my broken finger and want to roll my eyes at being forced to do something so stupidly girlie. Punching is more my thing.

"P-please," she begs, eyes wide and scared. "*Please, please. I didn't want to do it. He threatened to kill my family. He'll kill me!*"

"What the fuck do you think I'm going to do to you if you don't tell me what I want to know?" I reply with a deadly calm.

As I explained to Jax before we left Falcon Tower, Alejandro and Julio somehow got to the staff at the hospital. Sweet Nurse Stacy tried to inject Declan's IV with a syringe full of air to induce an arterial embolism. A syringe that was given to Stacy by the male orderly. But they failed.

Pearson had the men we'd assigned to guard Declan's room immediately transport Declan to the private hangar and put on a private jet where Mike was already waiting. The plane should arrive in Boston soon, where one of Cillian's men will meet them and take Declan to a McCarthy safehouse. The phone call from Pearson was to inform me the plane with Declan on it had taken off, and that Cillian would be flying to Boston from Ireland tomorrow.

I rise from my lowered position and go over to the man moaning on the floor. It seems that he's about to wake up and join the party.

Jax comes up behind me, his hot breath on my neck and his very hard cock pressing into my ass.

"Ready to play, Reaper?"

I feel his mouth curve on my skin. His hand slithers its way over my breast, fingers pulling and rolling my nipple through my shirt. I reach behind me and sink my nails into his shoulder, and my core tightens when he gives the tight nub one more hard tug.

"Jax, what are you doing?"

"Teaching you. Pain is pleasure, baby."

His tongue does wicked things to my ear at the same time his hand glides down my arm and his fingers wrap around the knife I'm holding. He guides my hand, lightly running the blade over me—thigh to pussy to stomach to chest. As he does, he explains in great detail the various ways I can use the knife that will cause the most amount of pain with the least amount of damage. Stacy watches in abject horror as Jax works my body with the knife, his touch sensual and his words filthy. I swear I could come if he keeps it up, I'm so turned on.

The man on the floor finally comes to, flopping around in the filth and dirt like a fish out of water.

Jax lets go of my hand and wrenches my lips to his. His kiss is full of sin.

"Now I'm ready to play, Angel."

Chapter 18

RAFE

I don't know what the fuck is going on, but Declan's men have closed off Andie's floor and won't allow anyone to enter, not even Liam. That didn't go over too well. Tessa accessed the security logs for the entire building since there are no cameras on Andie's floor other than the ones at the elevators and stairwell. All we know is that Andie and Jax left a couple of hours ago. Liam tried to reach out to Pearson. Nothing. We concluded that they were all at the hospital with Declan. That started another heated argument between Keane and Liam. Liam wanted to go and make sure she was okay, and Keane told him to chill the fuck out and give Andie some space and time with her father. I think Liam was pissed that Andie left with Jax and not with him.

Tessa reached her breaking point with Keane and Liam ten minutes ago. Their constant arguing finally got to the point where she insisted they go to the gym and beat the shit out of each other. I'm glad she did because I was getting a migraine from their nonstop bitching.

So, that's where I'm heading. I figure I can get in a light workout. I need to start rebuilding my strength after a week of bed rest.

Bypassing the elevators, I head straight for the stairs. Living here and working for Declan the past few weeks has been an adjustment, to say the least. The one good thing about the Rossi estate was all the land surrounding it. I hate this concrete and steel shit. I hate not being able to go outside and breathe in fresh air, and not the car exhaust that hangs like a perpetual shroud over the city.

"Rafael."

I look up to find Lochlan leaning over the railing of the landing. I like the guy. He reminds me a little of Enzo. I guess it's their similar personalities. Both are quick to laugh and make a joke. Unlike Liam, Lochlan accepted me into the Levine fold when I defected and switched sides after finding out that Max made a deal with my father to give Andie to Alejandro.

"What's up?" I ask, climbing the last few steps.

"My shift will end in an hour, and me and a few of the guys are going to the roof with a case of beer. Want to join?"

"Thanks, but I'll take a rain check. I'm going to get in a quick workout and watch Liam and Keane go at it."

"Yeah. I peeked inside a minute ago. My money's on Liam." He opens the stairwell door for me, and I'm immediately met by Mickey on the other side.

Hearing Lochlan's comment, Mickey says, "I'll take that bet. However, my money's on Keane."

"You're on," Lochlan agrees, and they bump fists before Mickey shuts the stairwell door.

"*Hola*, Rafe."

"*Hola*, Mick."

"*Buenas noches*," he says in the heaviest Bostonian accent I've ever heard.

"Getting better," I lie.

He started taking a free online language course to learn how to speak Spanish. He wants to impress some chick from Tomar he's infatuated with, and I don't have the heart to tell him that Spanish and Portuguese are similar but distinct languages.

A roar from the other side of the room has us both turning to see Liam delivering an uppercut that sends Keane stumbling back two steps. Keane gives back as good as he gets, smashing his fist into Liam's cheek.

I spot Tessa sitting on the floor with her laptop, half working and half watching the gladiatorial battle unfolding in front of her.

Walking over, I say, "They're not going to stop until the other is dead or in a coma."

"Sounds good to me."

Okay then.

Trying to be conversational, I ask, "What are you working on?" I don't understand any of the gibberish she's typing. Computer shit is Jax's domain.

"I'm taking another look at my face-recognition program. It should've flagged Alejandro at Spanks like it did Julio and Rita. It's my fault what happened to Andie."

"If it's anyone's fault, it's mine."

The guilt I feel about what Alejandro did to Andie is soul-crushing. If I never left Mexico, if I stayed and played the part my father was grooming me for, Andie wouldn't have been on Alejandro's radar to begin with.

Liam grunts loudly when Keane rams into his torso, lifting him off the mat and body-slamming him. Liam locks his legs around Keane's waist, and they roll across the floor.

I strip off my shirt, which gets Tessa's attention, and decide to hit the treadmill for some light cardio. I don't want to overdo it and pop another stitch. I've done that twice now, and both times have ended with me getting shot up with morphine. I went ballistic when I was told that was what they'd been giving me for the pain. That shit hits too close to home. Tylenol only, thank you very fucking much. I can live with the discomfort. What I can't live with is winding up like my mother, craving my next fix until I crave it too much and overdose.

Setting the incline to two and the speed to a brisk walk, I shout over to the guys, "Andie would kick both your asses if she were here."

Liam takes a swing at Keane, which he easily dodges.

"You're both being ridiculous," I tell them.

"Don't need your running commentary," Keane grunts, hooking his foot around Liam's leg and taking him to the mat. Liam's grip on Keane's arm pulls him down with him.

"The both of you need to deal with your shit and get over it."

Liam shoves Keane off him. "If I want your fucking opinion, *Rafael*, I'll ask for it."

Whatever. "Go fuck yourself."

"Nah, I'd rather fuck your girlfriend."

Goddammit! I walked right into that one.

He, Keane, and Jax have had more time to process how they feel about sharing Andie, but I'm still catching up, and it's a very sore spot with me.

Tessa bursts out laughing, and Keane joins her. "Nice one."

Liam's smile is a mile wide.

"You're all assholes," I grumble, increasing my speed on the treadmill.

Tessa gets up and cracks her back. "Alright boys, I'm out." She picks up her laptop and tucks it under her arm. "Gotta get my beauty rest and all. See you in the morning. Don't kill each other too badly. Mickey'll whine about cleaning up the mess."

She pats him on the chest and sends him a wink as she leaves. Mickey does a slow head turn, his eyes dropping and lingering on her ass.

"Be careful with that one. She's all piss and vinegar. And Andie will knife you in the balls if you touch her," Liam warns him.

"I can still look." Mickey throws a smirk at him, and Liam gives him the one-finger salute.

"Time?" Keane asks, collapsing back onto the mat and flinging his arm over his face.

I check my watch. "Half-past one. You think she and Jax are back yet?"

Liam pushes up on his forearms. "Any idea why he went with her and not one of us?"

Keane lifts his arm off his eyes and rolls his head toward Liam. "Jesus Christ, not this again. You rant at me about giving her space but won't stop whining like a dickhole that she didn't pick you."

I hop off the treadmill and hit the stop button. "I think Tessa had the right idea. I'm turning in."

Keane and Liam stop arguing and are quick to their feet when Andie suddenly walks out of the elevator, Jax right behind her.

And for a few short seconds, the whole fucking world stops.

"Can we have some privacy?" she calls over to Mickey.

"Uh, yes, ma'am." He slips through the door and joins Lochlan on the other side.

"Is that blood?" Liam bellows, his accusatory gaze slicing into Jax. "What the fuck did you do?"

Chapter 19

ANDIE

"Angel, we're home."

Angel.

My consciousness becomes aware and wakens at his voice, and I'm confused at first. When did Max build an underground garage? But I'm not at my childhood home. And Max is dead. Because I killed him. I killed those people tonight, too. But it was different. Jax made it different. He made *me* different. He made me *like* it. I'm still coming to terms regarding how I feel about that.

The passenger door opens, and the acrid fumes of car exhaust fill my nose. Jax reaches over me and unbuckles my seat belt.

"I think you have it wrong," I say.

Jax told me that he called me Angel because I saved him. There are many types of angels. Nine, in fact. Seraphim, Cherubim, Thrones, Dominions, Virtues, Powers, Principalities, Archangels, and Angels.

I disagree on the number. I think they're eleven. The last two being avenging angels and the Angel of Death. Jax has always been the latter one. I wonder which one I am. Maybe Powers. Those angels are warrior angels. Their job is to fight the demons and ensure the natural order. Or perhaps I'm a mix. Part Powers, avenging, and death. There's also Seraphim, which literally translates into "the burning ones." Pearson calls me *little flame.*

Jax lifts and lowers me from the seat of the SUV. I can smell the metallic notes of the sticky blood that clings to our skin and clothes.

"What do I have wrong?" he asks.

"The type of angel I am."

"The only type of angel you are, is mine."

I look into his gorgeous green eyes. The Reaper has retreated inside its cage, leaving only my sweet, vulnerable Jax staring down at me.

Another Range Rover pulls in and parks beside us. Pearson gets out. "Declan arrived safely in Boston."

The tight coil of worry I'd been carrying the last few hours unravels.

"Anything I should know?"

"He's in good hands."

Pearson of little words. He knows I'll be personally calling and checking in on Declan later.

I slip my hand into Jax's. "Let's go find the guys."

During the ride here, I thought about my next move. Alejandro will continue to strike out, putting the people I care about in his crosshairs in order to get me back. His ego is bruised. I was promised to him in the deal Max made with Julio. I was to be Alejandro's pliant, obedient wife. The vessel to bear his heir. The key to solidifying an alliance between the Rossis and the Ortizes in order to gain more power, more money, and more territory to run drugs through. Rafe and Declan thwarted those plans, which is why Alejandro went after them.

When I was brought to Alejandro after my unconscious body was taken from the car wreck, I could see the hubris of victory in his demented stare. He thought I was weak, but I defied him every step of the way. I didn't cower or grovel when he locked me in the cage. I fought him when he broke my finger and stole Keane's rings. I escaped. And for those things, he won't stop until he punishes me for my defiance. Until he shows he can break me. His sexist narcissism will be his ultimate downfall. Alejandro is like Max. And like Max, the oldest son of Julio Ortiz will also die by my hand. And I know just the thing to flush him out.

I tell Pearson to meet us in the conference room and send a

text to Tessa informing her the same thing. She's probably asleep and will bitch at me for waking her up.

Greeting the men and the guards we pass, a few of them do double takes when they see the drying blood covering my arms and clothes. I think there may be a smear or two on my face and neck, but that's more Jax's fault because he couldn't keep his hands off me.

Apparently, watching me cut people is a huge turn-on for him. After it was over and Pearson started cleaning up the mess and disposing of the bodies, Jax was barely able to control himself by the time we made it back to the car. And once we did, he slammed me against it and fucked me.

Jax and I get on the elevator, and I press the button for my floor. I lean into his body and rest my head on his upper arm. He angles his phone so I can see the video on the screen.

"Is that live?" I ask as I watch Keane and Liam go at each other.

"Yep."

I press the button on the panel for the elevator to stop on the floor for the gym.

"Do you think they're just blowing off steam or maybe sparring?"

Jax kisses the top of my head. "What do you think?"

That's what I was afraid of.

I'm off the elevator in a flash as soon as the doors open.

"Can we have some privacy?" I call over to Mickey when I see him in front of the door that leads to the stairwell. There should have been another guard at the elevator. Whoever left their post early better pray they have a good excuse.

When I was first introduced to Mickey, I was instantly intrigued by his curly red hair, golden-brown eyes, and quick laugh. Come to find out, Mickey and Seamus are my Levin cousins. Another man, Lochlan, is my fifth cousin on the McCarthy side. I went from learning the family I grew up knowing was all one big fucking lie, to finding my real father I knew nothing about, to discovering several newfound Irish cousins.

"Uh, yes, ma'am." Mickey slips through the door and closes it behind him.

I face my three men, and two of them are not happy.

"Is that blood?" Liam bellows, his gaze landing on Jax. "What the fuck did you do?"

I counter with, "Why are you and Keane fighting?"

Liam isn't amused with my turnaround. Neither is Keane. His entire demeanor hardens into a stony mask that could give Jax a run for his money.

"You going to explain where you went and why you look like that?" Keane asks. Like Liam, he aims his anger at Jax.

They should know by now that challenging Jax in any way only amuses him and brings out his crazy. As if he heard me, Jax tips my head to the side and swipes his tongue up my neck, licking the dried blood off.

Liam makes a face. "That's fucked up." He looks at Keane. "And you said I was worse than him. I call total bullshit. I don't do *that*." He points at a grinning Jax, who smacks his lips together like he just sampled the creamiest, most decadent chocolate mousse.

"Andie." This from Rafe.

Glancing over at him, I get a little lost in all his tanned, sweaty, gorgeously inked skin on display. He'd been on the treadmill when Jax pulled up the security feed. My sight follows a slow path down his body and back up again, briefly stopping on his bandage. He looks so much better. Vibrant, like the color of his blue eyes. Rafe has always been gorgeous as sin. The adrenaline from tonight hasn't fully abated, and it quickly changes to lust the longer I'm standing here. If there was no urgency for us to talk, and I wasn't also in desperate need of a shower, I'd be all over them.

Liam walks over to the corner of the mat and picks up a bottle of water, draining it empty. Funny how they haven't rushed me like they normally would have by now, wanting to check me over and make sure that I'm uninjured. I appreciate they're not treating me like I'm weak or fragile. They're treating me like an equal. I'm not Tinker Bell, or princess, or a sweet rose. I'm one of them. Capable and strong. Someone who can handle their own shit. A woman currently in control of an empire, who needs no man standing behind her because she's strong enough on her own.

"Declan's conference room in ten. I need a shower."

"I'm coming with you," Liam says.

"The last time she went anywhere with you, you were run off the road and she was kidnapped."

"Fuck you, Agosti!" Liam shouts and throws his water bottle at Keane's head, which Keane catches one-handed.

"Have they been like this all night?"

Rafe purses his lips. "Pretty much."

"Jax, handle that, please," I tell him and press a kiss to his cheek.

I take the exit for the stairs, my quota for being stuck in an elevator done for the day. As much as I want to, I don't know if I'll be able to call Falcon Tower my home, or let it be the place I want to set down roots in. I want to be surrounded by land and nature, not concrete, elevators, and millions of people.

I tell Lochlan and Mickey good night when I push through the door to the landing, then head up the six flights of stairs to my floor.

My phone vibrates against my outer thigh from inside the zippered pocket of my pants.

"You rang?" Tessa asks. "Well, you actually texted, but potatoes, po-tah-toes."

"You don't sound like you just woke up."

She fake yawns for my benefit. "That better?"

"Immensely." I smile.

"What's up?"

"Meeting in Declan's conference room in ten minutes. I have a plan."

"It scares me when you say that," she deadpans.

Without him even saying anything, I sense Rafe coming up behind me.

"Make that thirty," I amend.

She whines out a long groan. "Your vajayjay is going to fall off with all the dick it's getting."

"Vagina envy is not a good color on you." I bite the inside of my cheek when I spot Mattieu and Z, the two men guarding the stair access point to my floor. Z is dark and brooding, and exactly Tessa's type with his mocha skin, athletic physique, and light brown eyes. Not to mention the guy is a treat to look at with all his defined muscles and broad chest.

"Hey, Z, you know Tessa?" I ask him.

His hand hangs loosely on his sidearm. "The cute blonde? Yeah, I've seen her around," Z replies.

I size him up and immediately like the mischievous twinkle in his eye. "You good at giving oral?"

Matthieu starts choking, and Rafe's jaw drops at my forwardness.

Tessa hisses on the other end of the line. "You did not just order a man to come and service me!"

Z, however, takes it in stride and plays along, scratching his chin as if in deep thought. "I've had no complaints."

Tessa screeches over the phone. "Alex!"

"You just earned yourself a half-hour break."

"I'm going to kill you!"

I burst out laughing at my best friend's outburst. "You'll be too blissed out to even consider it."

She hums, and I can tell she's imagining the possibility. "Z is pretty hot," she whispers. "And my rabbit is out of commission because it needs new batteries."

"You're welcome." I hang up on her.

"Holy shit, I cannot believe you just did that," Rafe says as we enter my suite.

Once my feet hit the tile floor of the kitchen, I kick off my shoes and strip my shirt over my head, then shuffle out of my pants. I'll burn them later and have the clean-up crew come bleach the kitchen.

When I turn around, Rafe's scorching stare combusts me

where I stand.

I look down at the soiled clothes at my feet. "I know you and the guys have questions, and I promise to answer all of them. But right now, I want a shower. Preferably one with you in it."

His dimples pop with his grin. "I'm down with that."

Chapter 20

ANDIE

We approach the double doors that lead into the conference room.

"What?"

Rafe wears a Cheshire grin, one that has only gotten bigger since our shower. "Nothing."

My eyebrows raise, but then again, I'm wearing a similar goofy grin. Our twenty-minute shower was brief but handsy.

He stops me, lifts my face to his, and gives me the sweetest kiss. "I guess I'm just happy to have my girl back. I've really missed the fuck out of you."

Well, damn.

My arms go around his chest, and I breathe in his clean, soapy skin still warm from the shower.

"I've missed the fuck out of you, too."

A throat clears behind us. "You said ten minutes. It's been three times that much."

"Can you even count that high?" Rafe's chest vibrates as he talks.

"Cute." Keane says it sardonically, but I can hear a tinge of amusement.

They used to one-line each other with joking insults all the time. It's ridiculous how something as trivial as hearing their trash talk makes me stupidly happy. Since the whole "stabbing me in the neck with a needle," Rafe's friendship with the guys has been strained and tenuous at best. So, as dumb as it may sound, I'm happy to hear them exchange barbs.

Keane grips the back of my shirt and tugs me away from Rafe. "It's late. Let's get this over with so we can go to bed."

I don't miss the emphasis he puts on the *we* and *bed*, and my core clenches at the subtle innuendo. Keane taps me on the ass, nudging me through the doorway when I don't move because I'm staring at his mouth and thinking of all the wonderful things it can do.

I haven't been in this room before, and I take a quick survey of my surroundings. Declan's domain. The seat of the Levine organization. One of many branches tied to the Irish mob. The windowless room has padded walls to dampen sound from escaping its confines. A long dark wood table with an inlay of the Levin crest sits in the middle, its surface glossy and polished to a high shine.

I glance around the room. There are eleven leather chairs, five of them currently occupied by Pearson, Keane, Jax, Liam, and Tessa. The twelfth chair at the head of the table is larger in size, all black with intricate designs carved into the wood. The Levin crest, similar to the one on the table, adorns the top of the chair. It's a king's throne. *Or a queen's*, I think, when I walk over to it. This is the first thing I've seen belonging to Declan that blatantly flaunts his power, and it's hard for me to reconcile it with the man who wore button-down shirts and reading glasses.

Trailing a finger over the smooth wood of the family crest, another pang of guilt hits me. Instead of sitting down in Declan's chair, I beeline straight to Jax, his new black-hilted knife twirling between his fingers.

Without me having to ask, he pushes his chair back from the table, and I take a seat in his lap. This is my throne.

No one says a word. Not even Tessa, who hates uncomfortable silences and would usually be saying something snarky and witty by now to break the tension.

Jax curls an arm around my middle and pulls me farther back in his lap.

Tessa is slumped in her chair, her face relaxed and eyes

dreamy. She looks completely sated and blissed out.

Liam sits forward, forearms resting on the conference table, his patience apparently on empty. Just as he opens his mouth to speak, I jump in.

"Alejandro tried to get to Declan in the hospital. Had one of his men pretend to be an orderly and coerced a nurse into helping."

Rafe drops his head in his hands, mumbling something in Spanish.

With arms folded over his chest, Keane swivels his chair my way. "Where are they now?"

Goose bumps skitter from shoulder to fingertips when Jax runs the hilt of his knife down my arm. "Dead," he says.

"You took her with you? That's how she got all that blood on her?"

I reach over and cover Liam's hand with mine, his knuckles white as they dig into the armrests of his chair.

"I'm the one who asked Jax to help me." I don't have to tell Liam I'm the one who killed them. He sees the truth of what I did in my unrepentant expression.

"Princess."

I wave off Keane's worry. He doesn't want me getting my hands dirty. But I can't idly sit by, twiddling my damn thumbs. Declan chose me for a reason. He knew I could handle it.

"Is Declan okay?" Tessa asks.

I send her a gentle smile. "Yes." I flick my attention to Pearson.

"He'll stay in Boston at one of Cillian's safehouses," the quiet Russian says.

Declan will remain there until he heals and fully recovers, and who knows how the hell long that'll be.

Tessa's no longer relaxed. "Isn't there going to be a police investigation at least for what happened to Declan? I thought that was protocol for any gun-related shooting."

"No."

That's all Pearson says. No elaboration or further explanation. But Tessa makes a good point. However, I trust Pearson when he says no.

Keane uncrosses his arms. "Cillian? Why does that sound familiar?"

"New York," Liam replies.

"He's also one of my many cousins from the McCarthy side, and the person who taught me how to fight."

Keane's nostrils flare at my admission. Might as well lay it all out on the table.

"The day after Kellan's funeral, after I met Liam" —I look over at my angel-turned-devil— "I was so angry. I wanted revenge. On a whim, I reached out and contacted my McCarthy relatives. I knew who they were. I knew they were Irish mafia. I wasn't sure if anyone from that side of the family would even speak with me, but I was desperate."

They had banished my mother. Kicked her out of the family when she was in her twenties. I can't even recall my reasons for why I decided to take a chance and contact them. I don't regret it.

I relax back into his chest. "You wanted to know where I learned how to fight. Now you know."

The leather of Rafe's chair crackles when he stands up. "Any intel from the two you questioned?"

"Not much. Your dad is back in Mexico, letting Alejandro run the show."

Rafe presses his back to the wall, one knee bent. "That's not entirely true."

All eyes turn to him.

"The fuck that's supposed to mean?" Keane barks. "You still haven't told us who you called."

"Oh! The floo powder!" Tessa exclaims, and the book reference throws me.

I look across the table at her, completely at a loss as to what they're talking about. Whatever it is, it must be something that happened during the time Alejandro had me.

"My uncle," Rafe says.

"And?" Keane prods.

Rafe rubs the back of his neck, then his jaw, before blowing out a breath. "Alejandro has been *running the show* for a while.

Pushed Julio out and took over."

"Like an '*Et tu, Brute,*' without the stabbing and bloodshed because Julio is clearly alive and breathing," Tessa interjects.

All heads snap to Tessa, even Pearson's, and she shrugs in response.

I tap a fingernail on the tabletop. "Did that orgasm rattle your brain?"

Her face flushes a bright crimson.

"Trust me. Don't ask. You don't want to know," Rafe tells the guys.

"But I met with Julio right after you took Andie. Told me he wanted his property back." Keane's voice drops to a snarl, and nausea roils in my stomach at the reminder that I was sold off to Julio and Alejandro like a cheap whore. "Why would Max make a deal with Julio and not Alejandro if he was the one in control?"

"I have no fucking clue, Keane. Maybe Julio willingly stepped down and is helping Alejandro transition into the role. Maybe Alejandro is keeping Julio around as a figurehead to maintain stability and prevent infighting and a civil war. My older brother is not well-liked, as you can imagine."

Jax snorts.

"So, what now?" Liam asks.

I hop off Jax's lap and go to stand behind Declan's chair. My hands curl over the top, fingers touching the edge of the Levin crest. I take in every person in the room. My men. My family.

"I have a plan to make Alejandro come to us on our turf and our terms." My lips curve at Keane. "I think it's time we make an official wedding announcement."

Chapter 21

ANDIE

"Shit!" I curse, taken by surprise when I look up and see Keane. "I didn't hear you come back in."

I stayed behind after the meeting was over, my mind full of what's to come. I've been sitting in Declan's chair for who the hell knows how long, staring at the Levin crest on the table.

"That's because I never left."

I cover my face with my hands. "Seriously?"

He smirks, still sitting in the chair he was in earlier, and I never noticed.

"Well, that's embarrassing," I reply.

"You may want to add improving your situational awareness to your to-do list." He gets up from his chair.

"Ha ha," I deadpan. "How long was I 'situationally unaware?'"

He stalks toward me, his hazel eyes full of smug mischief. "Do you mean, how long were you completely oblivious and didn't notice that a six-foot-two man was five feet from you for over twenty minutes?"

He stops and leans over me in the chair, his thick, muscled arms caging me in. My hands instinctively mold to his biceps and squeeze, just like my pussy does at his nearness as I remember how he held me in his arms and fucked me standing up.

"Yeah, that."

Keane moves into my personal space, forcing my head to tilt back. His cologne sends my senses into a tizzy. Why does he always have to smell so damn good? His lips hover over mine, and my heart pounds in anticipation. Hazel eyes trace my face, lingering on my mouth for a few seconds before he steps back. I'd be irritated at how easily Keane flusters me with just one look, if I weren't so attracted to the domineering bastard.

"Do you really think Alejandro will come after you again once he finds out we're getting married?"

I inspect my nails and the chipped polish. I'll get Tessa to give me another manicure before we leave tomorrow. I'm going back to the Rossi estate with the guys. It wasn't an easy decision to make, but one I felt was necessary. Unlike here at Falcon Tower, I know every inch of the Rossi mansion—its hiding spots and its secrets. I know every tree and blade of grass that grows within the estate's walled perimeter.

"Not if, but when. Once he hears the announcement, he won't wait to make his next move. His ego and his hubris will force his hand. He'll want to punish me for lying to him. He lost it when I told him we were already married. Destroyed the cage he put me in, then broke my finger and took your rings."

Keane strangles the back of the chair, and it wouldn't surprise me if he picked it up and tossed it across the room with me still in it.

"Anyway, we're not talking about that. I'm actually glad you're still here. Saves me from tracking you down."

The anger subsides as desire takes over. "Ready for bed?" He strokes my neck.

"Yes." I press my legs together. "But also no. I want to talk to you about Liam."

I'm not amused at the groan he emits. It sounds like something a teenager would make when they're told to do their homework instead of playing video games.

"Keane, I can't have you and Liam at each other's throats all the time."

He paces a few feet, groans again, then turns around. "I don't like him," he says through clenched teeth.

"You don't have to like him, but you can stop needling and

picking fights with him."

His hands land on the table, and he scorches me with a glare. "It won't matter once we're married."

My jaw drops before I can shut it. Is he implying that I won't be allowed to see Liam anymore?

"Liam will always matter to me, regardless of whom I'm married to. And if you think for one second that this marriage between us meant to help *you* solidify your position as don will stop me from being with Liam, Jax, or Rafe, you're about to find out where you can shove it."

His glare turns pensive, then solemn. "That's not what I meant."

"I call liar, liar, pants on fire."

My juvenile reply has him snapping, "Now, wait a goddamn minute."

Not waiting, I continue, "I know this entire thing between me, and you, and the others is not normal. I *know* that. I also know how selfish it is on my end. How unfair it is to all of you. If the situations were reversed, I would murder you in your sleep if you wanted to bring in another woman and fuck her."

"You wouldn't wait for me to be asleep, Tinker Bell."

His quip takes all the metaphorical air from my sails, and I collapse back into Declan's chair.

Keane gestures a finger back and forth between us. "This *thing* between us happened because four men want the same woman, and we're lucky bastards that she wants us back. I don't give a shit if it's normal or not. If they can't handle it and want out, it's on them."

My throat swells with emotion. "Everybody leaves."

Nothing in my life has ever held permanence. And buried deep underneath the steel walls I was forced to build around my heart in order to survive, still lives a scared little girl who is desperate for someone, anyone, to love her.

Suddenly tired, I rub my temples. "Keane, I don't want to argue with you anymore."

Before I can protest further, he lifts me up and deposits me on top of the conference table.

"You love arguing with me, princess. And we're not arguing. We're discussing." I gasp when he roughly rubs between my legs. "I bet you're soaking wet right now."

My thighs clench together, locking his hand in place. He'd be absolutely correct.

"And our marriage won't be fake," he says, throwing my legs open and jerking me forward to the edge of the table. The long, hard length of him presses against my clit, and I moan.

He flattens a hand on my back to hold me in place and toys with a strand of my hair. "I promised Jax I would never take you away from him. Not after..." He pauses, blowing out a puff of air over my face.

"Not after..." I prod when he doesn't finish.

He pushes the strand of hair over my shoulder and kisses me behind my ear. "Hopefully one day, he'll tell you. But that's not the point I'm trying to make. It's about something he said to me about walking away."

He pauses again, and my insides twist painfully. "Is that what you want?"

My incessant insecurities I try so hard to hold back, niggle their way forward anyway.

He touches our foreheads together and cups my face. "No, baby. It's not what I want. What I want is you."

The painful twist unfurls, and I breathe in deeply, not realizing I'd been holding my breath while waiting for his answer.

"Good. Because as much as I want to strangle you half the time, I do love you. I think I've loved you since the moment we met, and you scowled at me."

His whole body shakes with laughter. "You were such a brat back then."

"Hey!" I smack his shoulder.

He catches my hand. "It's hard for me to say those three words, but I do feel them. Damn, do I feel them, Andie." He places a fingertip below my jugular notch and pushes with gentle pressure. "I'm about to defile you on this table, woman. My dick is aching to be inside of you. If you're too sore to take me, now's your chance to say no."

There is no way in hell I'll refuse him, and he knows it. I lie back on the hard wooden surface and raise my arms above my head, my back arching slightly, looking like a sacrificial virgin on a stone altar. He licks his lips, his hungry gaze roving over me. His hands slide underneath my shirt and up my stomach.

"There are no cameras in here, and it's soundproof." I curl my ankle around his backside and thrust my hips upward, grinding into him.

"Is that a challenge?" he asks, pushing a bra cup up and fondling my breast. "Want to see how loud I can make you scream my name?" He frees my other breast and pinches the nipple. Spikes of pleasure cascade over me like a waterfall.

"Just the opposite. You'll be screaming *my* name."

"Is that right?" he asks, tugging the hem of my shirt.

I sit up so he can peel it off me and am impressed when he easily unhooks my bra with a twist of his hand.

"Fuck, I love your tits." His large frame towers over me as he looks his fill, his eyes alight with need and want.

He palms the back of my head and brings our mouths together. Keane's kiss is as controlling and domineering as he is, but his lips are devastating with how soft they are. He owns me with his kiss. Breaks down every single one of my walls and has me forgetting that only a minute ago, we were arguing.

He bends over me, pelvis flush with my core at the edge of the table, his arms propped and braced on either side of my head. I get lost in the depths of his green-browns, as he pulls his bottom lip between his teeth in introspection.

"You are so fucking beautiful, it hurts. I wish I had my camera."

I haven't seen him behind a lens yet, so I'm curious. "I saw the picture you took of me hanging in your room at Kellan's cabin."

His mouth tips up at the corner. "When I caught you in there, I may have freaked a little."

"You don't say."

I giggle when Keane holds his index finger and thumb slightly apart.

"I haven't seen you take any photographs. Did you stop?"

He unzips my pants and slides them down my legs. He does it slowly, torturously. Strong, masculine fingers dig into the supple skin under my knee.

"My muse was in Switzerland," he answers, and something inside me melts at his words.

Gently bending my right leg, he places my foot on the table. My stomach muscles clench when the scruff of his stubble tickles as he roams open-mouthed kisses along my ankle and up my calf. He gives my right leg the same attention.

Stepping back, he examines his handiwork. I'm dripping wet and fully aroused. My clit is pulsing, and my naked breasts quiver with my shallow breaths.

"I need to know your boundaries, baby. If there's something you don't like or don't want me to do, tell me. You're safe with me, Andie. I swear I will never hurt you."

He means hurt me like Max did.

"No belts."

One of my one-night stands in Switzerland made the mistake of trying to bind my hands together to his bedpost with his belt. I broke his nose.

"No belts," Keane concedes and runs his hands up my arms, loosely circling my wrists. "What about tying you up? Bondage?"

I'm honest when I reply, "You'll have to ease me into it. I don't like feeling confined."

Keane French kisses my breast, his tongue swirling around my areola. God, that feels so good.

"Spankings?" he asks cautiously, wondering if being spanked might be a trigger for me. Rafe slapped my pussy, and I loved it.

"I trust you." His lips move over to the other breast. When he gently bites down on the taut nipple, the electric zip of pain it causes has me confessing, "I like a little bit of pain with sex."

Taking me at my word, he bites down harder. *Yes, just like that.*

He kisses where he bit, soothing the sting. "You liked it when Jax cut you," he states. Not a question.

"Yes." Keane saw how I responded to Jax when he nicked my chest with the knife while fucking me on the coffee table.

"Who knew my princess was such a dirty girl?" He lets go of my wrists, his touch creating a trail of goose bumps in their wake as he moves them to my belly button ring. He flicks the amethyst that dangles on the short link chain a few times. "This is incredibly sexy."

"So are you."

Keane is still fully clothed. He's wearing a black dress shirt, the top three buttons undone. The sleeves are rolled up, exposing his full sleeve of ink and the corded muscles in his forearms. His dark brown hair is longer and mussed in a just-rolled-out-of-bed way. But it's his hazel eyes that pull me in. The forest green flecks intermeshed in the light chocolate brown of his irises.

He dips a finger between my drenched folds, spreading my arousal over my clit, then down farther. His fingertip rubs a circle around my forbidden, puckered hole, and his eyes bore into me. He's testing my response to being touched back there. He had said he wanted to be the first to take my ass, and I know he must wonder about Max.

I look away, ashamed to tell him that Maximillian Rossi destroyed every part of me.

"I trust you," I repeat.

His finger stops moving when understanding hits.

"Jesus," he breathes, removing his hand and gathering me in his arms. He holds my face between his hands and kisses every inch of it. "I'm so sorry. I'm so fucking sorry," he says, over and over. "You are so strong, baby. So fucking strong."

Then he says the three words he thought he would never be able to voice out loud. "I fucking love you, Andie."

I turn my face into his neck and laugh. "That's a lot of 'fucking.'"

Not letting me go, he leans back, smiling, and it's a marvelous sight.

We stay wrapped around one another for a while. It's amazing how life-altering a simple hug can be. How safe I feel. Protected, loved, and cherished. The guys don't understand how much they've healed me and brought me back to life. And it's not just the incredible, hot, mind-blowing sex. It's love. Something I thought I didn't deserve. Something I thought I'd never find or have. And I've found it with four dangerous men. I'm a very grateful bitch.

My arms circle his neck. "Now, if you don't mind, I was guaranteed to be screaming your name by now, and I haven't said stop, *so*..."

My giggles turn into full-blown laughter when he rips his clothes off and climbs on top of the table with me underneath him.

Chapter 22

ANDIE

I dismiss the dresses and grab as many jeans, T-shirts, and yoga pants as I can, tossing them into the suitcase. A couple of pairs of tennis shoes and another pair of casual flats go in as well. I pick up my small bag of toiletries but leave the nail polish. Tessa just did my nails a little while ago. She passes me a Red Vine from the bag Keane left on my pillowcase, and I stick it in my mouth, letting the end dangle out.

"You know, you can take more than one suitcase," Tessa says while sitting on top of my overstuffed hard case, so I can zip it up.

"Not planning on staying that long," I reply with a grunt and give one last tug to the zipper.

"Then why go at all?"

"I've already explained why."

She clucks her tongue against her teeth.

It's past midnight when I finally finish packing. We'll be heading out after breakfast. We, as in everybody but Tessa, and she has made sure to let me know how unhappy she is about that.

I stand by every word I said to Keane. I know Alejandro won't wait much longer to come for me. I just need to make myself as open and available as possible to give him that chance. And I'd rather be on my home turf than here at Falcon Tower when it happens.

"You don't trust me to keep you safe."

I drop the underwear I take out of my dresser drawer into my carry bag. "Why would you think that? And it's not your job to keep me safe," I add, selecting a few bras to take with me.

She slides off the suitcase and onto the bed. "You're my best friend, Alex, which makes it my job."

I toss a bra at her head, and she bats it away.

"No, your job is to use that big, beautiful brain of yours and do amazing things at MIT. I want to be your first investor when you start up your all-female tech company."

She puckers her lips. "Is that what I'm going to do?"

"Yep."

Falling back into my pillows, she throws her hands up in the air. "Glad you have my life figured out because I sure as hell don't."

"Don't be a smart ass," I say, and sit down next to her.

Tessa doesn't want to return to England, and I don't want her to remain working for Declan. She deserves to live a normal, carefree life away from all this shit. I'm hoping once she's at MIT, she'll find her happy.

Tessa rolls onto her side and smacks her butt. "This ass is not only smart, it's cute and curvy."

"Is that what Z said?"

Yes, I'm fishing, and only because she hasn't told me what happened between the two of them. Which isn't like her because, at school, she used to tell me in graphic detail all about her sexcapades. Nothing would be left out, and my ears would usually be bleeding by the end of her descriptive recount. Tessa thoroughly educated me in many ways when it came to sex. She has no boundaries whatsoever, and some of the stuff she's into even shocked the hell out of me.

"Nice try," she says, still not giving me anything.

We squint narrowed eyes at each other.

She grins. "Your phone is ringing," she singsongs.

"Shit. I forgot." Seeing the time, I hop off the bed to retrieve my phone and swipe to accept the video call. "Hey, baby girl!"

Sarah's sweet, smiling face greets me. Her springy brown curls are tamed within two braided pigtails and tied at the ends with little pink bows. She looks adorable.

It's a six-hour time difference between here and Ireland, which puts it past six a.m. there. Sarah has been getting up early every day to help Hannah and Eoghan on the farm. I talk to her often, and it warms my fucking heart to hear her so happy. Seeing it lets me know my decision to send her away until this shitshow with Alejandro and Julio is finished was the right choice.

"Auntie Andie, Nutkins had her babies last night!" she shouts excitedly. Nutkins is Hannah's tabby cat.

I walk back over to the bed and get comfortable.

"Hey, Sarah." Tessa leans in to get into the camera with me.

"Tessy!" Sarah squeals, hopping up and down, so all we see is her bright blue jumper. In the background, Hannah asks her how many potato pancakes she wants for breakfast. "Ten!" Sarah replies, and I hear Hannah laugh.

Reeling Sarah back into our conversation before I lose her to breakfast and baby kittens, I say, "Wow. I bet that was exciting."

Her little nose scrunches. "It was gross. They came out slimy." She sticks her tongue out and shakes her head. "I want you to see them. When are you coming? I miss you."

Ah, hell. So freaking sweet.

"I miss you too, love bug. Me and your unkies will be there soon." I still get a kick whenever I hear her call the guys unkie.

Her little mouth draws down in the cutest pout. "Promise?"

I love this little girl more than anything. I don't care that she isn't my blood. In all the ways that matter, she's mine. What was it Keane had said? *We love her with everything we have in us. She may be Kellan's blood, but Sarah is ours."*

"Super duper pinkie promise," I assure her.

Sarah turns her attention to Tessa, and as they talk, my mind whirls with questions and doubts about whether she would be happier staying in Ireland permanently. Hannah and Eoghan live a simple life on a pastoral farm. Not one filled with guns and death and things a child should never see, let alone grow up around.

Hannah calling her for breakfast engages my brain back into our conversation. "Bye, Auntie Andie! Love you!"

"Love you to the moon and back," I tell her, and wait for her to log off before I toss my phone to the end of the bed.

"She is so freaking cute," Tessa says, then shoulder bumps me. "Lost you for a minute there. Where'd you go?"

I have no clue why it comes out of my mouth. "How badly do you think I'd screw up a child being its mother?"

Tessa blinks a few times and looks down at my stomach. Blinks again. "Holy shit! Are you pregnant?"

My ears are ringing from her shrill outburst. "What? No!"

Her eyebrows raise, not buying what I'm selling.

"I swear. There is no bun cooking in this oven."

However, the thought doesn't freak me out like I expected it would. It's also something I've started thinking about lately. A lot.

She pokes my abs. "You sure? Because you get more big dick than a porn star."

I can't stop my snort of laughter. "Positive. Ninety-nine percent."

Then she asks the big question I'd like nothing more than to ignore. "Do you want to be? A mom?"

My mouth hangs open, but nothing comes out.

Tessa reaches around and pulls me to her. Her hair smells like the strawberry and honey shampoo she uses. "Alex, you'd be the best damn mom ever. Any kid would be fucking lucky to have you."

Needing to change the subject before I do something stupid like get teary-eyed over the prospect of one of the guys knocking me up, I grab Tessa's arm and stand up.

"I need you to do something for me, and you're not going to like it."

Chapter 23

ANDIE

The house comes into view. Beautiful and majestic. Late afternoon sunlight scatters over the metamorphic quartzite stone façade, making the cream and beige color appear pinkish in hue. The house used to be the devil's home, but as I look at it, I no longer see the shadows that used to lurk along every wall and in every window. When the massive, ornately carved double oak doors open, I don't imagine myself walking through the gates of hell.

"Welcome ho—"

I rip the cherry sucker from my mouth. "Don't finish that sentence," I warn Dante, then continue to enjoy the lolli that Paul gave me when we stopped at the gatehouse for the usual undercarriage and weapons check. It's a precaution Max had implemented years ago because he was a paranoid fuck.

Rolling my shoulders back, I breathe deeply and hold my head high. I can't believe I'm back here. Again. By choice this time because it was my idea to return to the Rossi estate. Like I told the guys in the conference room, I'm going to fight Alejandro on my terms and on my turf. Kind of like the spider and the fly from that children's story.

Jax stops beside me and bends to my ear. "You gonna suck my dick like you're sucking that lollipop?"

His comment catches me by surprise, and I pull out the candy when I start choking.

"Not the only thing you'll be gagging on later," he says with a naughty smile and a wink. Jax steals my sucker right out of my hand and sticks it in his mouth, making a show of moving it up and down his tongue.

I roll my eyes. Lame comeback, I know, but the best I could come up with because all I can now think about is dropping to my knees and licking his cock. He knows it too by the shit-eating grin he's giving me.

His phone goes off and after reading whatever message he received, he says, "Give me an hour tops to take care of this, and then we'll head over to Bastard's." His forefinger brushes the side of my hip like an artist's paintbrush, as if he's already imagining what will be inked there.

Bastard Ink is where the guys get all their work done. The owner, Bastard—no one knows his real name—is originally from North Carolina. He does work for a lot of celebrities, and every design covering Keane, Jax, and Rafe's skin was by his hand. Keane already called him and set up a consult for me to discuss getting the flaming phoenix done on my back. For a piece that big, it'll take a few sessions to complete. I also have a special request for Bastard. Something the men don't know about, but something Bastard should be able to do tonight.

Dante chuckles and scratches his stubbled jaw. "There's nothing left on you to ink, man, unless you shave your head."

Alejandro flashes behind my eyes. His face leering at me through the cage bars. The tattoos crawling up his shaved head. The jagged scar crisscrossing his cheek. Those black, soulless eyes.

"Angel."

Jax scores his thumb over my mouth, tracing over my top Cupid's bow. I kiss it to let him know I'm okay, then tap the bridge piece of his glasses.

"One hour. Come get me if I don't find you first." He plants a swift kiss to my lips and jogs up the stairs, heading across the long mezzanine toward Max's office.

I pull my gaze from Jax and am met with Dante's smirking face.

"He seems happy, and not to sound like a dick, but it's weird as fuck." Dante opens his arms and I step forward into them. "It's good to have you back, Andie," he says, hugging me. "You look like you went twenty rounds with a Mack truck."

"Been a rough few days," I reply.

"I heard. I'm glad you're okay."

I get curious looks from a few men I recognize who worked for Max. Keane told me that he and Jax cleaned house, getting rid of the inside men Declan had planted. I hate that Matteo was one of the casualties. I never did get to talk to him about what he said regarding Kellan.

Dante gives me one final squeeze and lets go. I don't think any of the other men here know that I'm not Max's biological daughter. I doubt Keane has said anything. Doesn't matter anyway. Keane is the don now, and I'll soon be his wife. If anyone objects to either, they'll regret it.

"How's Enzo?" I ask Dante.

A trio of heavy footsteps climbs up the stone steps outside, and I glance behind me. I'm a little worried how Rafe and Liam will be treated while staying here once word gets out who Liam is, and that Rafe switched sides. Surely Rafe's absence has been noticed. And mine.

"Up and about. Bored as hell because he can't do much. Stupid fucker decorated his cane to look like a giant phallus. Bought a pair of those metal ball sacs you see hanging on the backs of trucks." Dante laughs, and I join him as I picture a pair of steel balls dangling from a walking cane. "They look stupid as hell. Not to mention, you can hear him coming from a mile away."

Dante's amusement dries up when Keane, Rafe, and Liam join us. I really like Dante, but if he tries anything or throws a punch, I'll lay him flat on his ass.

"Rafe."

"Dante."

Dante next eyes Liam for a tense second before thrusting his hand out in greeting. A handshake he didn't offer Rafe. The brush-off Dante just delivered couldn't be more obvious.

Keane barks a few orders at two of the men, telling them to take my luggage to his room. I brought clothes this time because there's no way in hell I'm walking around in the too-tight dresses from my teenage years like I had no choice doing the last time I was here.

"Who says I'm sleeping in your room?" I ask him. I'm only teasing. Kind of. The guys' rooms are in the east wing along with mine and Kellan's, and I don't know if I'll be able to sleep so close to those rooms that hold too many memories.

In front of Dante, the guys, and the rest of the men milling about, Keane wraps a long-fingered hand around my nape and brushes his thumb over my bottom lip, the heat in his hazel eyes making me breathless.

His voice lowers an octave. "My bed is the biggest."

Pornographic images of the last time I was in his bed fill every brain cell in my head. He and Jax and Liam. The things we did together. The things I want to do again.

"I'm not sleeping in your fucking room." Liam bends to pick up his black duffel where he dropped it on the floor, but Keane gives it a hard push with his foot, sending it sliding across the polished marble.

"Something we both can agree on," Keane replies. "Take that upstairs and drop it inside any of the guest rooms," he instructs one of the guards.

Rafe's head slowly rotates from side to side, his blue eyes introspective. "Looks like you've been doing some redecorating."

He wasn't here when I went postal with the crowbar. The foyer and entryway are empty of the tacky, expensive artwork and showy collectibles. No imposing portrait of Max hangs on the wall. I hated that damn thing the minute I saw it and am glad that it's gone.

"Andie thought it was time."

Rafe peers down at me with a questioning look, and I smile innocently.

"Got a minute, boss?" Dante shifts his weight, angling it slightly to indicate he needs to speak with Keane privately.

Pivoting around to face Keane, my hands circle his biceps, which instinctively flex under my touch. "Go. I'll get Rafe and Liam settled in."

I kiss each of his cheeks, then take his right hand between mine. I bring it to my lips, bowing slightly and kiss the ring on his finger, then press it lightly to my forehead.

My display of respect catches the attention of the other men around us. They just witnessed the daughter of the former Rossi don pledge her allegiance and support to the new don. Of course, I did it on purpose.

Placing a fingertip underneath my chin, he lifts my downturned face and brushes his mouth over mine, claiming me in front of his men, which must be confusing for those who saw Jax kiss me. They can get over it. I'm not going to hide how I feel about all four men.

"I won't be long."

"Jax said he had some stuff to take care of. Hour tops."

He lingers a moment, his eyes touching every part of my face before settling on my mouth. My face still bears several ugly bruises, but the right kind of makeup does wonders, and I used a ton of it to help cover the worst areas.

"Go," I insist.

Keane and Jax stayed away long enough to be with me at Falcon Tower. No matter how many times Keane assured me Dante was handling things in their absence, I knew better. The heavy crown of responsibility lies directly on Keane's head if he wants to remain don. There will always be someone trying to take what's yours unless you have the power to stop them. Our marriage will give him that power and a new ally—the Levines, and by association, the Irish mafia.

With a nod, he joins Dante at the bottom of the stairs. Keane stops briefly on the balcony landing and looks down at me. Max did the same thing the day the guys brought me back home after Kellan's cabin was destroyed.

I wait until they disappear up the stairs and head in the same direction Jax went before saying, "I need a drink." Something cold to help dispel the heat that Keane just ignited inside me.

"It feels weird being back," Rafe says.

As we head to the kitchen, I thread my arm under his, and he bends his elbow to support my injured hand. The house has two kitchens. One that is private for family use only, and a larger, industrial one used by the culinary staff to prepare meals. The family kitchen is where Kellan taught me how to bake. The place we would sit and talk while I did my homework. It's where Rafe kissed me for the first time.

Liam isn't familiar with the layout of the house, and I slow down my steps to give him a chance to check things out. I'm curious to know if he sees it the same way I do—ostentatious and gaudy. The last time we were here, he only saw a few of the rooms: the basement room with the cage, the dining room, my bedroom, and Keane's room. The house does have a few redeeming features. Liam is an avid reader like me and would love the library. It was one of my favorite places as a kid to escape. I could pretend, just for a short while, to live in the fictional worlds of the pages. I could become that character in my mind. Anything to give me reprieve from the abuse and pain I endured every fucking day of my life.

When we enter the private kitchen, I aim straight for the fridge and search its contents. Grabbing the pitcher of iced tea, I take a sniff and hum when I detect a sweet peach fragrance.

"When you said you needed a drink, I thought you meant something different."

Rafe hops up on top of the center island, and I hand him the tea pitcher so I can get three glasses from the upper cabinet.

I hold one glass out for Rafe to fill, then give it to Liam, who scowls at it.

"It's good. Trust me."

Europeans tend to turn their noses down at iced tea. To them, it's sacrilegious to drink tea that isn't piping hot.

"I'm pretty sure there's some honey whiskey or gin around," Rafe suggests.

Liam looks almost green. "God, no. That sounds even worse."

Stepping into Liam, I sip my tea, then crook my finger at him. As soon as our lips touch, I lick the seam of his mouth, and he opens for me on a hum. My tongue dips inside, slowly stroking his, so he can taste me. A hot ember of desire erupts into a full-blown fire as Liam deepens our kiss. He pushes me backward until I'm up against the counter island next to Rafe.

"You're not going to fuck her in front of me in the kitchen," Rafe says, setting his tea down on the granite hard enough to crack the glass.

Sooner or later, we're all going to need to sit down and have a discussion about our expectations—about what the guys want as well as what I need for this relationship to work. I already know Jax and Keane have no hang-ups when it comes to group sex. Would I want to be with all four of them? Hell, yes. I'd never experienced anything like the night I spent with Jax, Keane, and Liam. But that night was different. I needed them to help me bury the trauma of what Max did to me. Something that I chose for myself, and not something that was forced on me without my consent.

Spying a crystal dessert dome filled with colorful macaroons, I lift the lid and choose one of each color, immediately biting into the almond-flavored one. The light, airy cookie literally melts on my tongue.

"God, I forgot how much I missed these," I say with my mouth full.

I hold the pink raspberry one out for Rafe. He circles my wrist and brings the cookie to his mouth, biting it in half. A delicious tingle builds in my core when he stares at me like it's not the cookie he wants to be eating right now. Giving myself time to cool off, I finish off the other half, licking the sugar from my fingers and smile at Liam when I see him watching. The intense sexual pull between me and the guys is undeniable. But I don't question it, even though a part of me wonders, why me? What makes me so special? What is it about me that draws the interest of four different, yet equally dangerous men?

Rafe hops off the counter and takes my hand, pulling me

toward the French doors that lead out onto the back portico.

"Where are we going?"

"Want to take my girl for a stroll," he replies.

After being exposed to the full sun all day, I can feel the heat that radiates up from the stone pavers as soon as we step out into the back courtyard. The warm evening air smells of the climbing roses that are blooming on the arbor trellis we walk under. Rafe plucks a smaller red bloom from one of the thorny vines and tucks it behind my ear. The sweet gesture isn't lost on me. Liam comes up behind me, and I wrap his arms around my middle.

He drops his chin to the top of my head. "This is nice. Much better than inside."

"Cecelia designed it."

I don't add that my mother loved her garden more than her daughter. I used to despise this garden, but looking at it now, I can't deny how beautiful it is.

The grand feature of the Roman-inspired peristyle garden is the reflecting pool with a large fountain in the center of it. A beige stone portico and Corinthian pillars surround the garden's perimeter. The last time I was out here with Keane, I'd noticed the new addition of the butterfly mosaics along the paver stone pathway. *Maripositas*. Little butterflies. Which reminds me—

"I talked to Sarah last night. We should do another video call, so she can see all of us."

I make a point to lean farther back into Liam, so he knows he's included as well. Sarah will be thrilled to inherit a new "uncle," who will spoil her like Rafe, Keane, and Jax do. There's no doubt in my mind that Liam will love and protect her just like the other guys do.

"I miss her," Rafe says.

"Me too."

But Sarah's safety comes first, and she'll remain in Ireland with Declan's relatives for the time being. If Alejandro or Julio got their hands on her, they wouldn't hesitate to use her to get to me or the guys.

"Do you think our initials are still visible on the tree?"

The smile Rafe gives me is so fucking sexy. "Let's go find out."

There's a twenty-foot magnolia tree at the other end of the peristyle that Rafe carved our initials into. On the nights when Max was gone and I wasn't able to meet with Rafe at our spot in the park, I would come out here and sit beside the tree to feel close to the blue-eyed boy who stole my heart and never gave it back.

As we duck back under the trellis arch to take the path that leads to the tree, the hairs on my neck stand on end when I feel eyes on me. Being a young woman growing up in a house full of mafia soldiers and made men, I had to grow a thick skin real quick. I learned to block out all the nasty innuendos and not-so-funny propositions thrown my way from men who were much older than me. It was a constant battle.

I catch sight of two guards patrolling the garden, one of them vaguely familiar. It's not until I hear the low-mumbled "whore" and something that sounds like "stupid Mexican piece of shit" that it clicks who he is.

I'm reacting before my brain catches up, and I close the ten feet separating me from the two guards. In seconds, I have my nails digging into Mika's throat.

What the fuck is he still doing here? Mika is the guard who groped me at the gatehouse. He called me a whore. Rafe bashed his head in the car door for touching me.

"You're not a very smart man, Mika. You better be glad that it was me and not Rafe who heard you." I increase the pressure on his neck until the tips of my fingernails break the skin. A strange sensation overcomes me when I see the blood begin to ooze out in tiny tributaries along his neck, and suddenly, I'm back at the warehouse with my Grim Reaper, his hands touching me, his words guiding me.

"You stupid bi—"

I don't know how my knife gets in my hand, or why I do what I do next. All I remember is the feel of Mika's warm, red blood pouring out over my skin. How it seeps between my fingers and drips down my arm. How his curdled scream fills my ears.

And how much I like it.

Chapter 24

JAX

Antsy from waiting for Keane to begin the meeting he insisted we have right now, I light a joint and take a long drag.

"Do you have to do that now? I have shit to do and don't need your secondhand high," Dante says.

I blow smoke in his direction. If he doesn't like it, he can go fuck off. I briefly catch Keane's disapproving stare he sends me over his shoulder, and shrug.

Leaning back in my chair, legs outstretched in front of me, I ask Dante, "Who the fuck touched my computers?" He's the one Keane left in charge while we've been with Andie.

Dante sits up, elbows resting on his knees. "Enzo. Why?"

I'd throw something at him, but I don't think he'd appreciate having a lit joint bounced off his forehead.

"Three cameras are out, two of them along the south wall. That shit should've been noticed and dealt with immediately. And why the fuck would he be watching porn on *my* computers?"

I cleaned everything with disinfectant wipes once I saw the tracking log.

"Because he's bored out of his mind and can't do anything else after being shot in the gut?"

I flip him off, not amused.

Keane stands at the window, looking out at God knows what. He's been doing that for the last five minutes. Hands braced on his hips, he angles his head Dante's way. "Jax is right to be pissed."

Becoming frustrated, Dante scrubs a hand through his short hair. Even though he's about the same age as me and Keane, and we've known one another for years, Keane is now in charge. Dante is smart enough to realize that if he mouths off, he'll regret it.

Kellan was born and groomed by Max to be the next Rossi don, but Kellan never wanted the job. Not like Keane. Keane lived, breathed, and killed for Maximillian Rossi. For this life. Andie coming back was a complication he wasn't expecting. To be honest, none of us were prepared.

Keane may have wanted the Rossi throne, but he wants her more and would give it all up if she asked. But she hasn't, and I don't think she ever will. Declan was able to see what Max never could. Andie was born to be a queen. Strong. Fierce. Determined. Smart. Ruthless. It's why he handed everything over to her and not to Pearson or Liam. She'll be the reason why Keane will become one of the most powerful men in the country.

"I'm not going to make excuses for him, but we're a dozen men short, and no one else here is a computer genius," Dante replies, gesturing at me. There's an unspoken *and you both should've been here to handle this shit anyway, not me.*

Keane and I have been dropping in almost daily, but I can't argue that Dante is right. So was Andie when she told Keane he couldn't neglect his new duties or appear weak, especially during a transition of power. Add in the fact that we took out Carmine and Marcellus—the dons of the Ricci and Barone families, along with most of their men—in retaliation for Andie's kidnapping, and yeah, the whole thing is precarious as hell. We're living in a house of cards that needs rebuilding before Alejandro makes his next move.

Okay. That's not entirely correct. It's Andie who's running the show now, and it'll be her next move that determines the stakes in the cat-and-mouse game we've been playing with the Ortiz cartel.

I absentmindedly tap the joint on the desk, letting the ashes fall. Not like it's going to make it look any worse after Andie carved it up with her knife.

Rolling his head on his shoulders to relieve the tension, Keane blows out a breath. "We need to start recruiting new associates and soldiers. I have a few men in mind that I think will be good capos. I'd wanted you and Enzo to take over in New York, but clearly, Enzo isn't ready. And Jax, we should get someone else on board who has tech skills to shadow and learn from you."

I take another hit, hoping it helps dispel some of the annoyance at what he suggested. Me mentoring someone? I don't work well with others, and I definitely don't like anyone touching my stuff.

"Get Tessa to do it."

Keane faces the room, his back to the window. "Tessa doesn't work for me. You do."

Dante raps his knuckles against the open palm of his other hand. "Where are we going to find new recruits? It's not like we have a pool of men to choose from. Levine decimated us when he took out Max and the other capos. He killed even more when his men attacked the house. Once our guys find out she's *his* daughter and not Max's, some of them will turn on her."

I'm out of my chair, lifting Dante up by his shirt, and slamming him against the wall before Keane has a chance to do the same thing.

"Let them fucking try," I snarl.

Keane's hand grips my shoulder, and I release Dante with a shove, rattling a few framed pictures hanging on the wall.

Dante jerks down his now-ruffled shirt. "I was just pointing out a potential future problem."

Dante is the only person outside our small group who knows that Andie is Declan's.

"It won't make a difference after we're married. And if it does, we'll deal with it then. We have other things to worry about that need our immediate attention."

Dante's stunned look is almost comical. "You're getting married? To Andie?" Then his brows dip when he does a slow head turn my way. "But didn't she... you guys both fu—" He thinks about it, mulls it over, then says, "Never mind. Not my business. Congratulations."

Keane doesn't say thanks.

"I'm confused though," Dante continues.

Keane pulls out the leather executive chair and sits down. "About?"

"Where our allegiance lies."

"With me," Keane cuts in.

"What about Andie?"

"What about her?" I ask, taking out my knife. It's a tactile thing, the way I play with it. My version of a fidget spinner.

A loud crack of static erupts from Dante's earpiece. "Fuck!" He jumps at the sudden noise before lowering the volume to listen to whatever is being said. Pressing the mic, he says, "Repeat that?"

Snapping his fingers at me with urgency, he says, "Get to the courtyard."

I don't wait for an explanation. I rush out of the office, Keane right behind me, his Glock already out.

"Where's Andie?" I shout, hurdling down the stairs three at a time.

"She was in the foyer with Liam and Rafe when we came up," Keane replies, disengaging the safety on his gun as he jumps the last six steps and lands on his feet in a dead run.

My blood goes cold, my thoughts jumbled. If Alejandro's men are here...

Rafe and Liam won't let anything happen to her. My Angel will fight to her last breath. Why didn't anyone notice the fucking broken security cameras?

We don't know what's happened because we dashed out of the room before Dante could tell us.

"You got your comms on?" Keane asks, slightly winded.

"No."

"Me neither. Dammit." Spotting Garrett, Keane grabs my arm and pulls me to a stop, but I shake him off and sprint through the

French doors that'll lead out into the back garden.

I jump the hedgerow, searching for faces that don't belong. Hearing raised voices, I slow my steps and crouch down along the retaining wall of the reflecting pool. My sights lock on Rafe, who is a head taller, and profound relief crashes into me when I see Andie next to him. The relief is short-lived because Liam has his gun pointed at Johnny.

Doing a quick check of the area, I slowly rise and reveal myself, when I'm sure there are no immediate threats. "The fuck are you doing, Liam?"

"What did you do to her the other night?" he growls at me, lowering his gun, and my swift steps falter, not understanding.

At the sound of my voice, Andie turns toward me, but Rafe pulls her back and takes something from her hand. "Baby, let go."

It's then I see Mika's body on the ground, his throat slit.

Andie smiles at me, and it's the most beautiful thing I've ever seen.

And the deadliest.

What did you do to her the other night?

I dragged my Angel down into the darkness with me.

Chapter 25

ANDIE

The yelling starts immediately as soon as we enter the house. I ignore it and go to the kitchen sink, turn the faucet on, and begin scrubbing the blood off my hands.

"You are out of control."

I focus on the tiny soap bubbles that turn pink as they swirl down the drain and not my sudden desire to throat punch my soon-to-be husband.

Liam jabs an angry finger at Jax. "You should be saying that to your knife-happy pet psycho. She never did shit like that until *he* got his hands on her."

"Why the hell was Mika still working here?" Rafe demands to know.

I send him a silent, mental thank you for asking the same question I thought in the courtyard. I add more soap to my hands.

Keane's shoulders hike up and his hands fly wide. Kids make that gesture to say, "I don't know." Adults, however, do it to say, "What the fuck are you talking about?"

I attack the blood under my fingernails, scrubbing the cuticles with the same thoroughness as my hands.

Rafe slams his palms flat on the counter and leans in. My attention shifts from what I'm doing to how the muscles in his arms stretch the fabric of his shirt. So much arm porn on display. I hold my fingers under the spray to rinse them clean.

"That's the guard who felt her up. Guess he didn't learn his lesson the first time because he called her a whore and me a piece of Mexican shit."

I sigh, turning off the water. I'd hoped he hadn't heard that, but clearly, he did.

Liam's temper explodes. "I knew she shouldn't have come back here. *Bella*, come on. I'm taking you home."

"The hell you are!" Keane shouts, getting in his way. They shove one another.

I rip a paper towel off the holder and pat my hands dry, then toss it into the small trash bin under the sink. Leaning back against the counter, I find Jax. He's standing near the entryway and hasn't spoken a word. When our eyes meet, he quickly looks away, but not before I see the guilt. Does he believe what Liam said? I walk around the counter island and briefly stop next to him, kissing his shoulder since he's too tall for me to easily place one on his cheek.

"It's not your fault."

Just as I'm halfway out of the kitchen, Keane yells out, "Get your ass back here. We aren't finished."

Trying to avoid the fight Keane seems to want to have, I count to five before turning around. Keane is hot-tempered like me, and as alpha as they come. He's used to being in control and doesn't know how to handle it when he isn't.

"I disagree," I say.

"I don't know what's going on with you, but you're out of control."

My voice is low but steady. "I heard you the first time."

His jaw locks, and he seethes, "I don't need your smartass comments, Andie."

"And I don't need to stand here and listen to you chastise and berate me like a child, *Keane*."

"Then stop acting like one! You have no impulse control. Do you understand what you did and how fucked up it is? Just because Declan left you in charge doesn't give you the right to do whatever the hell you feel like here, in *my* fucking house—"

"Actually, it's *my* house," I mumble, but he rants right over me.

"—in front of my fucking men. You can't just kill someone because they pissed you off."

I want to clap back with, "If that were the case, you'd already be dead." But I hold my tongue.

Liam opens his mouth to say something, but I don't let him. "You're wrong," I tell him. "Jax didn't make me this way. I've always been like this. If you want to blame someone, blame Max."

Maximillian Rossi made me who I am. All the years he tormented me made me like this. I look at each man, one after another, before stopping on Keane. He's shaking his head in denial.

"It's unbelievable how hypocritical you're being. *All of you,*" I emphasize. "You dirty your hands every day. You kill and torture, justifying doing so because it's your job. A *job* you could've walked away from at any time. But none of you did. You chose to stay. I never had that choice. I didn't choose to be stolen from my real father and lied to all my life. I didn't choose to be whipped and violated almost daily. I didn't choose to be locked in a cage for days on end without food or water."

"Jesus Christ," Liam says brokenly.

Rafe and I, unfortunately, share the latter experience. I glance over at him. His blue eyes are full of regret because he still blames himself for what happened to me the night Max found us together.

Keane's hostile posture relents, and he takes a step back. "Andie, enough. You made your point."

"I'll decide when I've made my point. Not you. Mika got what he deserved. Don't expect me to regret what I did." I open my arms wide. "Take a good, long look because this is who I am, Keane. It's who I choose to be. And I'll never bow to any-fucking-one ever again. I see all your broken, ugly pieces, and I accept them. I love each of you even more because of them. Because that's *who you are.* If you can't accept me in the same way, that's your choice. I won't like it, but I'll understand."

I don't wait around for a reply. I walk away. Thankfully, no one follows me. Needing to be alone, I go to Keane's room, where my luggage should be, to change tops because I'd gotten a little bit of Mika's blood on the shirt I'm wearing. Instead of getting something of my own out of the suitcase, I open Keane's chest of drawers and pull out one of his soft cotton T-shirts. Holding it to my nose, I breathe in his unique scent of sandalwood, spice, and natural musk, then slip it over my head.

Sitting down on the bed, I pull off my shoes and socks, wanting the freedom of bare feet. Wiggling my toes, I collapse back onto the black satin bedspread, suddenly exhausted, my heart heavy as I think about what I said. I meant every word. But my resolve isn't strong enough to stop those niggly self-doubts from creeping in. Will I ever be good enough, strong enough, smart enough, sexy enough? Am I too damaged and fucked in the head for someone to really love me? The guys have told me they do, but are they just more lies I'm stupid enough to believe because I want it to be true?

Sitting up, I rake my fingers through my hair and shake it out. It's grown an inch in the last month and falls in haphazard waves to mid-back. The digital clock on Keane's nightstand tells me that I missed my appointment at Bastard Ink by over an hour. Hopefully, he won't hold it against me and will let me reschedule. I pull my phone from my back pocket to call Tessa, needing my best girl to talk to.

Things were kind of intense between us last night. She wanted to come with me, but I told her no. I asked her to do something for me, and she made it clear she wasn't happy about it.

Tessa reaches around and pulls me to her. Her hair smells like the strawberry and honey shampoo she uses. "Alex, you'd be the best damn mom ever. Any kid would be fucking lucky to have you."

Needing to change the subject before I do something stupid like get teary-eyed over the prospect of one of the guys knocking me up, I grab Tessa's arm and stand up.

"I need you to do something for me, and you're not going to like it."

163

When I pull Tessa into her room and close the door, I see her packed duffel on the bed.

"The answer is still no," I tell her before she can start in on me again about coming to the Rossi estate.

"Dammit, Alex." She makes sure to give me the biggest glower as possible.

"If I've never said it before, I like that you call me Alex." I give her fabric headband a tug and let go, messing up her perfectly smooth hairdo.

She slides down the headband over her eyes and pulls it back up into place. "Makes more sense than Andie."

"Andie comes from the 'andria' part of my name. It's what Kellan always called me."

"Like I said, Alex makes more sense," she replies, digging through her things and pulling out a hard case. She shifts over so I can sit beside her on the bed.

"Is that it?" I ask, pointing to what looks like a plastic first aid kit in her hands.

"Yep."

She opens the box and pulls out a weird-looking syringe with a huge-ass hollow needle. She holds up a tiny, clear canister, unscrews the top, and carefully deposits a miniature oblong pill-shaped capsule into her hand. She picks it up with her index finger and thumb, so I can get a closer look at the epidermal GPS tracking microchip. Amazing how I had one of these in me for years without my knowledge.

In one of our late-night girl gabs, Tessa mentioned she made some for Declan, and I told her to procure one, just in case.

"Where do you want it?" she asks.

I take my shirt off and drop it in my lap. "Under the arm."

Tessa sucks in air through her teeth when I lift my right arm above my head. "That's a sensitive area. It's going to hurt when I put it in."

"You know I can handle pain. And please don't tell the guys about this unless the situation calls for it."

Her eyes snap to mine and hold for a long minute before she rips open a couple of rubbing alcohol packets and starts to clean a small *area of skin.*

The guys saw how devastated I was when I found out that Max had—somehow, at some point in my life without me knowing—inserted a tracker in my arm. After Jax told me about it, I cut my arm open and dug it out with my fingers, then hurled it at Max with a "fuck you." So getting another one implanted is a big deal.

Tessa inserts the capsule into the syringe, and I give her a small nod to proceed. I can't look at her as she does it, so I turn my head and focus on the wall.

I hiss when Tessa slowly pierces my skin. Holy shit, that hurts worse than having my finger broken. As much as I hate the idea of having another tracking chip inside me, I need the assurance that if Alejandro ever gets his hands on me again, Tessa and the guys will be able to find me.

Thinking about it now makes the injection site itch, so I type out a text to Tessa to help distract me.

GirlUpHigh: You busy? Need to rant.

Before I hit send, something familiar catches my attention on the nightstand. Kellan's journal. In all the craziness of the past week, it slipped my mind that Keane still had it. What doesn't slip my mind is remembering how Keane wouldn't give it back, nor would he or Jax tell me what the coded messages meant.

Sliding my phone back inside my pocket, I swipe the journal, take a left out of Keane's room, and head to the storage closet at the end of the hallway. There's an access panel in the back of the closet that opens to a metal ladder railing that leads to the roof. I take a quick glance behind me to make sure the coast is clear, before opening the door and stepping inside. My movements are automatic now. I flick on the light switch, push the maid's cart with cleaning supplies to the side, and get down on my knees. The access panel is easy to jimmy open; something I've done a hundred times before. Propping the metal grate to the side, I reach through the opening.

There are no lights to rely on, so it takes me a few seconds to find the ladder by touch. My heart beats a little faster as I shove Kellan's journal in my waistband and pull myself through. I'm not a wispish teenager anymore, but at least I'm still as flexible. Grasping on to the ladder, I feel with my foot until it lands securely on another rung below. Then I climb.

When I get to the top, I push up with my shoulder to dislodge the hatch for the roof, years of unuse and rust making it stick and not easy to get open. This section of the roof is flat, not angled, and is gray concrete, not interlocking terracotta tiles. It was another one of my secret quiet spots I found when I was little. I'd come up here to look at the stars when the night sky was clear. When I was older, it became one of the places I would meet Rafe.

Climbing the last rung, I heft myself out, wincing only slightly when my broken finger protests. It's become easier to ignore the pain to the point where I don't notice anymore. The concrete surface is overly warm under my hands and bare feet, even though clouds are obscuring the sun's radiant energy. Finding a spot with the best view of the forests surrounding the property, I remove Kellan's journal from my waistband, sit down, and cross my legs into a comfortable position.

The fingertips of my right hand caress over the worn leather encasing the paper pages. How many more secrets are written inside that I don't know about? I open to the first page and am met with the same cryptic letters, numbers, and symbols as before.

"Kellan, what were you hiding?" I mumble, flipping the pages.

I stop on a detailed pencil sketch... of me. It's the same picture Keane had a photograph of in his room at Kellan's cabin —well, a drawing of it anyway. I keep flipping pages and find more drawings of me interspersed between the odd words and numbers. It's like looking through a family photo album a parent would make chronicling their child's development. The later sketches are of me in Switzerland. I recognize the mountains in the background. My dorm room. The school campus.

The last dozen pages or so in the journal are blank. Are they intentional because he no longer had anything he wanted to write down? Or because he died? A familiar melancholy hits me as I remember the last time I spoke with Kellan and listened to him gasp his final breaths.

I about jump out of my skin when the roof access clanks open, and a raven-haired Rafe pops up.

"Jesus. You scared the shit out of me." I put Kellan's journal down and help him climb the rest of the way out.

Standing, he bends over and vigorously brushes his hair. "You don't see a spider on me, do you? I went through a fucking cobweb." He briskly frisks his arms and legs.

I can't help but smile as I check him over. "The badass criminal who's not afraid to take on anyone, but the thought of a tiny spider crawling on him freaks him out. I don't see anything."

"Good." He mock shivers in relief.

"How did you know where to find me?"

"I didn't. This is the sixth place I checked." His arms come around me, holding me loosely, giving me the choice to either stay or step away. I choose to stay.

Choices. It's one of the points I made to Keane in the kitchen.

Rafe rotates his shoulder a few times, his hand covering the area of his chest where he was shot.

I throw my hands on my hips and say, "Please don't tell me that you popped your stitches again."

"I didn't. Just sore. I swear," he promises when he sees my you're-full-of-shit face. He looks down and points to the journal. "What are you reading?"

My hands move from my hips to cross at my chest in exasperation. "Rafe, you didn't come find me so we could start a book club. Just spit it out already."

"They're worried about you."

"Are you?" I deflect. It's a common interrogation technique. Avoid answering a question by asking one of your own.

"I'll always worry about you, *rosa*. But that's not what you're asking, is it?"

I don't respond.

"If I asked you to come back inside with me so we could sit down and talk, would you?"

"Not yet."

"Figured as much." He scuffs the sole of his work boot against the gritty, leaf-littered concrete. "You were right, you know." He waits a beat to see if I'll reply, but when I remain silent, he continues. "We are being hypocritical. Kind of like the old 'do as I say and not as I do' thing kids hear all the time from adults."

A very unladylike snort of agreement comes out just as the wind picks up, blowing my hair in front of my face. Rafe steps in front of me and wraps the strands back behind my ears.

"You are so beautiful, Andie."

I wasn't ready for his abrupt change of subject, and a blush spreads up my cheeks at the compliment at the same time as I deny it. "Purple and green bruises and split lips are not beautiful."

"Every part of you is beautiful."

I decide to poke that statement with a metaphorical stick. "Even the ugly, dark parts?"

He gathers me close and tucks my head under his chin. "Especially those."

Another eddy of wind swirls around us just as a spear of sunlight breaks through the clouds. If I was overly religious or superstitious, I'd think it was a sign.

Our bodies gently rock from side to side in a lazy sway. Just one of many slow dances we've shared on this small section of roof.

"Being up here brings back a lot of good memories."

"A lot of sex memories, you mean."

His light laughter vibrates his chest under my cheek. "That reminds me, I still owe you a date night."

It's my turn to laugh. "Sweaty quickies on the roof remind you that you owe me a date?"

My laughter increases when he dips me low in a dancer's pose. "What do you think will happen at the end of the date? Except it won't be quick."

He nips my bottom lip and pulls me back up, then turns me a quarter way around. Our bodies press together again in our silly, impromptu dance.

The solid thump of his heart lulls me into a serenity I rarely get to experience. I bury my face in his chest, enjoying the fleeting moment I'm about to ruin with my next question.

"Did you love her?"

I promised myself I wouldn't ask him about Rita. About her or about any of the other women he, Jax, and Keane have fucked since I've been gone. Jax said they didn't matter. Liam said he didn't love Sophia. But the argument with Keane in the kitchen has ripped the scab off old wounds. Wounds that never seem to fully heal and continuously ooze my insecurities no matter how many Band-Aids I slap over them.

Rafe stops our slow dance and leans back to look me in the eye. "The only woman I have or will ever love, Andie, is you. It's the same for Keane and Jax. We've all been in love with you since we were kids. Just proves how much smarter *I* am that I made the first move."

God, that dimpled, cocky grin does deliciously wicked things to me.

"You did the first *everything* to me," I say, voice husky as I reach down and pop the button on his low-hanging jeans.

Being up here with him brings to mind so many nights together, necking and laughing. Being in love. Being foolish. His crystal blue irises disappear when his pupils expand, and a low rumble builds in the back of his throat when I painstakingly pull his zipper down.

My hand stills when he says, "I wish it was my ring on your finger. That's a first I won't be able to give you. I won't be the man waiting for you at the end of the aisle."

Chapter 26

RAFE

Andie's hand falls away from my open fly, and my dick calls me every curse word in history for ruining his chance to get balls deep inside her.

I don't like that she backs up a few feet, putting distance between us. There's been too much fucking distance between us the last five years. An ocean's worth. I'll never let that happen again. Even if it means watching her marry Keane and not me. Take his last name and not mine.

Keane originally came up with the idea of marrying Andie to stop the deal Max had made where she was to be given to my brother. That's what Keane claimed was his intent at the time, but he was lying. He wanted her—wants her—just as badly as I do.

"I'm sorry," I tell her. And I am.

The guys and I keep messing up with her. Well, me and Keane more so than Liam and Jax. I know the marriage to Keane doesn't change how she feels about me. The whole concept is new for me, but I can accept that to be a part of her life again, to be with her again, means I'm sharing her with three other men.

Andie has lived a hell that none of us will ever be able to fully understand or relate to. Not only lived it but survived it. She's so much stronger than all of us combined. And yeah, what happened today with Mika was disturbing in some ways to see, but how is what she did different than me bashing his head in like a squished grape with the car door? Or Jax when he goes on one of his happy murder sprees and walks around the house afterward, naked and covered in blood? Or Keane when he shoots someone in the head like he did in front of Andie at the warehouse where she was being held?

"Me too," she says softly.

I look at her like a man dying of thirst, and she's my oasis. A few wavy wisps of her hair lift in the wind and kiss her face before floating back down. My perusal drops to her bare feet and baby-blue painted toenails before roving back up her body. I hadn't noticed what she was wearing before. A men's shirt. I can tell it's Keane's from the Randy's Custom Auto logo emblazoned on the front. I tell the flicker of jealousy that rises at seeing her wearing his clothes to fuck off.

She wipes her hair off her face and pushes the thick mass to one side and over her shoulder. "Keane and I haven't really talked much about what our marriage will entail and what comes after or how it's going to affect you, Jax, or Liam. It's something we should all sit down and discuss. You will always be my first and forever love, Rafael."

I'm man enough to let her see the sappy emotions that fill my eyes when I hear her say that.

Her head tilts back, soaking up the small sliver of sunlight that shines around her, the light playing over her face and pinking her cheeks.

"I had this crazy idea." She lifts her right hand and turns it over, flipping it front to back to front again. "I was planning on getting your name tattooed here." She points to her ring finger on her right hand, and my damn chest constricts. "Jax's name would go on my middle finger."

"Of course."

"Of course." She smiles. "Liam's would go on my index finger. Keane's on my pinkie finger. Then, when my broken finger heals, I'd get all your names inked around it like a wedding band. I'd belong to all of you. Committed to all of you."

I take her hand and kiss the finger that will soon bear my mark. "I like that idea. Jax and Liam will too."

"Maybe. It was just an idea. I was going to talk to you guys about it when we got to Bastard Ink. Guess it'll have to wait a little longer." She tries to shrug it off, but I can see the disappointment behind it.

"Nothing on your thumb?" I'm only teasing, but her answer has my dick hard and throbbing in an instant.

"Maybe our children's names?" She says it so softly, so quietly.

The neanderthal in me wants to throw her down and rip off her clothes. Fuck her and fill her with my cum. Give her as many babies as she wants.

I need to touch her. I grab her and pull her to me.

"You want children?" I ask in a calm I don't feel because I'm about to have a heart attack at the thought of her pregnant.

She touches my mouth, staring at it, and licks her lips. "I do, but it scares me. I don't want to mess my kid up. I don't want them growing up around violence and accepting it as a normal way of life. Or even worse, turn out like me."

Hearing her fears breaks my damn heart. "Any kid would be fucking lucky to have you as their mama."

"That's what Tessa said."

I'm sure she can feel the violent thud behind my chest. "You talked to Tessa about it?" She nods yes. "Baby, our kids would know nothing but love because they'd have you, *mi dulce rosa*. I want a little girl," I blurt, getting it out there. "A little girl with your violet eyes."

Her breath catches as she pictures it. Then she says, "Rafe, if you don't make love to me right now, I'll die."

With fucking pleasure. My hands grab her ass, and I pick her up. Her legs wrap around me like a vise, and her lips attack my neck, biting and sucking the skin like she's ravenous. My dick is so hard, the tip pokes out from where Andie left my fly unzipped, a divining rod pointing straight at her pussy. She wiggles in my arms, and the friction caused by her jeans over the exposed, sensitive tip has me almost coming. I need inside her right flipping now.

"Wall?" she pants, her tongue swirling in my ear and driving me out of my mind.

"Too hot."

Her back would get first-degree burns if I fucked her up against the wall. The few times we had sex up here were at night when the temperatures were cool.

"Floor?" She bites the fleshy lobe of my ear, and my dick jerks excitedly.

I turn my head and capture her lips, licking inside her sweet mouth. She takes over and sucks my tongue like the cherry lollipop she had earlier.

"Too hot."

She growls in frustration. "Bend me over the goddamn roof then."

"Baby, you'd burn your hands."

She bites my lower lip and pulls. The jolt it creates travels through my entire body like it's one giant exposed wire.

"Fine." Unlocking her ankles, she drops to her feet, picks up the book she was reading, shoves it in the waistband of her jeans, and starts climbing down the ladder.

"You coming?"

I blow out a breath laced with sexual discontent. "Wrong thing to ask me right now."

Her smile is luminous. "Don't pout. You're about to get very lucky in the storage closet."

Well, fuck. Can't argue with that.

I follow her like an eager puppy, making sure to close the hatch door before carefully descending. The light spilling in from the closet below helps dispel the darkness enough for me to see. There are so many more secret passages like this one throughout the house. Max may have been a paranoid son of a bitch, but I do have to admit he was also a smart one.

By the time I come through the opening into the storage closet, secure the metal grate back into place, and stand up, Andie is naked and waiting. I don't waste any time. I toe off my boots and reach behind me to tug at my shirt, tossing it to the floor. She helps shed my jeans, and I kick them off. She cups me through my underwear and rubs the length of my cock a few times before pushing down my briefs to join my jeans in a pile at our feet.

Her eyes travel over me in appreciation. She wets her lips with her tongue. "You're... bigger," she says breathily, and my ego does a fist pump in celebration.

I give her the same inspection. When I took her from behind against the window, it was fast and over way too quickly. This time around, we take a moment to eye-fuck each other. Andie as a woman is curvier, more voluptuous at the hips and chest. Her contours have more muscle definition and are a testament to her strength. She's a fucking sex goddess with her tussled hair falling down over her chest and her gorgeous purple eyes shining bright.

Something in the way she's looking at me has my heart trying to pound through my rib cage. Heat. Fire. Lust. Desire. Want. Need. The tension between us pulls tauter and tauter, until it finally breaks like an overstretched rubber band.

We crash together, mouths fused and tongues tangling, my cock in her hand and her breast in mine. We've devolved into two horny teenagers trying their best to get to third base as fast as they can. Our bodies stumble and crash into the cleaning cart. A few towels fall off.

"You okay?"

"Yep," she says, taking my nipple in her mouth. She fondles and pinches the other one with her fingers.

Men's nipples are just as sensitive as women's, and I love that she remembers how much I like to have mine sucked and played with.

"I love touching you. Tasting you," she whispers across my skin as her mouth roams my chest.

My head falls back on a moan and hits the wall when she takes my cock and pumps it a few times, then swirls the precum around the bulbous head with her thumb. The handle of a mop careens sideways and clatters to the floor.

She giggles, then says, "*Shh*," bringing her thumb up and

sucking it into her mouth.

I go feral at the sight and push her back until her spine flattens on the wall. I cup her breast and roughly knead it, enjoying how it fills my hand perfectly. Her bruises are faded although still visible, but all I can think is how fucking soft her skin is. I stroke her all over like a cat, and she literally purrs like one as my hands map her every curve.

Her chest is flushed with arousal, her lips are bee-stung, her nipples both swollen and red. The scent of her infuses the air around us and fills the small space of the closet. Roses and the sweet, delicious smell of Andie's arousal.

I kiss her, stealing the breath from her lungs.

"Now, Rafe. Please," she begs, gripping my hair and pulling.

"Need to make sure you're ready." I slide a finger through her soaking wet folds, and her legs tremble. She's more than ready.

I want her to come on my tongue first, but my cock has other ideas. He won't be made to wait any longer. Andie feels the same way. She lifts her leg and hooks it around my hip, then grabs my cock and guides it to her entrance.

"Trust me, I'm ready."

"I love you," I tell her, thrusting into her at the same time my tongue thrusts into her mouth.

The entire closet seems to shake as I hammer into her, the sound of skin slapping and our grunts and moans getting louder and louder. She grabs on to the ledge of the shelf above her head and holds on. Her tits bounce as I drive into her again and again. It's too much of a temptation. I bury my face between them.

I bite her. Staking my claim. *Mine.*

"*Oh, God.*" Her nails score my back, marking me just like I marked her.

"Who do you belong to?" I demand.

"You, Rafe!" she cries.

Damn straight.

Her walls convulse around me, and I groan, pounding into her harder, faster, deeper.

I wait until I can't hold back my orgasm any longer, then slide my hand between us and pinch her clit in the way I know will have her chanting my name and flying apart. She does, and I explode along with her.

Mine.

On a sultry, sated sigh, she goes limp in my arms. I don't pull out, my dick happy as can be right where it is.

Sweat glistens our skin, our lungs sawing in air. She buries her face in my neck, and I do the same in hers. I never thought I'd have this again. Hold her like this again. For the first time in five years, I can breathe. The profound happiness I'm feeling right now with Andie in my arms, her lips swollen from my kisses, my cock buried deep inside her, and my cum dripping down her legs, is painfully intense.

She hums. "I don't want to move. I want to stay here just like this."

Me too.

I kiss her thoroughly, tenderly, taking my time to reacquaint myself with the taste and feel of her mouth.

"Can I make a suggestion?"

She nods.

"How about we take a nice, long shower, get something from the kitchen to eat—"

"A hot fudge brownie sundae with extra whipped cream," she says.

"—and find the guys so we can have that talk."

Her smile falls. Keane's going to have a lot of groveling to do. Is it bad that I'm looking forward to seeing that?

"Okay."

I use one of the freshly laundered washcloths from the maid's cart to clean Andie. We unhurriedly put our clothes on and walk hand-in-hand out of the storage closet. Just as we get to my room, Keane appears at the end of the hallway.

"Where the hell have you been?" he says when he sees her, and I'm tempted to throw him down the stairs he just walked up.

Andie arches her eyebrows at him.

"Well?" he says.

She rolls her eyes, opens the door to my room, and disappears inside.

It takes him all of a second to eat up the length of the hallway from the stairs to where I'm standing.

"Where was she?" he asks, and I block him to stop him from barging into the room.

"On the roof." I take a quick glance into the room. Andie is sitting on the bed, the book she was carrying open in her hand.

The jackass actually sniffs me. "You fucked her?"

"Why? You jealous?"

His nostrils flare, and his fists clench. "No."

Andie looks over at us, but the daggers her eyes are throwing are directed at him.

"Liar." I cross my arms over my chest. "If all you're going to do is yell at her again, I'd strongly reconsider."

His head hangs, chin to chest, and he tugs on the short ends of his hair. "She pissed?"

"You think?"

He cranes his neck to look past me, and I swear his face blanches of all color right before I'm tossed to the side, and he rushes into the room.

"Keane, what the hell?!" Andie shouts when he almost tackles her on the bed.

He makes a grab for the book, but she goes ass over end and rolls off the side of the bed with the book still clutched tightly in her hand.

She gets back on her feet, her hair a tousled mess. "What is your problem?"

Keane gets off the bed and thrusts his arm out. "Give it to me."

She hides the book behind her back.

"Give me the goddamn journal," he snarls.

Her mouth turns down, and her eyes go deadly. "Fuck you."

I have no clue what's going on, but I dart around the foot of the bed and stand next to Andie.

"Are you high?"

He pins me with wild eyes. "She can't read that."

I slide in front of Andie so she's half behind me. "She's not allowed to read a book?"

Keane shifts, like he's preparing to leap across the bed. "It's not a book. It's Kellan's journal."

"So?"

"She can't know what's in it!" he yells, a mixture of anger, desperation, and fear rolling off him.

"I think it's way past time I know what's in it," Andie tells him.

"Keane, if it's Kellan's journal, she has a right to read it."

She says to me, "It's written in some kind of code. Keane and Jax were able to read it, but they refused to tell me what it said. Maybe you can figure out what it all means."

I know I'm missing a huge chunk of backstory, but I go with my gut which is firmly on Team Andie.

When she places the journal in my hand, Keane's eyes fly to mine, pleading with me.

"Tinker Bell, please trust me."

"Trust goes both ways, and clearly, you don't trust me at all."

He comes forward, but this time, Andie pushes me behind her and takes a protective stance, ready to go to battle with him.

I stare at the book in my hand. The leather binding is old and faded.

Keane closes his eyes and swallows thickly. "All it will do is bring her more pain."

I hesitate, the uncertainty killing me. On the one hand, I'm curious to know what Kellan wrote down and how it could be that bad that Keane is literally freaking the fuck out. On the other hand, I believe Keane. *Jesus, Kellan, what did you do now?*

Andie has been lied to enough. Whatever secrets are contained inside the journal, she deserves to know.

I pull the leather cord and open it.

"Rafe, man, don't."

"Get out," Andie tells him, the tone of her voice cold and just... dead.

I've seen Andie angry before, but this is something else. Anger is born of fire. But the way Andie is looking at Keane is nothing short of downright glacial.

Keane goes from shocked to livid to resigned in a space of three seconds. He must see it too, because for the first time in his life, Keane backs down from a fight and walks out of the room without saying another word.

Chapter 27

ANDIE

"I miss you so fucking much. You promised me that you would never leave me," I angrily tell him. Kellan left me alone in a world I don't know how to navigate, in a life that has no purpose without him.

I stand and cry silent tears that fall like the rain beating down on me from above. My shoes are soaked and covered in rivulets of brown, as are both my legs. The late May temperature is already hot and muggy, the humidity made even worse from the liquid precipitation that has been relentlessly falling all day long. I fucking hate this city. I hate this life.

"I hate you for leaving me!" I scream at Kellan's grave. My eyes widen when I realize what I'd said. "Oh, God. I'm so sorry. I didn't mean it."

I drop to my knees in the slick mud, my umbrella flying away in a gust of wind.

"I didn't mean it. Take me with you. I want to be with you," I beg him, clawing at the ground, flinging clods of wet, slimy mud every which way. My desperation to be with my brother leading me into darkness. I wish I had died with him.

I kneel at Kellan's tombstone, his journal heavy in my hands. It's the first time I've visited his gravesite, and it will be my last. Early morning dew clings to the blades of grass and soaks into the thick fabric of my blue jeans at the knees. The first peek of the rising sun has barely crested the eastern horizon, setting the sky ablaze in bright yellows and oranges. Unlike the other gravesites adjacent to Kellan's, his plot is bare and colorless. No flowers have been left. No evidence that anyone has visited his grave since the day he was buried.

My eyes feel gritty and raw after staying up all night, listening to Rafe read me every word Kellan wrote in his journal. Keane was right. The pain I'm in is worse than any lash of the belt Max gave me. Lashes that Rafe never noticed when we were together because I made sure he didn't see the evidence of them. Every time we made love was under the cloak of darkness. At night at the park or on the roof. With the lights off in my bedroom. If he felt the raised, rough scars when he touched my naked torso or thighs, he never said anything. Max was very deliberate and meticulous where he hurt me. Couldn't have a daughter show up to school with a black eye or scabbed arms.

The white quartzite feels cold to the touch as I trace each letter of Kellan's name engraved into it. There are no words in memoriam chiseled into the hard stone, like beloved son or an epitaph that describes what kind of person Kellan Maximillian Rossi was. I always hated his middle name for obvious reasons.

So, what kind of person was Kellan Rossi, the brother I adored and was willing to give up my life for?

He was a fucking liar.

The secret bank account he set up for me was paid for by Ortiz blood money and the drugs Julio funneled into the country using the shipping channels and ports Max controlled. Kellan was clever in how he stole from the Ortiz cartel. So clever, in fact, that Julio and Alejandro never noticed. I wouldn't have touched that money if I knew where it came from.

But that wasn't Kellan's only secret. He knew. Kellan knew I wasn't his sister. He knew Maximillian Rossi wasn't my real father. He wasn't even my half brother. His real mother was one of Max's whores. As soon as she gave birth to Kellan, Max killed her.

But the worst secret of all? Kellan was in love with me. Or so he said, over and over, in his journal. Coded, rambling sentences that made my skin crawl as I listened to Rafe read those sickening words out loud. Made nausea churn my stomach as I looked at the hundreds of sketches of me drawn on almost every page.

Kellan recorded videos of Max abusing me. Kept them as a kind of twisted life insurance policy to herald over Max as blackmail. He used Max's abuse as a way to keep me close to him. Dependent on him. Needing him. All the times I would crawl into Kellan's bed seeking comfort from my nightmares. All the times he would hold me or touch me or kiss me to help soothe away the aches and pains of Max's latest beating. It explains why Kellan always insisted I tag along with him and the guys wherever they went. Or why he liked staying home and spending time with me. Having me close was a way for him to feed his growing obsession. An obsession that began when I was four. The same age Max started coming to my room at night. It makes me sick to learn that the brother I loved was the same as the father I hated.

My miscarriage was Kellan's apparent turning point. That's when he started stealing from the Ortiz drug shipments and funneling the money into the offshore account. That's why he kept those videos to use as blackmail against Max, and why I was sent to Switzerland. Kellan was building a nest egg for the two of us to live on. Together. It's fucked up.

The day I left with Cecelia for Europe, Kellan and the guys went out to a bar. It's where he met Sarah's mother, Daniela. At least now I know her name. And I know why she caught Kellan's eye that night. She looked like me. Kellan wrote that he hated her eyes. Hated the dull brown color of them. Hated that they weren't violet like mine. Whenever he would fuck her, he would blindfold her so he wouldn't have to look into her eyes.

The final entry in Kellan's journal contained his last secret. It was written a week before he died. Even though Kellan had discovered early on that Max wasn't my biological father, he didn't find out until two years ago that Declan Levine was. A meeting was arranged. The details were few, but I have no problem filling in the blanks. Declan's men infiltrated their way into the Rossi organization. Kellan figuratively opened the door for them to march right in under Max's nose. Kellan was planning to kill Max and take over. I guess Max found out and took Kellan out first. His own son. The son he groomed from birth to be the next don.

Mom must have been in on Kellan's plan. It explains why she suddenly took me to Switzerland and deposited me in the Swiss boarding school, and why she went to Declan for protection. Cecelia made a huge mistake though. She let it slip that I was his daughter; a secret Kellan never wanted him to know. Declan killed her because of it.

I pluck a small, yellow dandelion from the ground and pull a few individual petals off. "Amazing how an ugly weed can produce such beautiful flowers."

The symbolism isn't lost on me. I crush the flower in my hand and wipe the remains on the pants leg of my jeans.

"Thank you, Kellan, for giving me another weapon to use against Alejandro and Julio." I clutch Kellan's journal to my chest. "In a way, I guess I should also thank you for giving me Jax, Keane, and Rafe. They were your friends first, and I never would've met them otherwise."

I stand up and look down at my brother's name etched into stone. And then I spit on his grave.

"Goodbye, Kellan Rossi."

With those final words, I walk up the grassy hill to where the SUV is parked. Liam meets me halfway, and I walk straight into his arms. Where I belong. Where I'm safe and cherished. My angel-turned-devil with the moonlight eyes who always knows exactly what I need.

"I don't know what to say to help make it better."

I kiss his short beard. The whiskers are rough and scratchy now because it's only been a few days since he started growing it. It's going to feel fucking fantastic between my legs, and I can't wait.

"Honestly? There really isn't anything that can be said to make it better. But thank you."

"I think you can guess who's been blowing up my damn phone."

Mine too. Calls from Keane. Texts from Jax. Both from Rafe. I wouldn't let them come with me. I needed some air and some time to deal with my feelings about the revelations Kellan wrote in his journal.

Liam never knew Kellan, so he was my neutral ground. He's also my second since I'm in charge of Declan's organization, and according to Liam, he's still my bodyguard. Where I go, he goes —along with four other guards. It's something that I'll have to, unfortunately, get used to.

Z is standing beside the second SUV with Seamus, both men wearing casual clothes and displaying dual fuck-off expressions on their faces. A step up from the matching dark suits and dark aviators the guards at the Rossi estate wear that make them look like extras from *The Matrix*. I give a hand signal to let them know Liam and I are going for a short walk but will remain within sight.

"Cillian called. Declan's awake and wants to see you. Fancy a trip up to Boston?"

Every time I called to check on Declan, he was asleep.

I take Liam's hand as we stroll along the paved sidewalk that circles the cemetery. The sun is behind us, slowly rising to start a new day. The bright red of a male Northern cardinal flies across from one oak tree to another, chirping loudly to compete with the squawk of an irate Blue Jay.

"I'd like that. Did he sound alright? Is he in any pain?"

Liam stops us and brushes his knuckles down my cheek. "He's good, *bella*."

Good. But I won't stop worrying until I can hear Declan say that.

I turn us back toward the Range Rover and take out my phone when it vibrates with an incoming message.

"Want me to tell them to fuck off?" Liam asks, assuming it's one of the guys.

I frown when I see the text.

Unknown: Want to play a game, *mascota pequeña*?

I know what it means now because I looked it up. Little pet. It's what Alejandro called me when I was locked in his cage. Adrenaline floods my bloodstream, and all my senses become hyperaware. Another message comes through.

Unknown: Guess who's buried in that grave? I'll give you a hint. It's not Kellan Rossi.

I stare at the message in disbelief. The fuck?

My eyes dart around. Is Alejandro here?

"Liam," I whisper, tilting my phone to show him the messages.

He quickly reads them and takes out his gun. Z and Seamus notice, and they go on high alert. The other two guards get out of the Rover. Liam and I look around, searching our surroundings. It's all manicured grass, tall trees, and colorful flowers visitors have left at the gravestones of their loved ones.

"Anything?" I ask.

"Nothing. Stay close. I have an extra gun in my left holster under my shirt if you can get to it easily."

With both our heads on a cursory swivel because of having to scan everywhere at once, we swiftly walk toward the SUV. It's armored and has bulletproof glass. Right now, we're sitting ducks out in the open, and I don't like it. I crowd around Liam almost tripping him. I won't let what happened to Rafe happen to him. If Alejandro is shooting anyone today, it's going to be me, not my man.

Seamus rushes over to flank my side. I hold down the number seven on my phone. It's programmed to directly call Tessa's number.

Pick up. Pick up. Pick up.

"Hey, babe. I'm actually at the gatehouse waiting for Paul to let me in. He gave me a lolli—"

I cut her off. "Tessa, Liam and I are at Kellan's—"

I don't get a chance to finish. I'm hit with a scorching blast of heat seconds before being violently thrown backward.

BOOM.

Chapter 28

KEANE

Standing next to the wet bar in the living room, I tip my glass back. The whiskey stopped burning three shots ago.

"How drunk are you planning to get?" Rafe asks from where he's sitting on the couch.

I grab the bottle of vodka since the whiskey isn't working fast enough.

She and Rafe were holed up in her room for hours reading that damn journal. When they finally emerged, she destroyed Kellan's bedroom looking for the thumb drive that contained the videos Kellan recorded. Thank fuck for small miracles, because Jax and I had already destroyed it.

"She hates me for not telling her."

Rafe looks at me like I'm the dumbest person on the planet. Perhaps, I am, but only when it comes to Andie. Every attempt I make to protect her backfires stupendously. When I ripped into her in the kitchen, I expected her to fight back with her bitchy one-liners that make me hard as hell. Instead, I got a composed Andie handing me my ass with a heartfelt speech about acceptance and love. I didn't think I could feel worse after that, but then she found Kellan's journal.

"No, she doesn't."

I take a slug from the vodka bottle, wanting nothing more than to smash it over his head.

"Who did she fuck last night?"

Andie spent the night with them, not me. I was shut out, and it fucking hurts. Andie meted out my punishment, and I had no other choice than to take it. My punishment? I had to watch as Jax and Rafe each took her right in front of me. They gave her pleasure. Kissed her and touched her. Made her moan and come over and over again. Then she spent the night with Liam in his bed. It was absolute torture knowing she was with him.

But if that was my penance, so be it.

I'm ticked that Jax didn't get the same blowback as I did. He also didn't tell her what was in Kellan's journal. Didn't stop her from riding his dick like the world was ending. Bastard. I can guarantee there won't be a second night of that shit. Andie will be screaming my name and gagging on my cock tonight. And these motherfuckers aren't invited.

Needing an outlet for the anger directed solely at myself, I turn on Jax. He's leaning against the back wall, joint between his lips. He hasn't lit up yet because Rafe would beat his ass.

"What the hell is wrong with you? I blame you for what happened in the courtyard."

He pushes his glasses up his nose with his middle finger.

"We agreed she wouldn't see that shit, and then you just take her to one of your torture parties. Do you want her to end up as fucked in the head as you are?"

I knew my words would cut him open before I said them. Knowing that didn't stop me. I'm livid that he had Andie participate in one of his torture playdates. I've seen Jax at his worst. The gruesome things he enjoys doing to people. How he gets off on others' pain and suffering. It's a good quality to have if you're an enforcer for the mob. Not one I want in the woman I love. A woman who has been the recipient of the kind of torture Jax inflicts on others.

"Keane, it wasn't Jax's fault. It was Andie's choice. And her arguments are valid," Rafe says.

I slam the vodka bottle down. "She killed a man like it was nothing."

"She did what any of us would've done in her place," he counters.

"She's not one of us. She's better than us."

Rafe gets up and walks over. "Damn straight she is. But you're wrong about the first part. Love her enough to accept all of her, even the parts you disagree with."

Fuck. I hate it when he's right. I jerk my chin at Jax in apology. He rolls his damn eyes at me, but I know we're good.

"I want to talk to you both about what happens next." I gesture for Jax to sit on the couch. Of course, he takes his sweet-ass time.

Rafe puts one foot up on the coffee table and relaxes back into the leather cushion. "Is this a discussion Liam should be included in?"

"No," I say a little too quickly.

When Jax sits down, Rafe reaches over and snatches the joint from his mouth. "You'll get it back later."

"Good thing I have a spare," Jax says, reaching into his pocket and pulling out a pre-rolled one that's bent in two. He looks at it in disgust and tosses it. Rafe grins.

"Are you coming back?" I ask Rafe.

"Do you want me to?"

I rub my hand over the back of my head a few times. "You've made it clear that you want out, so this is me giving you the choice to stay or to go."

He thinks about it, then asks Jax, "You got an opinion?"

"I want us all together. But my opinion doesn't mean shit if that's not what Andie wants. Honestly? I think she's finally found where she belongs. Declan handed her the reins for a reason. Is the wedding still happening?"

"Unless she says otherwise," I reply. After what happened yesterday, I wouldn't be surprised if she called it off. Just means I'll have to hog-tie her and carry her to the altar myself.

Jax takes out his knife and taps it against the arm of the couch. "Are you prepared to align the Rossis with the Levines? It'll piss off a lot of the other families we do business with. You know how they feel about the Irish."

I hate how old cultural prejudices get in the way of progress.

"They can think whatever they want. They won't do anything about it, unless it affects their bottom line. We no longer have the New York families to contend with. I'll assimilate them under the Agosti name."

Rafe sits up. "Wait. You're dismantling the Rossi family? The business?"

I laugh at the irony. "What family? There's no one left. Andie isn't a Rossi, and she sure as fuck doesn't want to run the family business. Kellan, Dom, and everyone else with blood ties to Max are all dead. It would be more of a rebranding, not a dismantling." All semantics, but whatever.

"Then walk away from it. Let it die. Let Andie burn the house to the ground," Jax suggests. It doesn't help.

I lean my head back and look up at the ceiling. "And do what? I don't know anything other than this life. Neither do you, Jax. Besides, my family has been intertwined with the Rossis since my great-grandfather was the underboss for Vino Rossi."

"So what?" Rafe argues. "You say you want Andie to have a better life than this one? Build one for her. She wants it. A family of her own. Kids. Us. We can give it to her. We can be happy and not have to look over our shoulders all the damn time. Aren't you tired of always fighting? Always waiting for the next turf war to arrive or the next power-hungry asshole to decide he wants what's yours."

"She wants kids?" My cock wakes up at the thought of Andie round with my child growing inside her. With all the bare fucking we're giving her, she may already be pregnant. She said she gets the birth control shot, but like all forms of contraception, there's never a hundred percent guarantee. "*Is she pregnant?*"

Rafe's exasperation is apparent. "That's all you got out of what I just said?"

Any thought of fucking Andie overrides everything else, but I reply, "I heard you."

A commotion erupts somewhere in the house before we hear Tessa's voice scream our names.

Chapter 29

ANDIE

Cold water hits my face.

"Damn it, Keane!" I splutter, blinking my eyes open. But it's not Keane holding a bucket of water over my head to wake me up like he did at Kellan's cabin.

"Ah, yes, the man you said was your husband. I despise liars, *mi mascota*."

Alejandro's black, soulless eyes glitter when I look up at him. He tosses the empty water bottle to the side and squats down in front of me. I try to move, but my hands and feet are zip tied. Figures.

Alejandro's scarred face gapes open with a smile, that stupid diamond in his front tooth winking at me. We both lurch to the side at the same time. He catches himself with an outstretched arm, but I'm not so fortunate. I go rolling and smash into hard metal. We're in a moving van.

He angrily shouts something in Spanish to the driver. With his attention distracted, I take those few precious seconds to regroup. The explosion came from the second SUV. I don't know if Z, Seamus, or the other men are okay. *Liam*.

I get my answer when I hear a grunt next to me. The relief I feel that he's alive is indescribable. The back of the van is dimly lit from the light coming in through the windshield. Liam's tall, prone form is lying across from me on the other side of the van. Like me, he's also bound. Unlike me, he's gagged and can't talk.

A headache pounds inside my skull and my ears keep ringing

off and on. That's all I need is yet another concussion. I don't think anything in my body is newly broken, but then again, I can't feel anything other than the pure, unadulterated, murderous rage that is currently consuming me. A charred, smokey smell wafts up from my shirt and wrinkles my nose. God willing, I hope Liam and I were far enough away from the explosion to avoid being burned. Shrapnel is a different story.

I don't have time to prepare for the kick to the stomach before a hand grabs my shirt and pulls me upright. I suck in a sharp breath at the flare of pain, then cough as I try to hold back the vomit that wants to come. Liam thrashes, trying to escape his bindings, and another man suddenly appears like a wraith from behind Alejandro. He smashes his fist in Liam's face a few times to subdue him, but that only makes Liam fight against his tethers more.

"For fuck's sake," Alejandro says in clipped English. "The money I would get for your useless head isn't worth it." I hear the click of a gun.

"What money?" I ask, wiggling like an earthworm on a hot sidewalk. Keep him talking. Make sure his focus is on me and not on Liam. Anything to buy us more time.

"Levine would pay a pretty penny for *El Arma del Diablo*."

I give him a droll look. "You know I don't understand," I tell him. However, that's a lie. He called Liam the Devil's Weapon. My Spanish may be sparse, but I do know a few words.

The van makes another turn, and I'm able to stay sitting up this time.

"Your father would be ashamed how easily you switched sides to the enemy, *mi mascota pequeña*."

I tamp down my grin. He doesn't know Declan is my father, not Max. He and Julio must think I left with Rafe and changed allegiances. I'm a woman, so naturally, I would seek the protection and help of the top alpha male in the city since Max was dead. Keane would be hurt knowing Alejandro doesn't view him as a threat. I can't wait for him to find out how wrong he is.

As discreetly as I can, I twist the Levin ring around on my

finger to hide the family crest. If Alejandro had seen it, I'm sure it'd be missing and I'd have another broken finger.

Liam's swollen eyes are locked on Alejandro and murdering him a thousand different ways. Other than the two shiners he's sporting from the beating he just took, he looks better than I expected.

Alejandro slides his gun into his front waistband. I beg for the powers of karma to have it discharge and shoot his dick off.

I don't know how much time I have before the cavalry arrives, because they will most definitely be arriving. Tessa would've told the guys about the tracker I had her implant under my arm. I hope the car bomb or me flying through the air like a popped helium balloon didn't damage it. Shit. What if it did?

"What did you mean about Kellan?"

His last text insinuated something I don't want to think about, because it would be utterly impossible for it to be true. Kellan can't be alive. Alejandro must've meant something else.

Liam stills his struggles. He's as interested in hearing the answer as much as I am. I wonder if he still has that extra gun on him that he said was under his shirt.

Alejandro makes a *tsk* sound. "I'm not going to share all my secrets, Alexandria."

God, I hate hearing that fucking name being spoken from his lips.

I wiggle around some more to give me time to think. Then it comes to me.

I'm able to bend my knees and awkwardly bring my bound feet up to my chest. My wrists are thankfully zip tied in front of me. I discreetly feel around my right ankle for my knife. My thumb catches on the outline of the top of the handle. Alejandro will never learn.

"How about I share a few of mine?" I reply. "Like how Kellan stole five million dollars from you along with a shit-ton of drugs, and you and your asshole of a father never even noticed."

I enjoy the constipated look on Alejandro's face as he works out if what I said was the truth.

"*Mentirosa*," he spits, anger flushing his face and mottling it red.

Whatever he said, I don't think it was anything nice, but I plaster a smug smirk on my lips and wait. Alejandro is so easy to bait.

His black gaze bores into me. For once, I'm not lying, so it's easy to meet his stare and hold it.

"Where is my money?" he finally demands.

My smirk widens to a grin. See? So fucking easy.

"Where is my heroin?" he barks, spittle flying from his lips.

"How about we ask Kellan?" I continue to bait him, partly to keep him talking and to waste time, but also because I'm desperate for an answer to the riddle he texted me.

Alejandro's shouts and curses in Spanish boom inside the small confines of the back of the van. He leans over and yanks me up by my hair. I'm thrown against the side of the van with such force, the large vehicle rocks on its tires as it drives down the road. Liam growls through his gag and renews his efforts to break free from the zip ties.

"I want my money."

"Tell me where Kellan is," I demand, not backing down.

Alejandro backhands me across the face. He wants me to cower and beg for my life, tell him whatever he wants to know so he doesn't hurt me. He wants to get off on my tears and my whimpers for mercy. My life has been full of men like him. I've survived men like him. And I've killed men like him.

"I'm going to break you, just like I broke your fucking *hermano*. You'll be begging me to end your suffering, just like he did."

That can't be right. He's lying. Isn't he? Kellan died in an alleyway after being shot. I heard it. I heard everything.

Swiping up to accept the call, I answer, "Hey, Kel." But instead of hearing him say hi back, I'm met with a muffled, scraping sound, then loud bangs that sound like firecrackers exploding. Are they gunshots? What the hell is going on?

"Kellan, answer me. Kellan!" I yell into the phone.

Several voices are shouting over one another, the cacophony a mess to understand. My heart is thundering in my chest and tears fill my eyes and spill over as I hear Kellan brokenly say my name, the sound garbled like he's choking.

"I'm so sorry, Tinker Bell," he rasps quietly.

"Kellan, can you hear me? Please! Please tell me what's going on. Where are you?"

I hear him wheeze a stuttered breath.

"Kellan!"

Pounding footsteps can be heard over the line, and then a voice I recognize.

"Fuck!" the voice shouts as more gunfire explodes in a staccato rhythm. The voice belongs to Rafe.

Wailing sirens punch through the line from far off in the distance. With a trembling hand, I press the phone closer to my ear, trying to hear everything I can.

"Goddamnit!" That's Keane's voice.

More pounding footsteps. Some grunts of pain. People yelling. And gunfire that never seems to end. Then nothing. A whimper escapes me as I'm frozen in place. Where's my brother?

"I love you, Andie." The sound, so soft now, I wouldn't have heard it if I hadn't had the phone plastered to my ear. Relief spreads through me. He's alive. Whatever just happened, my brother is alive.

"Kellan? Thank God," I breathe. The guys will get him out of there.

"I'm so sorry," he garbles again.

Those are the last words my brother said to me. I listened to Kellan take his final breath. I listened to my brother die and was helpless to do anything. I listened as police officers showed up ten minutes later, one saying what I already knew. Kellan was gone.

Then my memories flash to what Jax told me as we lay in bed and listened to the rain.

"We were under heavy fire. We circled around and were coming back when we were told Kellan had been extracted and was being taken to Hollis," Jax says.

Now it's my turn to look confused. Because that's not what happened.

"Who told you that?"

Jax's full lips thin to a grim line. "Your father."

Like pieces of a mangled jigsaw puzzle made from years of lies and deceit, I finally put together what happened. The police that showed up that night must have been men on the Rossi payroll. Max handed Kellan over to the Ortiz cartel. Punishment for his betrayal and blackmail—Kellan's plans that he wrote in his journal are still fresh in my mind.

Max had to keep his hands clean and make Kellan's shooting look like a job gone bad. If the guys found out Max arranged for Kellan's murder, they would have retaliated. Keane, Jax, and Rafe may have worked for my not-father, but he knew their loyalties would always remain with Kellan.

Max used Rafe to open talks with Julio. Under the table deals are made all the time between crime families. You take care of this problem for me, and I'll do a favor for you. The Ortizes took care of Max's problem, and in return, Max gave Julio exclusivity to run his drugs through Rossi-controlled ports and territory.

But Alejandro was making his own moves to push Julio out and take over. After that happened, I was added to the original deal. Alejandro decided he wanted me, and Max was more than happy to hand me over to keep the deal intact. Which means Kellan might still be alive.

An icy cold settles over me, and my voice is deadly when I say, "Where's my brother?"

The driver shouts something just as the van swerves. There's an explosion of sound like a tire blowing out, and he slams on the brakes, sending Alejandro and me crashing together in a forward momentum that flings us between the driver and passenger seats. Luckily, I land on top of him, and he takes the brunt of the collision with the center console. A bullet pierces the left side of the windshield, spider-webbing the glass and leaving a circular hole in its wake. Brain matter and blood splatter over the headrest of the seat, and the driver falls forward onto the horn.

Fight, Tinker Bell! Move. Now. The voice talking to me isn't

Kellan's. Somehow, it's Keane's.

I smash my forehead into Alejandro's thick skull, momentarily dazing both of us. *Motherfucker*, that hurt. Not doing that ever again.

Hobbling off him as best as I can without 'timbering' sideways like a damn tree, I raise my bound hands above my head, then swiftly bring them down while locking my elbows at my sides. The zip tie breaks at the head and falls off. Another trick Cillian taught me.

Alejandro snarls and grabs at me. I throw myself backward and fall to the floor, trying to get to my knife so I can cut through the ties around my ankles.

The other man trips over Liam's outstretched legs, and Liam does a reverse donkey kick into the side of his head with such brute force, it knocks out several of his teeth. The man crumples to the floor and doesn't move.

"Liam, hold on!" I yell, struggling to get my knife out of its ankle holster.

Alejandro pulls his gun from his front waistband and aims it at me. I freeze. Then I see a thin beam of red light refracting through the shattered windshield and focused on Alejandro's back.

My grin is savage. "You're not the only one who's good at making things go *boom*."

Another bullet flies through the windshield and hits Alejandro in the shoulder. His body jerks at the impact, and he stumbles forward.

Fucking finally! I don't waste any time. Using the knife, I quickly sever through the zip tie binding my ankles together. Now to get to Liam.

"You fucking cunt," Alejandro growls out, staggering on his feet, blood pouring down the left side of his body from his shoulder where the sniper's bullet hit.

With my limbs untethered, I don't wait for him to raise the gun still clutched in his right hand. I react. Pushing off the side of the van with every bit of strength I have left, I barrel into him like a linebacker. The force of our momentum smashes open the back doors, and we hit the black asphalt of the road. The jarring impact steals the air from my lungs in a violent *whoosh* and spots dance behind my closed eyelids. *Aw, fuck.*

Both moaning, Alejandro and I roll to our sides and slowly stand up, mirror images of one another. The gun must have slipped from his hand when we fell out the back of the van. But then again, so did my knife.

"It's over," I tell him, my abused muscles protesting as I straighten up to my full height.

My guys will be here soon. Maybe they already are, but I'm not going to look around to find out. My gaze stays focused directly on the man I'm going to enjoy kicking the shit out of. As much as I want to kill him right now, I won't. The questions I need him to answer override my desire for revenge.

Alejandro licks the blood from his mouth. "I think I may have underestimated you."

"Most usually do." I get into a fighter's stance and crook my finger at him. "Let's see how much of a man you really are, *mascota*," I taunt him.

Taking the bait like I knew he would, Alejandro snarls at me and lunges. We meet like wrestlers, arms outstretched, hands gripping shoulders. He thinks because he's bigger and stronger, I'll be easy to subdue, but I know how to fight dirty.

I find the bullet hole on the back of his shoulder at his trapezius and dig my middle finger into it. He howls in pain, his grip on me loosening, and that's all the advantage I need.

I kick at his kneecap and thrust my palm upward under his chin. The crunch of teeth and bone sound loud to my ears which are filled with a buzzing of rage. Eyes wide in stunned disbelief, his body folds in on itself like a paper accordion, and we drop to the ground. I lock my thighs on either side of his chest, curl my right hand, and punch his ugly face. I let the memories of him flood into my brain and fuel each strike of my fist. The deal Max made. *Hit.* The bullet hitting Rafe. *Hit.* Liam and I getting pushed off the road. *Hit.* The cage. *Hit.* My broken finger. *Hit.* Keane's

197

rings. *Hit.* The chains. *Hit.* Declan. *Hit.* The car bomb. *Hit.* That fucking stupid diamond on his front tooth when he smiled.

When his face looks like I took a meat cleaver to it, I grab the sides of his head, holding it steady. Alejandro isn't moving anymore underneath me, but he's still alive as evidenced by his eye movement and shallow breathing.

Making sure he hears my next words, I bend over to his ear. "Death is only the beginning," I whisper.

He moans low, a hand twitching and grabbing my hip as he tries to push me off him. Can't have that.

"Lights out, motherfucker." I slam his head on the tarmac.

Shouts and rapid footfalls pull me back to the present. I look over my shoulder and the most beautiful sight I've ever seen greets me.

"Took you long enough," I say to Keane, Jax, and Rafe.

"Fucking hell, princess," Keane says, just as Jax grabs for me, lifting me off Alejandro and crushing the ever-living shit out of me.

"You did so good, Angel."

I slump against him and steal his warmth.

"Can someone help Liam?" I ask since Jax isn't letting me go.

Keane clambers inside the van, and he must remove Liam's gag first because I hear him cursing, English mixed with Gaelic.

Rafe walks over to me, and Jax stares down at an unconscious Alejandro. I can't even imagine the tumult of emotions Rafe must be feeling right now. I reach out and touch his face. His blue eyes meet mine. Jax finally lets go, and I immediately wrap my arms around Rafe.

"It's almost over," I tell him, and he nods.

Something glints in the sunlight, catching my attention. I look around, my gaze finally dropping to the body at my feet. It's then I see it. A gold chain hanging outside the collar of Alejandro's shirt. And on it are Keane's mother's rings.

Bending over, I rip the necklace from Alejandro's neck and turn around with a triumphant smile just as Keane helps Liam out of the van.

"Look what I just found."

Chapter 30

ANDIE

I drag the tip of my knife. Slowly. Precisely. Meticulously. Like a scalpel in a surgeon's steady hands.

"Wakey, wakey, asshole," I say, carving the beginnings of a letter X into Alejandro's chest.

He's been barely conscious the entire time I've been sitting on his bent knees, slicing my name into his flesh. It wasn't until I was finishing the E that he started to struggle. Keane must have damaged some vital brain cells when he punched him.

Focusing on the task at hand, I tell Liam, "I never did thank you."

He comes up behind me and brushes the hair off my neck, kissing my shoulder. "For what?"

I tip my head back to look at him. The swelling around his eye has gone down thanks to a poultice Hollis made. Whatever herbs and other shit he used to make it with smelled rancid, but it worked.

I stab my blade deeper into the pectoral muscle. Alejandro thrashes about but isn't able to move one inch. Jax did a very good job with the restraints. Alejandro's shouts are muffled by the cloth I shoved in his mouth because he was hemorrhaging bloody drool all over me after I ripped out that stupidly ugly tooth with the diamond in it with a pair of pliers.

"My name in Max's chest," I reply.

Liam looks to his right. "That was Rafael, not me."

It's messed up how much I like hearing Rafe did that for me.

I search for the man in question. "I love you," I tell him.

Rafe has been quietly watching me carve up his brother. His dimples pop with his smile, before disappearing. The intensity in Rafe's blue eyes when he looks at Alejandro makes them glow with an anger I haven't seen since the night Rafe was forced to watch as Max beat me.

Rafe says something in Spanish, which causes a fierce reaction in his brother. Alejandro grunts with effort, trying to break out of his restraints.

I slide my knife up his neck to his ear and nick the lobe. "If you don't stop, I'm going to shove this in your ear canal."

The fucker growls and tries to headbutt me, so I throat punch him. He convulses as he chokes, forgetting he has to breathe through his nose since he can't breathe through the gag in his mouth.

Alejandro glares at me, but I can see the fear lurking beneath the surface. His eyes dart sideways toward Jax. My Grim Reaper with the manic smile.

I tap Alejandro's cheek. "He'll get to you soon, but I have a few questions for you before I let Jax have his fun."

Keane hasn't tried to stop me from what I'm doing, and I'm appreciative that he has let me take my pound of flesh. I wish I hadn't destroyed the cage down here with the crowbar. It would have been a fitting place to put Alejandro.

I seek Keane out, and he gives me a barely perceptible nod. I know how hard it is for him to watch me do this, and only because he never wanted this part of the business to touch me. And as upset as I was that he kept Kellan's journal from me, I get it. I may not like how Keane tries to protect me sometimes, but I can't stay mad at a man who will do anything for me because he loves me.

I bring the knife back to the letter X on Alejandro's chest, which looks more like a crooked Y since I hadn't finished.

"You're going to answer every question I ask. Those answers will determine whether your death is drawn out over weeks, or over quickly. Trust me," I say, leaning in close to whisper in his ear. "You don't want to be Jax's plaything for long."

Alejandro's eyes bulge when the knife pierces his skin again, and I drag it down to finish the X I'd begun. Grunting in pain, capillaries burst in the whites of his eyes, giving them a pinkish hue. Unlike before, he's fully awake now to feel every single thing I'm doing.

"I'm going to remove your gag. If you spit on me or do anything else other than answer my question, I'll cut your tongue out," I warn him.

Alejandro goes very still.

Taking that as my answer that he'll cooperate, I snag the cloth jammed into his mouth with the tip of my blade and pull it out.

"Is Kellan alive?"

Alejandro chuckles huskily. "What do you think, *mascota*?"

"I think you're a lying asshole."

"Then it doesn't matter what I say. It doesn't matter that your father paid me to kill him. Did you enjoy hearing his pitiful pleas?"

I keep my face unemotive when he drops that bomb. He was there that night in the alley when Kellan called me? Holy shit, he's telling the truth. He couldn't have known that otherwise.

Alejandro's voice pulls me back, and I hate the crooked smirk on his face. "That's nothing compared to how your precious Kellan screamed your name while I gutted him open right here in this room while your father watched."

Nausea spikes heavily in my stomach. Kellan made a lot of mistakes in his life where I was concerned, but I loved him as only a little sister could love the man who she thought was her brother.

Needing to have the last word, I slowly slide off his bent knees and impale the knife into his thigh. I smile at Alejandro's shrill, pain-filled scream.

"Kellan wasn't my brother, you stupid prick. Maximillian Rossi wasn't my father. Declan Levine is. And I'm done listening to you."

Leaving my men to their fun, I head up the stairs into the

main part of the house and find Tessa anxiously waiting in the living room.

"Fancy a trip to Mexico?" I ask her.

Chapter 31

Two days later

ANDIE

I'm overly warm, but I refuse to move. A hand dips under my panties and teases the sensitive skin just above my mons. Plush lips kiss me. The hand stroking my pubic hair moves lower, and a finger strums my clit like the plucking of a guitar string. My sleepy, pleasure-filled sigh is the music to the song being played. When I come, it's a sweet release that has me floating and my muscles going lax.

Fingers lace with mine, and I roll my head where it's resting on someone's shoulder.

"How long was I out?" I ask no one in particular. It's a two-hour flight to Mexico, so I couldn't have been asleep that long.

"We're about to land," Rafe says, and I open one eye, then shut it again when a finger slips inside me, pumping slowly and drawing out my orgasm.

Fully awake now, I arch my back, seeking more of what Jax is giving me. "Why do you wake me up with orgasms? Not that I'm complaining," I add quickly, not wanting him to stop.

"Angel, making you come is my fucking pleasure."

When I become too sensitive, I tap his arm, and he slides his finger out, then sucks it clean. Rafe pulls me sideways in his lap until I'm draped over both him and Jax on the three-cushion sofa.

Declan's private jet is more like a luxury motorcoach with wings. There's sleeping quarters in the back with a king-sized bed and a mid-sized bathroom. The middle of the plane is partitioned, with the forward section nearest to the cockpit equipped with a desk and individual seating. In the back of the plane where we are, there's a living area with a couch and reclining seats. The rear galley is similar to the ones you see on Dreamliners, just smaller in size.

"I can't believe you did that," Rafe says, feathering his thumb over the small, red, raised bump on my arm where Tessa implanted the tracking chip.

"Be glad that I did."

If I hadn't gotten the tracker reimplanted, who the hell knows what would've happened with Alejandro. My plan to draw him out worked, but Liam and several of the men were injured.

Jax lifts my foot onto his lap, digs his thumb into the sole, and I moan like a whore.

"You better not be fucking back there because I'm coming in and don't need to see that shit," Tessa calls out.

"You are such a drama queen," I yell back.

She walks in and stops to make sure there's no orgy happening. "Oh, come on. That's even worse!" she exclaims when she sees Jax rubbing my feet. "You are such a lucky bitch."

"Everything in place?" I ask her when she drops into the chair across from us.

"Yep."

"Z doing good?"

I know she's been keeping tabs. My grin turns smug when I see the rosy blush staining her cheeks that gives her away.

Fortunately, Z and Seamus weren't badly hurt when the bomb went off in the second SUV. Unfortunately, the state authorities and FBI are now involved. There really isn't much we can do to stop an investigation from happening this time; however, we can plant misleading information and guide authorities in the direction we want them to look.

A yawning Liam walks out of the bedroom, looking deliciously mussy, and heads straight for the coffee machine. Guess I wasn't the only one who had a nap.

Keane walks in and takes his seat, clipping the seat belt over his lap. "No time for coffee. Lochlan said to buckle up," he tells Liam, who gives him the bird while pouring himself a cup. He dumps the rest from the pot and makes sure everything is properly stored away.

Lochlan was the one to shoot the driver and Alejandro. My distant cousin is not only an excellent sniper, but he's also a pilot.

The large plane seems very, very small now with everyone crowded into one place. The groan of the landing gear coming down fills the cabin.

In the end, it took less than twenty hours for Alejandro to break. He would've done anything to stop the torture. I believe what Alejandro said about Kellan. Then again, the man is a liar. Do I want to exhume the body buried in Kellan's grave? Then what? I can't keep living my life forever chasing a revenge for a man who lied to me.

Sitting up, I reach for Rafe's hand and examine it. He used this hand to pluck out his brother's eye with a screwdriver.

"You ready for this?"

His blue eyes dim slightly as the wheels make contact with the uneven tarmac of the private airstrip.

The elaborate chess game we've been playing is almost finished. We're about to call checkmate.

Chapter 32

RAFE

I'm the only one to disembark the plane, and I'm immediately overcome with nostalgia when I lay eyes on my home country. That nostalgia quickly fades when the sweltering sun beats down on me. The air smells just as I remember when I was a child, if dry and dusty could be considered smells. It's already pushing close to a hundred degrees Fahrenheit, something I don't miss not one fucking bit. Between the intense sun and the heat radiating up from the black asphalt, it feels like I'm being cooked in an oven.

My father's compound is located near the town of Monclova, the "steel capital" of Mexico, or so it's been coined. My childhood growing up here holds few good memories. I never thought I'd ever come back. Luckily, we'll be leaving very soon.

Without sunglasses, I'm forced to shield my eyes with a hand as I look around at nothing. The private airstrip we landed on is out in the middle of nowhere. My uncle is standing next to a blacked-out Hummer parked at the side of the narrow runway. Six men carrying semi-automatics and wearing Sinner's Fury cuts surround the large SUV.

Luis Echeverria is the oldest brother of my mother, and the bastard son of Dirk "Sinner" Carmichael, the president of the San Salamacha Sinner's Fury motorcycle club. The Sinners, along with several other MCs, run drugs across the border for various cartels and gangs. One of Dirk's side pieces he would fuck on the regular while passing through was my grandmother. There was no denying my mother and Luis were his kids because they got his blue eyes. So did I. When I was old enough to understand the significance of that particular genetic trait, it made me wonder about Alejandro. He has dark brown eyes. Or he did.

Luis flicks a finger at one of the men wearing a prospect patch on the back of his cut, then slowly heads my way. He looks exactly the same as the last time I saw him a decade ago. Tall like me, broad-shouldered and thick-muscled. His hair is peppered with gray, as is his beard. Wrinkles crease his face, unlike my father, who has tried to hold back the natural aging process with plastic surgery and collagen injections.

I meet Luis halfway.

Smiling broadly, he refrains from embracing me in a familial hug. Eyes are watching us from the Hummer.

Speaking in Spanish, he says, "You've grown into a man, Rafael. No longer a little boy." He steps back and looks me over.

"And you look just the same," I reply.

He laughs at that and pats his stomach. "With old age comes a wider girth. Not that I'm complaining. Carmella's cooking is too good."

"Carmella?" I ask, not knowing who she is.

"Wife number three."

"Ah." I know better than to ask what happened to wife number two. I barely remember wife number one. Like my mother, she died of a drug overdose when I was little.

"Your old man is frothing at the mouth to have you back." He spits on the ground, but it evaporates within seconds.

There's no love lost between Luis and Julio. They used to be friends once upon a time. But that all ended when my mother died.

I recall our phone call days ago when I reached out to him, feeling like I had no other choice because the guys hadn't been able to find Andie. If I'd only waited five more minutes, that call would've never happened because Andie was able to escape Alejandro and had stumbled her beaten body into the lobby of Falcon Tower. By then, it was too late. My promise to my uncle was already set in stone.

Jerking my chin at the Hummer, I ask, "Does he suspect anything?"

Luis stifles his laughter but not his calculating toothy grin. "Not a damn thing, the stupid cunt. Alejandro?" he asks about my brother.

"It's done," I reply emotionlessly.

He strokes his beard a few times. The silver rings adorning his fingers glint in the oppressive sunshine. His skin is much darker than mine, attesting to the amount of time he rides his hog every day.

"You sure you want to do this? Because once it's done, there's no going back," Luis says, scrutinizing me intensely.

Fuck. I scrape a hand over my face and exhale loudly. *Fuck. Fuck!* Andie will never truly be safe until both Alejandro and my father are dead.

Luis has been waiting for a chance to take my father down but hasn't been able to make a move against him because the cartel is much more powerful than the MC and has many more friends in low places. I'm about to hand my uncle his wish on a silver platter.

"Yeah, I'm sure."

Luis flicks a hand, and the man next to the back passenger door of the Hummer opens it.

There always comes a time in a man's life when he makes a choice of the type of man he will be. It doesn't matter the environment he grew up in, the parents he had, the friends, the education—whether it was book-learned in a school or lessons learned on the streets. It doesn't matter the religion or the god he believes in, or whether he is rich or poor. When the time comes to choose which path in life to take, he will have to make a choice. To walk the path of angels or delve into the depths with the devil.

And staring into the eyes of my father for the first time in almost a decade, I realize that I made my choice when I watched my mother die, and I ran away from home. I made a choice when I first picked up a gun and killed a man. I made a choice when I first laid eyes on Andie and promised her my heart and my love. And now it's time for me to be that man; the one who walks in the footsteps of my namesake. Except, instead of the path of light that the Archangel Rafael adhered to, I'm one of the fallen.

Luis takes a few steps back when Julio approaches.

"Rafael," my father says, looking polished in his thousand-dollar suit.

Due to the copious amounts of plastic surgery, he looks like he's made of wax, like one of those creepy as fuck figures in a museum. I wouldn't be surprised if he started melting right before my eyes. It's that fucking hot.

His gaze rakes over me, searching for something, and I meet it with a blank expression that Jax would be proud of. I refuse to appear weak in front of this man.

"I forget how much you look like your mother."

I hold in my *fuck you*, knowing this entire charade will be over soon. Uncle Luis schools his features quickly enough, but not before I see the fleeting rage pass over his face at the mention of his sister.

Julio reaches into his jacket pocket and pulls out a white linen handkerchief, using it to dab across his brow line where sweat has gathered. His black eyes drift behind me where the plane is taxied.

"Where's Ale?" he asks Luis.

"Fucking his whore." The lie flows out of my uncle like a leaky hole in a dam.

The mere thought of Alejandro fucking Andie makes me want to vomit. I curl my fists, putting a leash on the immense urge to grab Luis's gun and shoot my father where he stands. Luis was right. My father hasn't a damn clue what's actually going on. He really is a stupid cunt.

Julio smirks. "He can play with the Rossi bitch when we get back to the compound."

When he starts to walk toward the plane, I stop him by saying, "The only bitch I see here is you. Heard Alejandro pushed you out, and you didn't put up much of a fight."

My cheek stings when my father backhands me, but I was prepared for it. I stand there and take every hit he gives.

"You know nothing, boy." Another backhand. "You thought Rossi could protect you from me?" Another slap. "And then you go and hide behind Levine's skirts instead of coming home where you belong."

When he finishes, he's breathing heavily and sweating profusely. *It's almost over.*

The humid, soupy air becomes electric, and the fine hairs on my neck and arms raise. I feel her presence before I see her. Andie comes to stand beside me, her face a mask of stolid beauty, her long hair flowing over her shoulders like spun gold. A small red rose is tucked behind her ear that matches the color of the dress she's wearing.

I do a slight double take because she wasn't wearing that when we landed. And where in the hell did she get the rose?

She looks up at me and sees the handprints on both my cheeks, and a fire lights behind her violet gaze.

My father's eyes, on the other hand, fill with lust at the sight of her. "*Muy hermosa.*" He switches to English. "Come, let me have a look," he tells her, signaling her with a hand gesture to come closer.

It takes all of my self-control not to punch him in his smug, victorious face. *It's almost over.*

"I can see why Ale was obsessed with having you," he says. He leers at her, taking in every gorgeous inch of her curves. He turns to speak to Luis. "We will put her to good use, *sí*? The Rossi girl —"

"Actually," Andie says, cutting him off, her red-handled knife suddenly appearing in her hand.

My father never sees my beautiful *ángel de la muerte* coming. She slits his throat open in one clean line. Her smile grows wide when he clutches at his neck, mouth agape in utter disbelief.

"My name is Andie *Levine*, motherfucker."

Julio stumbles back, mouth open but no sound coming out, blood percolating in his throat like a pot of water coming to boil.

Luis and the other armed men circle around us. My father isn't leaving here alive or in one piece. I can see the instant he finally realizes what's going on, but that realization comes too late.

Andie hands me her knife.

"Just so you know," I tell him. "Alejandro is dead. He died on his knees, screaming like a weak little bitch."

I throw a sealed sandwich bag that contains the eye I cut out of my brother at his feet.

"An eye for an eye," I tell my father, right before I grab his head and do the same thing to him.

My father's death is played out on a shitty airstrip in the middle of an arid landscape, like a scene from a dystopian Shakespearean play.

As I watch the men in Sinners cuts bag up the dismembered pieces of the man whose DNA I carry, Luis steps in front of me, hand outstretched and a grin pulled across his face behind his beard. My blood-soaked hand takes his, and we shake.

"Your mother would be proud, *mi sobrino*. Or should I call you *jefe*?" Luis smirks like an asshole, and a wide grin stretches under his thick beard.

My chuckle is devoid of humor. "Let's not."

My reign as the head of the Ortiz cartel is going to be very short-lived. I sure as fuck don't want the position. I'm going to burn the Ortiz compound down to ashes. If the Sinner's Fury MC wants to pick up the leftover mangled dregs of the drug business, they're more than welcome, but I doubt Luis would be interested.

Luis raises Andie's hand—the one she slit Julio's throat with— to his lips. "It was a pleasure to meet you, Andie. I look forward to doing business with the Levines."

She gives him one of her genuine smiles, and I swear to God, his breath hitches. I snatch her hand back, and he laughs. The guy is already on wife number three. He doesn't need to make a play for a fourth. And definitely not with my woman.

"Likewise. I'll have Pearson contact you soon," she replies.

Andie has been quietly standing beside me. Just her presence is enough of a balm to calm my inner chaos. I pluck the rose from her hair and twirl it between my fingers.

"Ready to go home?"

Her smile is brilliant and beautiful. "Absolutely."

"Jax!" I shout, my voice carrying over the tarmac.

He and the guys have been waiting inside the plane the entire time.

"What?" he yells, coming to the open cabin entry door, wearing only a loose pair of jeans that hang low. I'm about to ask him what happened to his shirt but decide to let it go.

Andie notices, however, and her low, lusty hum has my dick perking up. Once we get airborne again, we can initiate her into the mile high club.

I swirl my finger in the air. "Send in the drones," I tell him.

Even from here, I can see the maniacal glint in his eyes behind his glasses.

"Fuck, yeah!"

Andie came up with the idea of equipping explosives to drones and has been eager to see her idea come to fruition.

Minutes later, as the plane rises in altitude, we watch from one of the small windows as smoke plumes and hot licks of red and orange flames engulf my childhood home below.

Chapter 33

ANDIE

I rap my knuckles lightly on the partition that separates the rear galley from the private bedroom in the back of the plane. Taking out his earbuds, Keane sits up in the bed when he sees me standing there.

"Hey."

"Hey," he says back.

The plane hits some turbulence, and I grip the doorframe to stop from being bounced around.

"You have a minute?" I ask.

I hate how things have been so tense between us the past few days. I know bickering and fighting are our things, but I miss him.

His eyes fuck me where I stand, so I know everything is going to be okay when he says, "You talking to me now?"

"You going to be a dick about everything?"

"Pretty much."

We both smile at one another.

"Come here, princess."

It takes four steps before I'm climbing on the bed and straddling his lap. His hands slide under the skirt of my dress, and he grabs hold of my ass, settling me down over his already hard length. I spear my fingers through his thick, dark brown hair and tilt his head, so our eyes are aligned as I look down at him. His fingers glide up and down my back, and my skin erupts in a shiver of gooseflesh.

"I'm sorry."

I bend over almost in half so I can snuggle his chest. I love the way he smells. "Me too."

"We good?"

I give him a chaste kiss, soft and sweet. "More than good," I assure him.

His hands pause their soothing motion, when I whisper into the cotton of his T-shirt, "It's finally over."

Keane's arms band around me, and he holds me close. So close.

It hasn't hit me until right now that it really is truly, finally over. No more Max, Alejandro, or Julio. No more secrets. No more revenge. The relief is almost painful.

Keane kisses the top of my head. "I'm so damn proud of you, Andie."

Confused, I use his chest for purchase and push myself up. "For what?"

He brushes my hair behind my shoulders, and his eyes flit over my face like he's seeing me for the first time. Maybe he is, in a way.

"For the woman you've become."

Something huge and elemental swells inside my chest. Keane's proud of me. It means more to me than any declaration of love he could have said. The worry that had been eating at me, fades away.

He strokes the rose tucked safely in my hair. "I remember seeing you a few times with a flower in your hair, but I never understood the significance of it. *Mi dulce rosa*. It's what Rafe calls you," he says in contemplation. "Jax calls you Angel, and Liam calls you *bella*. Guess I need to up my game and devise something better than princess."

"How about wife?"

His cock jerks and thickens beneath me, and my pussy clenches in response. He definitely liked hearing me say that.

"Is that what you still want?" he asks, playing with his mother's rings on my right hand.

I almost started crying when he slipped them on my finger

once he got out of the van. I was just so fucking happy that Alejandro hadn't destroyed them. Once the swelling goes down on my broken finger, I'll transfer them to where they belong.

I hover my lips directly over his. "I want it all."

I want everything these men can give me. Every-fucking-thing. Our relationships won't be easy, but damn, they will be so worth it. Now it's up to me to make the next move. To grab hold of that future I want with the man beneath me and the three men sitting outside this room.

Movement catches my attention. Rafe is standing in the entryway, watching, a look of contentment on his handsome face. He feels it too. Freedom. A future of open possibilities.

I'm so happy we found each other again. A second chance for first love, I guess you could say. But also, a first chance to build something spectacular with my savage kings.

I watch Rafe's lips move as he quietly says, "I love you."

"I love you, too."

Keane lifts his head to see who I'm talking to, just as Rafe sends me a wink and pulls the privacy curtain closed.

"He can join us if you want."

I kiss Keane's neck, his skin hot against my lips. "Right now, I just want you." I kiss up his neck, then softly nibble on his earlobe. "Did you know the body has over thirty erogenous zones? Most people have heard of the G-spot, but there's also an A-spot."

His hands caress up my thighs, fingers digging into the flesh. "I didn't know that," he replies, his voice husky and thick.

"Want to try and find mine?" I whisper, blowing a teasing breath in his ear.

"Hell yes, I do." He sits up and rends my dress in two right down the middle, unzips his pants, pushes my panties to the side, and impales me on his cock faster than my mind can process what's happening.

"*Oh, God*," I moan as his thick girth stretches me. The man's dick is a monster that wants to rip me in half. So damn good. A full-body shudder overtakes me.

"Missed this pussy. Don't you ever shut me out of your bed again. We fight, we talk, we get the hell over it." He drives home every word with a sharp jerk of his hips, his cock slamming into me with punishing brutality. "Got it?"

"*Yes*," I hiss, the throbbing in my core building rapidly.

I'm flipped over onto my stomach, and Keane re-enters me from behind. My face is smashed into a pillow, and I use it to muffle my scream when he slams forward, going so deep, my vision tunnels. I'm wrenched up onto my spread knees. Keane's arm holds me to his chest as his thrusts become wilder.

I turn my head and our mouths meet, tongues wild and tangling, our kiss carnal and full of sin. He pushes me forward again, and I reach out to catch myself on the wall at the head of the bed.

"*Keane.*"

His hand shoves my bra aside, so he can palm a breast. "Yeah, baby."

"My birth control shot expired a few days ago."

Suddenly, I'm tossed on my back, and Keane is hovering over me, a huge, Cheshire smile blinding me.

"Oh yeah?" He thrusts into me once again, then kisses the ever-living hell out of me before saying, "Baby, I'm going to fill you with so much cum, you'll be pregnant by the time this plane lands."

I wait in breathless expectation for him to fuck me into oblivion and fulfill that promise, so I'm not prepared for him to loudly shout, "Hey, fuckers! Andie wants us to knock her up!"

I hear a loud commotion outside the room and dissolve into a fit of giggles when Tessa wails, "Oh, hell no! I'm sitting up front with Lochlan with my noise-canceling headphones on."

Chapter 34

ANDIE

I bite my bottom lip at the sharp, incessant sting of the tattoo needle as it scores the sensitive skin of my lower back, my eyes glued to the colorful drawings and images hanging on the wall as I sweat through the pain. Bastard wipes the area he just did, then continues. Holy mother of hell. This hurts. And because the piece will cover most of my back, it has to be done in multiple sessions. I'm glad he did the guys' names on my fingers first.

"Going to finish the outline of the phoenix, then we'll call it a day," Bastard says.

I'd never met the man before today. He looks like a cross between an MMA fighter and a member of a motorcycle club. He wears silver skull rings on his fingers, is covered from neck to thigh in colorful ink, and has a long, black beard. He reminds me a little of Rafe's uncle Luis.

"Good. My butt's falling asleep."

I thought I'd be lying down on my stomach for this, but nope. I've been sitting backward in a special chair that stopped being comfortable an hour ago.

"Feel free to name drop any hot celebrity you've inked," I tell him.

I've been dropping those not-so-subtle hints the entire time I've been here. Bastard is the on-demand tattoo artist for a lot of high-profile musicians and movie stars. I'm surprised he had an opening to fit me into his schedule so quickly after I was a no-show the other day.

"Still not telling you, babe. I don't care if you're a big badass mafia queen. Celebrities can be much scarier, and they love to sic lawyers on you if you break NDAs."

"Looks good, *bella*," Liam says as he comes in, holding a to-go cup with the local coffee house on it, and sits down right in front of me.

I eye the cup in his hand with greed. "You going to share?"

He takes a sip and leans in to kiss me. I can taste the icy cinnamon on his lips.

"Did you get me a cinnamon roll iced coffee?"

My angel-turned-devil actually blushes. "I may have overheard Rafael mention it was one of your favorites, then bribed a certain barista to make my order first so I could bring it to you before he did."

Speak of the devil. Rafe saunters in, holding a matching to-go cup, and scowls at Liam. "You're an asshole, you know that?"

Liam shrugs. "Brownie points get me extra blowjobs," he quips.

"You know you can suck it."

"That's her job," Liam replies, and Rafe curses.

"Damn it! I always walk right into those."

Bastard quietly chuckles as he continues to work. Rafe shoves his cup into Liam's free hand and walks around to see the progress Bastard has made.

"That looks fucking phenomenal."

If Rafe says it looks good, then it must look fantastic. It's his design.

It's been three days since we came back from Mexico, and things have been so busy that, with the exception of Liam, I haven't seen much of the guys. Because Liam isn't comfortable sleeping in the same bed at night with me and the other three, I've been doing a little bed hopping, switching off between the two. One night with Liam. The next with Rafe, Jax, and Keane. Thank God for California king beds. We'll need to get a custom one made soon. I love the guys but being smooshed between three very large men who are all bed hogs is a little much. I woke up this morning on top of Jax because Keane encroached on my sliver of sleep space. Rafe was sleeping soundly on his other side.

Bastard finishes up, puts the tattoo gun away, and rips off his nitrile gloves. I'm able to take my first true breath that's not sucked in between gritted teeth. He puts on a fresh pair of gloves and applies ointment and protective tattoo film over the area he worked on.

"Sit tight, sweetheart. I'll be right back, and then we'll go over your aftercare instructions and set up your next appointment."

"Thanks, Bastard."

He winks at me. "Anytime, sweetheart." He bumps fists with Rafe as he steps out.

Stretching my arms up high, I roll my head from side to side while ignoring the stinging burn on my back. Taking a shower and cleaning the tattoo every day are going to be major pains in the butt, but at least I have four men who will be more than happy to help.

"Jax is going to lose his mind when he sees it." Rafe's finger trails down my neck, then back up again.

"Are Jax and Keane on their way?" I ask.

"Um, no. We're meeting them." Rafe gets distracted when an incoming text message chimes on his phone.

Liam nudges Rafe out of the way and slips the sleeves of a loose men's long-sleeved shirt over my arms, then spins me around and does up each small button, one at a time.

"You know, I've been able to fasten my own buttons since I was three."

"I know."

I pop up on tiptoe to kiss him.

Bastard returns to go over my aftercare instructions, and we schedule my next appointment.

"What's that look for?" Bastard asks me, when he notices me staring at him and not the sheet of paper he handed me.

"You have a woman?"

"For fuck's sake." Rafe's hand flies over my mouth.

I bite his palm, and he removes it. "But Tessa would love him."

"Baby, you gotta stop pimping out your best friend."

"But—"

"Ignore her."

Not giving up, I tick off on my fingers Tessa's amazing qualities like a used car salesman. "She's gorgeous. Blonde. Genius-level smart. Can do anything with a computer, and I mean anything. Got accepted to MIT. Has a sexy British accent..."

"She does not," Rafe interjects.

"Yes, she does. She's from England."

His head cocks slightly, brow pinched. "She says, *y'all*."

"Doesn't negate the fact that she was born and bred in the UK, babe. And her accent is most definitely as English as they come."

"Huh," he grunts.

Bastard throws his head back and laughs, then gives my shoulder a squeeze. "See ya soon, sweetheart. Call if you have any questions or concerns. The guys know what to do. I gotta set up for my next appointment."

"Thanks again, Bastard," I tell him.

"And give your friend my number," he says, walking away, still chuckling.

Feeling triumphant about that, I do a celebratory shimmy and smile up at my guys.

Liam taps the tip of my nose. "Woman, you are trouble with a capital T."

"Damn straight." I take the iced coffee he offers me.

As soon as we step out of Bastard Ink, we're greeted with the blacked-out SUV that's waiting for us alongside the curb, engine idling. Even though there's no longer a threat from Alejandro or Julio, we're still cognizant of our surroundings. If the past month has taught me anything, it's that we can't afford to *ever* let our guard down.

Mickey opens the back passenger door for us when we approach. Rafe climbs in first.

"Miss Levine," Mickey says as he takes my elbow and helps me in.

"You're so full of shit," I tell my cousin. He likes to call me that to get a rise out of me.

As I get situated in the middle seat, Liam settles in on my other side.

"Why are you fidgeting?" he asks when I can't get comfortable.

I huff in annoyance. Sitting with my back touching the seat is making my tattoo burn like crazy.

"My back," I reply, then give up and unclip my seat belt. I crawl into his lap. "Much better."

Liam is careful to only put his hands where it doesn't cause me discomfort. They settle on the curves of my ass. My forearms bend around his neck, so my fingers can play with the ends of his hair.

"Where are we meeting Keane and Jax?" I ask Rafe.

He reaches over to rest his open palm on my thigh. I love the easy intimacy I have with the guys. Spontaneous touches or kisses. Little things that come naturally, but mean so much to me.

"It's a surprise," Rafe replies, tipping his head back against the headrest and closing his eyes.

The past few days have been rough for him. A couple of issues had to be dealt with in Mexico, but they weren't anything his uncle couldn't eventually handle. Pearson is working the contract negotiations with the Sinner's Fury MC, while Keane and I are negotiating a contract of our own: how to combine the Rossi and New York families together under the house of Levine. It was an easy decision to make. One that will expand our territory and reach, while also allowing us to work together, not separately.

"I hope this surprise includes food, because I'm hungry."

"It does now," Rafe says, rousing to take out his phone.

I yawn and settle into Liam, the back-and-forth strokes of his hand through my hair making me sleepy.

"If you're doing a DoorDash, order from that place that sells burgers with sweet potato fries."

I must have passed right the fuck out after I said that because the next thing I know, the car door is opened wide, and Jax is helping Liam lift my dead weight.

"Her back is still tender," Liam tells him.

"I got her. Wrap your legs around me, Angel."

"What's going on?" I slur, still half asleep, but doing what he said.

"Welcome home, princess," Keane says behind me.

I hate those two words as much as I hate it when they call me by my full first name.

I force my eyes to open when I hear the calls of nature, not the hollow echoes of an underground parking garage.

What the hell?

We're standing in the middle of an open, grassy field surrounded by thick forest. And I swear I hear running water, like the burbling of a nearby creek. Several swallowtail and sulfur butterflies flit around the scattering of red and white wildflowers that are in bloom.

"Where are we?" I ask, absentmindedly kissing Jax and dropping my feet to the soft grass.

The men gather around me as I take everything in. Or lack thereof, because we're in the middle of nowhere with nothing but summer foliage and pristine natural beauty as far as the eye can see.

"Home. Or what it will be once we build it," Keane says, threading our fingers together as he takes my hand.

Home.

"You're building me a house?" A lump forms in my throat and emotion swells my chest.

Jax hooks his arm around me. "*We're* building a house. Your dream house."

I look down at the wavy green grass and weeds, picturing us standing in our future kitchen as I make homemade biscuits, our kids sitting and laughing at the counter island. I can see the enormous Christmas tree we'll put up every year, decorated with silly ornaments crafted by our children's hands. The large, expansive backyard our kids will chase the dogs in. The garden I'll plant to grow vegetables. The rocking chairs on the wraparound porch I'll spend countless mornings in, sipping coffee and watching the sun rise. And in every one of those wonderful images, I see a lifetime of happiness with these four men.

Chapter 35

ANDIE

"The poor delivery guy thought he was being punked."

Rafe snickers.

The guy who brought our food thought he was lost when he drove up to a field and not a house. If I knew that was where Rafe and Liam were taking me, I would've made Mickey find a fast-food joint to stop at.

"The yam fries were good," Keane says.

"Sweet potato," Liam corrects.

"That's what I said."

"Yams and sweet potatoes are not the same."

"Yes, they are."

"Seriously?" I ask, needing the elevator ride to be over with before I pull my hair out.

Jax flips his phone around, showing an infographic from online. "Liam is right."

Keane grabs the phone. "Then why the hell does the grocery store say they're yams?"

"Why does America still use feet instead of meters, or Fahrenheit instead of Celsius?" Liam quips.

Rafe looks at Keane quizzically. "When in the hell have you ever bought a yam, let alone stepped foot in a grocery store?"

Oh, my God. I mash the button for my floor in rapid succession, willing the elevator doors to open.

Jax pushes me back against the wall.

"What are you doing?" I ask, even though I'm already

climbing him.

"Distracting you." He states the obvious, right before his lips meet mine just as the elevator dings and the doors whoosh open.

I cling to him, not breaking our kiss, as he hefts me up and carries me out of the lift.

I briefly register that no one is standing guard, but I'll deal with that later.

"Bedroom," I whisper against his mouth, just as a small, familiar voice asks, "Why is Auntie Andie kissing Unkie Jax?"

Jax freezes in place. I go rigid. Keane and Liam looked stunned.

"*Mariposita!*"

Sarah squeals and runs over to jump into Rafe's outstretched arms.

And then my eyes slide past Pearson and land on the man sitting on the couch ten feet away from me.

"Dad?"

"Shoot! I'm so sorry," I yelp, when I walk in on Pearson and Declan in a lip lock. "Your door was open, and I wanted to check on you before I turned in, and... shit." I quickly turn on my heel to leave.

"Get back here," Declan says with a chuckle. When I come back into the room, he pats the bedcovers. "Come. Sit with me."

I glance at Pearson. "I didn't mean to interrupt. I can come back."

Declan pats the bed again. "Stay, sweetheart."

Pearson nudges me forward when he passes by to leave. "Mike just left. I'll be back with his pain meds," he says, and it only serves to remind me that Declan was shot. Four times.

I nod and look over at my father. The stubborn man. He looks frailer. Thinner. But he's alive. And he's here. Back home. I've missed him.

The flight from Boston took a toll on him. He had Cillian bring Sarah from Ireland once Pearson informed him Julio and

Alejandro were dead.

I still can't believe he and Sarah are *here*.

Padding barefoot over to the bed, I carefully slide in next to him. He opens an arm for me, and I snuggle in, resting my head on his good shoulder.

"We're quite the pair," he says.

Declan was livid when he saw the new bruises I'd acquired. He wasn't pleased about the back tattoo either.

"Do you need anything?"

"Just some alone time with my daughter," he replies.

My daughter.

"Thank you for bringing Sarah."

He kisses the top of my head. "My pleasure. I'm proud of you, Andie."

I'm not a crier, but tears gather as his words slam right into my heart. My whole life, I never received praise from Cecelia or Max. Hearing it from my real father is overwhelming, in the best way.

He lifts my right hand, inspecting the names inked on my fingers. "I think it's time we had that talk now."

I feel like a teenager who just got caught sneaking back into the house after midnight on a school night.

"I love them," I blurt. *Fuck me. Shut up, Andie.*

"I know."

What?

"You do?"

He kisses the tips of my fingers and places my hand in my lap. "A father knows these things."

"You don't hate me or think it's wrong?" Or think I'm a slut? But I don't voice that out loud.

He tips my chin up. "Loving someone is never wrong, Andie."

He taps Keane's mother's rings. I had to transfer them over to the middle finger of my left hand. It's a tight fit, but nothing I can do about it. My ring finger on my left hand is broken, and four of my fingers on my right are freshly inked.

"Which one is the lucky man?"

Oh, dear lord. "All of them."

His sharp bark of laughter echoes in the room. "That's going to be an interesting wedding ceremony."

"Uhh…"

Taking pity on me, he says, "I think we'll postpone the rest of this conversation for the morning, after I have a talk with my future sons-in-law."

I'm going to make sure to wake up nice and early and take Sarah out to the park.

Sliding his family crest off my thumb, I hold it out to him. With him back, it's time for me to step down.

"Thank you for trusting me with this."

He covers my hand and gently pushes it back. "Keep it. It belongs to the head of the family."

Brows furrowed, not understanding, I reply, "Exactly. That's you."

With a small shake of his head and a soft smile, he looks me dead in the eyes and says, "No, Andie. You're the future of this family. If you want it," he quietly adds.

Do I want it?

"Can I think about it?"

He kisses me on the forehead. "Take as long as you need. I love you, my sweet, precious girl. No matter your choice, I'll always love you. Your happiness is my first priority. Not this job, or the money, or the power. *You* are what matters most."

He couldn't have said anything more perfect.

"I love you, too, Dad."

He breathes in deeply and smiles broadly, as I slide the ring back onto my thumb.

"That means everything to me, Andie."

We lie in silence for a minute and enjoy the peace of being reunited. I try to memorize this moment and how it feels. It feels pretty fucking good. I came home with a singular goal in mind: avenge Kellan's death. I never expected to find love and family along the way.

Stirring slightly, I sit up and face Declan. "I'd like to talk to you about something."

"Is it about Mexico and how you slit that bastard's throat open? Now that's a story I'd love to hear over and over."

His smile drops when I don't return it.

"I found out something about Kellan."

Declan's blond brow hikes in interest, then dips when he sees the intensity on my face. "You know about the deal he made with me?"

I nod slowly. "I do."

He rubs his thumb across his mouth in contemplation. Declan could lie or try to evade, but instead says, "Do you have any questions about it?"

I nod again. "Not about that, but about something else."

My father joins our hands together between us, his warmth seeping into me and giving me strength.

"Kellan kept a journal. A coded journal that Keane and I found. There was a lot of... stuff in it. Bad stuff."

Declan's grip tightens but his expression remains impassive. "Anything you'd like to talk about?"

"No... yes. It's going to be difficult to say. It was difficult to hear when Rafe read it to me." I don't go into detail about how the guys knew Kellan's code or that Keane and Jax tried to keep it from me.

"Whenever you're ready. If that time is never, that's alright too."

I don't think I'll ever get used to his unconditional support. His trust. Two things I wanted so badly my entire life that Declan now gives to me so easily.

Just to confirm what Kellan wrote, I ask, "He never told you that I was your daughter, did he?"

Declan's entire demeanor transforms before my eyes. He is the ruthless king of an empire and wears it well.

"No. Fecking hell, Andie, I wish he did tell me. I would have come for you sooner and taken immense pleasure in gutting that lowlife son of a bitch," he vehemently states about Max.

"Kellan knew."

Declan's heated violet gaze snaps to mine. "What do you mean, he knew?"

"He knew I was yours. That's why he never told you. He didn't want you to take me away from him."

"Tell me everything," Declan declares.

He's not going to like hearing it. Hell, I don't even want to repeat a lot of it. But I do because both Declan and I need closure. To acknowledge it, then lock it away where it belongs, never to see the light of day again. I'm not going to live in the past any longer. For the first time, I'm looking forward to the future.

Chapter 36

ANDIE

When I return to my floor, I'm greeted with the sight of my four men in various positions of manspreading on the leather sectional. The television is playing some random football game.

Keane holds up seven fingers. "That's how many stories we had to read before Sarah fell asleep."

"She was excited to see her unkies," I say with a smile, walking over and kissing his welcoming lips.

Before I left to check on Declan, Sarah had already gotten me to read her three before the guys came in to kiss her good night and tuck her in. Even Liam, who Sarah immediately took a shine to. I think she has a crush on him. Can't blame her one damn bit.

I'm glad I had one of the guest rooms already prepared for her. I made sure there were unicorns everywhere. Bedspread. Pillows. Nightlight. Plushies. Lampshade. Shower curtain. Her room looks like a fairy threw up in it. She absolutely loved it.

Jax grabs me and pulls me into his lap. His hand immediately slips under my button-up and cups my breast. The tiredness I'd been feeling seconds ago, quickly dissipates as his lips find the area behind my ear that I fucking love having nibbled.

"Declan doing okay?" Liam asks, sliding his hand along my outer thigh to my hip.

"Better than I expected, actually," I say with a breathy hitch when I catch Rafe's topaz-blue gaze eye-fucking me. "Expect to get interrogated tomorrow."

Liam leans forward and rests his elbows on his knees.

"Interrogated? Why?"

Keane takes my hand and helps me to stand, kicking Jax in the shin when he tries to pull me back.

"Bedtime, princess."

Two words and I'm instantly wet.

Licking my lips, I drag my attention from Keane's heated smirk to Liam. "He knows about us."

"Good," Rafe says, taking my other hand and pulling me down the hall to my bedroom.

We stop briefly at Sarah's room. She's curled up on her side, clutching one of the unicorn stuffed toys I bought her, a smile on her face as she sleeps.

"It's good to have our girl back," Keane says in a whisper.

Yes, it is.

As soon as we enter my room, Jax is helping me out of my shirt, while Rafe and Keane remove their clothes.

Liam closes and locks the door, then turns around, his fingers unbuckling the belt around his waist.

It takes a minute for my brain to engage, but when it does, my heart throws itself against my chest, trying to burst free.

All four of them. In my bedroom. Clothes being shed. Is this really happening? Please, let this be happening.

"Liam?"

Without a word, he steps out of his trousers.

Jax walks around me, his hands touching the edges of the waterproof bandage on my back. "Are you sore?"

"No." Right now, all I can feel is my core pulsing like mad, desperate to be filled.

"Do you want this, Angel?"

Fuck, yes, I do.

"More than anything."

Everything has been leading up to this. The five of us. I was made to be theirs, and they were meant to be mine.

"Six," I say, hungrily taking in their naked chests, legs, arms, cocks. It's eye candy overload.

"Six what, baby?" Rafe asks, dragging his knuckle down the

column of my neck as he leads me backward toward the bed.

"Kids, I want six kids."

I gasp as I'm picked up and thrown onto the mattress. My gasp turns into a moan when Jax falls on top of me and immediately thrusts his tongue inside my mouth. I fucking love how the metal barbell of his piercing feels. On my skin, my nipples, and most definitely, my clit.

The kiss doesn't last long before he's rolling off me to make room for Liam.

"Hi."

Liam smiles down at me, his hands cupping either side of my face. "Love you, *bella*."

"Love you more."

Sappy as shit, I know, but I want him to understand how much it means to me that he's here. Liam doesn't like to share me with the other guys, but he's done it twice. Three times if you count now.

I've been with Jax, Keane, and Liam. Then Liam, Jax, and Rafe. But never the four of them together. Just the thought of it—touching, tasting, kissing, fucking all four men at once sends me into a spiral of intense euphoria, and I cry out when an orgasm flies out of me without warning.

The mattress dips when Keane crawls onto the bed. "Damn, man, how did you do that so fast? I didn't even see you touch her."

Liam's stunned face peers down at me, and I dissolve into a mess of breathless giggles.

"I didn't do anything. I hadn't even kissed her yet."

Sobering, I wrap my legs around his waist. "Then shut up and kiss me," I tell him, reaching down to mold my fingers around his thick erection.

Like with Jax's tongue stud, Liam's Jacob's ladder feels incredible. I run my thumb up each rung until I get to the tip of his cock. He inhales sharply, his pupils blown wide, then he's kissing me. Liam fucks my fist in the same way his tongue fucks my mouth.

A low rumble draws my attention when Liam carefully extracts himself off me. Jax is watching with heated eyes, his heavy cock in his hand.

"Come here, Reaper," I beckon him, catching Rafe's smirk when Jax stalks to the end of the bed and tugs me down by my ankles.

"Going to eat this pussy, while you suck Rafe off."

Scenes from the night I kneeled at Keane's feet, my lips around his cock, while Jax fingered me from behind, wash over me and blend in with every image I have of Jax's head buried between my thighs.

I'm suddenly spun around at the foot of the bed until I'm lying with my head hanging off the mattress. Jax comes around to the headboard and tosses the pillows to the side to make extra room for his long frame.

"Spread her wide," Jax instructs, throwing my right leg over his shoulder.

Keane grips the underside of my left knee and bends my leg up, opening me up more for Jax to settle in.

Lightning bolts rock through me when Jax's fingers open my folds, and he inhales deeply, then groans. "I can smell how much you want us. So fucking wet for us already."

I know I am because I can feel it dripping down my labia.

"Can you take me like this?"

I look up to see an upside-down Rafe, his erect cock bobbing right above my mouth. His tanned skin glistens in the moonlit room, and I can make out the thorned rose vine tattoo that snakes around his upper thigh.

"Yes," I reply, greedy to taste him.

I bend my arm and take him in my hand. His length is satiny smooth and hot to the touch.

Liam slides in next to me on my other side, cupping a breast and drawing a nipple into his mouth. Keane bends to my other breast and teases it with a scrape of teeth.

Each man's touch is different, but every bit as wonderful. Keane's mouth is firmer, Liam's softer. Jax's touch delivers a pinch of pain, whereas Rafe's is reverent. They all combine together to create an explosion of hedonistic desire; one so powerful, I'm coming again, back arched and muscles locked, their names exploding out of me in a guttural scream.

"Goddamn," Keane exclaims in wonder, pinching my nipple.

"Oh, God." I writhe on top of the silk sheets, which only adds to the multitude of sensations I'm experiencing.

"Fuck, baby. You're incredible," Rafe says, stepping closer, and I pull his dick to my lips, licking up the underside.

Rafe moans, his gaze boring into mine as I tease his slit, lapping up the precum beading out. He cradles the back of my head, easing the pressure on my neck, so I can take him deeper.

My cries are muffled around Rafe's cock when Jax's mouth devours me, pummeling my clit with hard swipes of his tongue. Keane and Liam kiss, suck, and caress my breasts, my stomach, my arms. Everything is too much, and not enough. Sex with each of them individually is incredible. But together, it's a whole other experience. Four mouths, eight hands. All combined to give me a pleasure like I've never experienced before. It's indescribable. And I want nothing more than to reciprocate. I want them to feel what I feel.

I reach around Rafe and score my nails into the meat of his ass, tugging him forward, so I can take him deeper until I'm gagging.

"Oh, fuck. Fuck, Andie. So good, *rosa*."

The hand supporting the back of my head fists my hair, creating tiny spikes of pain. He pumps wildly inside my mouth, the wet sounds being made turning me on even more. I hollow my cheeks and suck as hard as I can. I want him to come down my throat. Need to see him when he does.

I undulate my hips, letting Jax know how much I love what his mouth is doing. My fingers thread through the silky strands of Keane and Liam's hair on either side of me.

They work my body, gradually building me up for another climax, this one more powerful than the two I've already had.

Keane bends low to my ear, his filthy words making me moan. Spurring me on.

"Andie, baby, I'm going to come," is the only warning I get before Rafe erupts down my throat, shouting my name to the ceiling.

He drops to his knees when they give out and kisses me. "I love you. So much."

I want to tell him I love him, too, but I need to come. So. Fucking. Badly.

I break our kiss and beg, "Please, someone fuck me."

Jax growls and spears me with two fingers, crooking them to raze my inner walls, and I detonate.

Convulse.

Scream.

Maybe even black out.

Holy shit.

A goofy, sated smile spreads across my face. "Mmmm."

"I think we broke her. She sure as hell broke me," Rafe says, resting his head on the back of the bed where mine is hanging down.

I hear the sounds of the guys moving around as they shift positions.

"Ready to be ruined, Angel?"

Too late. They ruined me a long time ago.

Keane gently lifts my limp, sweat-soaked body, and my head lolls against his shoulder.

"You always smell so good," I sigh into his neck.

Carrying me around to the side of the bed, he kisses my forehead and hands me over to Liam, who cradles me in his thick, muscled arms like a coveted possession.

"I need you," I implore, cupping his face and melting into his soft, gray eyes.

Jax scoots over and makes room for Liam to lay me down. As soon as my back touches the mattress, my thighs part and I welcome my angel-turned-devil inside me.

I'm sensitive and swollen from the orgasms I've already had, but his cock feels wonderful when he slowly slides in, inch by excruciating inch.

"You feel amazing, *bella*."

I wrap my arms around him, holding on, as he grinds down against me with each slow thrust. Liam usually takes me hard and fast, so the soft, tender way he's making love to me is delicious. I feel airy and weightless, like I'm floating.

"So do you," I breathe, my hips meeting his in a sybaritic rhythm.

He steals my lips in a kiss as sensuous as the way he's fucking me. Several hands make contact and roam my body, leaving a trail of goose bumps in their wake. It takes longer for me to build up to another orgasm, and when Liam and I crest over the edge and come together, pleasure pulses through me like warm sunshine, leaving me punch-drunk with endorphins.

Something soft touches my forearm when my hands are lifted above my head. I don't have the strength at the moment to move a muscle. My bones are liquid.

Keane's dark head comes into focus. "Ready for more?"

"Yes, please."

He smiles into our kiss. "That's my girl."

Supple fabric brushes down my arm. Curious, I raise my head with effort to see what he's doing. Making direct eye contact, Keane shows me the silk binding held in his hand. I'm at a loss how he knew where to find it. Tessa gave it to me last week, laughing when I shoved it in the back of my underwear drawer. I nod to let him know I'm okay with it.

Taking his time, he secures the silk around one wrist, then loops it around my other wrist and pulls the material taut.

"Anytime you say stop, we will. You're safe with us."

I know I am. These men would die for me.

"Please don't stop," I reply with anticipation.

Liam moves off the bed, and Keane turns me over onto my stomach, then bands an arm around my waist and pulls my back flush with his chest. The light scattering of his chest hair tickles along my spine, his breath hot on my neck. I'm already panting, and he hasn't done anything yet but bind my hands.

"I'm going to fuck you so hard." He slaps my ass. "Your voice will be raw from screaming my name." Another slap.

God, yes.

I push my hips back, wanting more. His palm connects again, alternating between each cheek. Heat blooms higher with every slap, until I'm dripping with need.

Keane's hand soothes the abused skin as he croons words of love to me.

"More?" he asks.

"More," I answer.

Jax positions himself in front of me, a wicked gleam in his green eyes behind his black-rimmed glasses. The light catches on the red-handled knife, and I whimper. Not in fear, but in need.

"Make it hurt," I tell him.

"Pain is pleasure, Angel," he says and cuts a thin line across the skin above my heart.

I moan when he bends to lick the drop of blood that oozes out, then moan louder when he presses his lips to mine.

He rubs his thumb along the seam of my mouth. "Exquisite."

I want more. With my hands bound, I can't touch him.

"Jax, Keane, please." I pull on the restraint, and Keane's low chuckle fans across my ear.

"So impatient." He bites down hard on the dip of my neck where it meets the shoulder, and I throw my head back, seeking more.

Jax tosses his knife to the floor and cups my pussy. He scissors my clit, then dips a finger inside. "Think your sweet cunt can take both of us?" he asks, pumping a lazy finger in and out.

I writhe in Keane's arms, my core clenching at the thought of being stretched and filled by both of them.

Keane's hand circles my throat, his lips nipping the column of my neck to my ear. "We need your words, princess."

I can feel the pulse of Keane's cock where it's pressed against my buttocks. I can see Jax's chest rise and fall in rapid succession as he waits for my answer. I see Liam and Rafe standing at the side of the bed, stroking their cocks as they watch us. This is everything I've dreamed about. A culmination of the desire and love we share.

"*Yes.*"

Once I give my permission, Keane and Jax take me together. It's brutal and beautiful being fucked by two men at once. The sex is dirty and hard. Jax comes first, followed by Keane. Then I'm reaching for Rafe and Liam.

I don't know how much time passes as I take each of my men, over and over. The bed, the wall, the floor, the shower. Two at a time. Three. Four. My mouth, my pussy, my hand. My jaw muscles hurt, my clit is swollen and raw, and I'm covered in cum and bite marks from head to toe. I probably won't be able to walk for a week. And I fucking *love* it.

When I finally collapse from exhaustion with Jax, Rafe, Keane, and Liam wrapped around me on the bed, a feeling I've only experienced once in my life crashes through me and settles deep in my chest.

True happiness.

Epilogue

Six Years Later

My toes curl into the warm sand, the hot sun kissing my skin as it beats down from the midday sky. The aquamarine waters of the Caribbean Sea gracefully roll onto shore; small, frothy bubbles of sea foam pop as the gentle breakers wash over my feet.

Five years ago, Keane and I bought this tiny, private island paradise, and every June and July, we spend two months doing nothing but enjoying the long, lazy days of summer.

"Mama! Watch me!" Callum shouts to get my attention.

A very sexy, shirtless Jax tosses our four-year-old son into the air. It took all of one second after giving birth to Callum to know he was all Jaxson West. Callum is a miniature version of his father. Dark blond hair, moss-green eyes, and a fuck-you attitude only a boy his age could have. God help us when he hits his teenage years.

Callum squeals with joy as he flies in an arc and splashes down into the water where Liam is standing, Sarah sitting on his shoulders. Sarah throws back her head and laughs when Liam gets drenched by the splash. She's grown up so much and is blossoming into a beautiful pre-teen. Hopefully without all the teenage angst that hormones bring.

Callum pops out of the water and swims back over to Jax. "Mama, did you see?"

"That was brilliant, baby!"

Rafe wraps his arm around me, and I lean into his side, looking into the sea-blue eyes of the first man who stole my heart so long ago.

"He's growing up so fast."

He kisses the tip of my nose. "Feeling a little mushy today, *rosa*?"

"It's these damn hormones," I grumble, covering my swollen belly.

I can't wait to see who this little one looks like. Three more months to go before we greet our little girl.

Thick-fingered, masculine hands glide over mine, and lips press a kiss to my cheek.

Keane bends to my ear. "I like your baby hormones. They make you super horny."

I roll my eyes, but he's absolutely right.

The baby kicks, and I grab Rafe's hand to join ours, so he can feel it.

"That's our baby girl. Strong and fierce like her mama," Rafe says when she kicks again.

"I still think it looks like one of those creatures trying to burst out of my stomach like in the movie *Alien*, whenever she does that." It freaked me the fuck out when Callum did it the first time.

Keane laughs into my shoulder as he and Rafe rub my belly, their hands following our girl's movement. He does that a lot now. Laugh. All my guys do. Shielding my eyes, I look out into the water and watch Liam as he holds Sarah's hand and helps her jump the small breakers. He and Keane finally buried whatever discontent they had with one another and are actually friends now, if you can believe it.

I reach behind me and pull Keane's lips to mine, kissing him deeply. Then I grab Rafe and kiss him just as passionately. That's something that never lacks between us and only gets better with time. Passion. I'm so fucking in love with my four men, it's ridiculous. And they show me every damn day how much they love me, too.

Over the last six years, we've created a good life together, and we work hard at maintaining a balance. Family first. Always.

Everything else comes second. Declan taught me that.

Joining the houses together wasn't easy, but Keane and I make a great team. The Levine-Agosti family now controls most of the Central and East Coast territories. We have a good support network—Declan, Pearson, and the McCarthys—who can step in for us when we need downtime, like during the two months we spend here every summer.

Speaking of Dad—

"Dad called this morning. He, Pearson, and Cillian will be flying in later this afternoon."

"Good. They can babysit. We're taking our wife out. I'll let Lochlan know to get the boat ready."

He means luxury yacht, but whatever.

I lean into Rafe. "Bring your guitar, so you can serenade me under the stars."

"Already thought of that, *rosa*."

Each man takes a hand, and we begin slowly strolling back along the beach to where our cabana is set up on the sand.

"We head out on Monday, right?"

"Tuesday," I reply.

Tessa will be receiving her Master's degree in Computational Science and Engineering, and there is no way I'm missing it. The kids will stay here with their granddad since we'll only be gone for a couple of days.

A tiny blond blur comes flying out of the water, kicking sand up as he runs straight at my legs, wrapping around them like a koala.

Callum's cute face tips up at me. "Mama, I'm hungry."

Keane gives me a quick kiss on the lips. "Going to grab something from the cabana. Be right back."

Rafe plucks Callum up and tosses him high in the air, and Callum screams out a belly laugh. "You're always hungry, *Principito*." Little prince.

"I'm not little." Callum sticks his bottom lip out in the cutest pout. "And I'm a king, *un rey*, just like my daddies."

I take him in my arms, kissing his face all over until he's

giggling for me to stop. "Yes, you are. A Savage King."

Callum smacks a wet kiss to my cheek. "And you're our Savage Queen."

Sarah skips over, Liam following closely behind, scrubbing his hair dry with a towel.

"Mom, I'm hungry."

"Me, too!" Callum wiggles in my arms to be let down and immediately hops on Sarah's back.

Sarah started calling me Mom five and a half years ago. I cried my fucking eyes out when she first said it.

"We're heading in right now. Maria should already have lunch waiting for us," I tell them.

"Alright, family, gather in," Keane says, setting his tripod in the sand so his camera is facing out at the cerulean waters.

We all smoosh together for a family photo, one of many that Keane has taken over the years. Each one special. Our walls back home are covered in framed photographs.

Keane sets the timer, waits a beat, then rushes over to join our huddle.

"Okay, on the count of three. One. Two..."

Keane, Jax, Rafe, and Liam lean in at the same time and kiss me.

Click.

Keep reading to check out the first two chapters for my next dark reverse harem/why choose romance, **Beautiful Sin (Beautiful Sin Series Book 1)**. Are you ready for Syn (pronounced 'sin'), Tristan, Hendrix, and Constantine?

One more special bonus! I've included the Prologue to **Forever His (Forever M/M Romance Series Book 1)** and a link in the back matter where you can read an exclusive excerpt from the book. The Forever M/M Series is Julien and Elijah's story, two of my fan favs from my Fallen Brook Series. Steamy, angsty, and oh, so good.

Sneak Peek at Beautiful Sin

Prologue

Ten Years Ago

I'm not here.

I'm not here.

I'm not here.

The scream that fills my ears is unworldly, like the gates of hell have opened up, letting loose the demons to rip flesh from human bone. My hands grip the sides of my head until it feels like I'm trying to crush in my own skull.

Block out the sounds.

Block out the screams.

But the screams are coming from me. And they won't stop.

"Shut the fuck up!" the man snarls in my face, his spit splashing across my nose and mouth.

A harsh hand grips my long hair and wrenches my head back. I couldn't look anymore as the man, the other one with a scar down the left side of his face, defiled my mother in the cruelest of ways.

When my eyes find her again, her body is unnaturally contorted, bent at an odd angle on the living room's red floral Chateau rug. Her head is turned in my direction, her once beautiful, clover-green eyes are black, like a doll's soulless eyes. I think she's dead.

They already killed Papa. They killed him first. And I'm next.

Because the Society demands it for my father's betrayal. That's what the guy with the constellations drawn on his neck said right before he shot my father in the head.

A strange odor, both acrid and sweet, assaults my nose, but I'm not able to process it over the searing pain of the knife being shoved in my side. The pain comes again and again, each time hurting a little less until there's no pain at all.

A whoosh whispers in my ear as a bright light erupts behind my closed eyelids. Heat scorches all around me, tiny licks of fire dancing across my body like magical forest sprites.

I wonder if I'll become a phoenix once the fire burns me to ash, like the one in the story Papa reads to me at bedtime. I'd like that. I'd like to be able to spread my wings and fly.

I feel like I'm flying now. Higher and higher toward a bright light. It's beautiful. Peaceful. I am the phoenix.

Right before the light surrounds me, I'm pulled back down to earth, my wings clipped and useless. As life courses through my body once again, the pain comes. My torn, damaged vocal cords cry out a sound much like that of a kitten's strangled mewl.

I don't want to come back. I want to be the phoenix and fly into the bright light like Icarus did the sun.

But I can't because the person who saved me won't let me go.

"You're safe now. You're safe. I've got you."

Chapter 1

Slamming the employee locker room door open, I yank the shirt and jeans from the hook in my small cubicle and head to the one-stall bathroom in the back. I've only worked at the Bierkeller for three weeks, but I'm quickly coming to hate my Saturday night shifts at the bar. It's the third Saturday in a row where some drunk asshole who can't hold his liquor—literally—has spilled his beer all over me. Hence why, after the second time it happened in as many weeks, I started bringing an extra set of clothes with me to work. The stupid dumbass even managed to get it in my hair. So even with a change of clothes, I'm going to smell like a distillery for the rest of my shift until I can get home to shower.

As soon as I enter the bathroom, I shut and lock the door and quickly strip out of the sodden cotton tee before the motion sensor triggers the overhead strip lights to flicker on. I wince as the harsh fluorescent light punches a fist through the once inky darkness of the small room and slices across my scarred, bra-covered torso.

My reflection mocks me as I stare into the rectangular mirror secured to the wall above the sink. Every imperfection, every burn and red, raised ridge that mars my pale skin are exposed and illuminated in all their ugly, horrifying glory. Not able to stop myself, I touch the razor-thin lines left by the knife the man used on me. Those ugly reminders are inconsequential when compared to the burned, melted skin that scores down my left arm and side, the end of the gory patchwork stopping on my upper thigh.

And like with every other time I'm greeted with my mirror image, I ignore the gruesome reminders of the night ten years ago when I lost everything.

Don't look. Don't remember.

Mumbling under my breath, I drape the clean clothes over the closed toilet seat and wrench the faucet knob at the sink to turn on the water. The guy who spilled his beer on me was also the same guy who palmed my ass when I walked by his table.

Taking my anger out on the paper towel dispenser, I rip out several sheets and wet them, then do a quick wipe down over my arms, neck, face, and chest. My cornflower blue eyes take stock of the state of my hair.

Fantastic.

I look like a sad, drowned rat. Finger combing through the damp tresses, I remove the elastic band I always wear around my wrist and pile the mass of red, wavy hair into a top bun, not bothering to tame the loose wisps that escape.

It's not like I'm trying to impress anyone. My job is to deliver food to the tables, not look pretty. There's nothing pretty about my appearance. One peek at my scars is enough to send guys running the other way. Or stare with morbid curiosity. I get that a lot from both men and women. I used to wear long-sleeved shirts, even in the summer, to hide my burns. Not anymore. If people can't handle how I look, then don't fucking look at me.

"Yeah?" I call out when there's a knock at the bathroom door.

"Hey, country girl. Keith said to go ahead and clock out," Shelby says through the pressed wood.

Country girl is the nickname she started calling me when she found out I grew up on a farm in the Shenandoah Valley of Virginia. She's a few years older than I am and a city girl through-and-through. Tall and gorgeous, with the clearest blue eyes. Paired with her jet-black hair, it creates a stunning contrast that has every man who comes in to the Bierkeller turning his head in interest. Unfortunately for them, Shelby only has eyes for one man in her life: her three-year old son, Christian.

I look down at the pink plastic watch on my wrist. "I don't get off for another thirty minutes."

Clocking out now computes to thirty minutes of missed tips and wages. Money I need because my scholarship to the prestigious Darlington Founders College only covers the cost of tuition.

"I'm just the messenger, babe."

Sighing deeply, I hang my head. "Thanks for letting me know. Let me get dressed. Tell Keith I'll be right out to cash in my tips."

There's a repetition of three taps on the door. "You got it."

Toeing off my black Sketchers that somehow missed the beer dousing my clothes got, I quickly slip into the dry, black Randy's Custom Auto tee emblazoned with the name of my favorite Motocross racer, Seamus Knox, before taking off my trousers. I bundle the wet clothes together into a ball and place them in the sink. Reaching for the clean pair of jeans, the soft, worn denim slides easily up my legs. Once I put my sneakers back on, I gather my clothes and hurry out of the bathroom to collect my bag and head out to the main area.

The Bierkeller is actually a very cool place. It was built in 1875 around the same time as the college. The walls are the original red brick, but the bar is the best feature by far. It's handcrafted mahogany with 'flame' panels stained a deep, dark brown. During Prohibition, the underground cellars were converted into a speakeasy. Keith gave me the mini history lesson on my first day.

The cacophonic racket of people talking over one another and the pervasive aroma of burgers sizzling on the kitchen's large griddle hit me as soon as I step out into the hallway—and careen directly into a wall of tall, muscled man coming out of the men's restroom.

Well, shit. Is anything going to go right tonight?

"I am so sorry!" I apologize to the guy's dark blue dress shirt.

I'm tall at five-foot-nine, so for me to be eye level with his chest puts him a couple of inches over six feet.

Firm hands steady my shoulders when I teeter backward.

"No apologies needed."

His voice is as smooth and sophisticated as a whiskey neat. Cultured, with a slight accent. Bostonian, maybe? My gaze trails up the broad chest of a swimmer's body to meet eyes the same color as the simile I used for his voice: a light, golden brown.

I've never been struck stupid by a guy before, but *this guy* is hands down the most gorgeous man I've ever seen. Even his imperfections—a slight bend in his nose where it looks like it was broken not once, but twice, and the faint line of an old scar that runs through one dark brown eyebrow, slicing it in half—are intriguingly gorgeous.

He must have just arrived or was sitting in the section at the other end of the bar because I definitely would have noticed him.

When I continue to stare, his mouth spreads slowly in a lopsided, dimpled smile.

"I could say something inappropriate, like the only time I render a woman speechless is when she's choking on my massive co—"

And he just ruined the moment.

I cut him off by abruptly walking away. "You can keep the rest of that to yourself," I throw over my shoulder.

"Not what they usually say," he replies, his amused chuckle following behind me.

It takes me a second to get the double entendre. Why are cute guys such assholes?

From the tailored, expensive look of his clothes to his albeit gorgeous, Gen-Z, manscaped appearance, he must be one of the trust-fund frat babies that goes to Darlington Founders. Which means I'll probably run into him again at some point on campus, or here at work.

Determined to forget the stunning jerk and go home, I scan the main floor for Keith until I spot him behind the bar, pouring a draft. When I approach, he glances up at me, giving my new attire a once-over before he slides the full pint glass of beer down the bar to the customer who ordered it. Without missing a beat, he starts mixing the ingredients for some fruity-looking cocktail.

"Shelby said you wanted me to clock out early?"

He stops for a second in his movements and jerks his chin at a plain white envelope sitting to the side of the register.

"Tips for the night are in there. I'll add a little extra to your next paycheck to help cover the cost of some new clothes."

Wow. That's really... nice of him.

Keith hired me on a part-time basis since, starting Monday, I'll have a full course load during the week. I'm scheduled to work every Wednesday night, as well as the six-to-eleven evening shifts on Fridays and Saturdays. Tomorrow is Sunday, which means I get to do nothing but sleep in and be lazy.

I'd moved to Darlington at the beginning of the month, wanting time to acclimate to my new surroundings and look for a job before the fall semester began. Because of my severe aversion to having people in my personal space, I chose not to live in the dorms with the rest of the freshman. It took a couple of weeks of scouring online listings for places to rent or lease before I found a cute, little, one-bedroom studio apartment located within walking distance of campus. My adoptive mom insisted on paying the monthly rent; hence, the second reason for needing gainful employment, even if it is only part-time. I'm determined to pay her back every penny. It's difficult for me when she gives me money or buys me things. It always has been, even when I was younger. She's done so much for me already. Alana took me in and gave me a home. Paid for my surgeries and skin grafts. She loved me like I was her flesh and blood. I owe her.

"Thanks, but you don't have to do that," I tell Keith.

His bald head gleams and his gray eyes twinkle under the bar lights. "Already done, sweetheart. You walking home tonight?"

"That's the plan."

"Got your mace handy?"

Keith has two teenage daughters, which makes sense why he's so overprotective of his female employees.

I pat my bag. "Yep."

I also carry a switchblade. It's similar to the one the man used on me. I keep it as a morbid reminder of the night that changed my life forever. But I'm not going to tell him that.

"Always be—"

"—situationally aware. I know. I don't have to walk far. I'll be fine," I assure him.

Stuffing the envelope in my carry bag, I give Keith a wave good night and head out the back, deciding to cut through the alleyway over to Chesterton Street. Once on Chesterton, it's only a short two-block walk to my apartment.

When I push the door open and step out into the night, a cool breeze caresses my face, rejuvenating me after a long five-hour shift. I inhale deeply, needing to breathe air that isn't infused with cloying perfume, body odor, and beer. Unfortunately, I can still smell it in my hair.

The service door closes with a resounding click when the inside locking mechanism automatically engages. But I don't notice because I can't stop staring at the bloodied body crumpled on the ground in front of me, his face bruised and stained crimson.

I jolt when a muffled pop sounds next to my ear. Tiny shards of brick strike my face, leaving stings of pain in their wake. I touch a tentative finger to my cheek and feel something wet and warm. I think I'm bleeding.

What the fuck? Was that a *bullet*? Shouldn't there have been a loud bang or something if a gun was fired?

"Get down!"

Wait. I recognize that voice with the Bostonian lilt. It's the gorgeous asshole from the bar.

Like being hit by a wrecking ball made from granite, his body crashes into my side, slamming me back against the wall of the Bierkeller. Pain explodes in my left shoulder which took the brunt of the impact.

Motherfucker!

But before my brain can even process what's going on, all hell breaks loose.

There's an old saying: Beware the devil that disguises itself as an angel of light. The problem with angels is that they can also fall.

Prepare to enter the dark world of Darlington Founders where nothing is as it seems. Are you ready for Synthia (aka Syn, pronounced 'sin'), Tristan, Hendrix, and Constantine? *(Did you like the reference to the phoenix and the knife? I enjoy throwing in little Easter eggs from past stories into all my books.)*

Beautiful Sin will release summer of 2023. Keep informed of release dates, pre-orders, and enjoy other awesome perks such as monthly giveaways, by joining my private Facebook group, the J-Crew at https://www.facebook.com/groups/190212596147435, or by signing up to my newsletter at https://forms.gle/BJLEKcDqU6wXigEi8.

Beautiful Sin Series

#1 Beautiful Sin
#2 Beautiful Sinners
#3 Beautiful Chaos

Sneak Peek at Forever His

PROLOGUE

My best friend, Liz, once said, "*It's funny how life plays out sometimes. I think the ancient Greeks had it right with their belief that the Fates controlled everyone's destinies. Those fickle Fate bitches. They've been pulling the strings of my life and tying them into twisted knots since the day I was born.*"

She was right.

I'd always categorized my life as a series of what I called "Life-Altering Moments."

Some moments were good. Some bad. All of them had guided me on my path to where I was today and had changed my life in unimaginable ways.

But to understand my story, I had to start from the beginning.

The day I met *him*.

You can read an extended excerpt from
the book on **Verve Romance**.

Forever His is a Contemporary Romance Writers Stiletto Finalist!

Love was hard. Loving him was easy.

Soccer center forward for Fallen Brook High. Best friends with Elizabeth Fairchild and Ryder Cutton. Twin brother of Jayson Jameson.

We all know the story. Boy meets girl. Boy falls in love with girl. It's a tale as old as time.

Well, it was until I met **him**. Elijah Barnes.

My name is Julien Jameson, and this is my love story.

Reader's Note: Intended for mature audiences due to sexual and mature content. All sexual intimacy is consensual.

Forever M/M Romance Series (A Fallen Brook Spin-off)

#1 Forever His (Julian's POV) Pre-order now. Releasing April 4, 2023.
* A Contemporary Romance Writers 2021 Stiletto Finalist
#2 Forever Yours (Elijah's POV)
#3 Forever Mine (Dual POV)

About That Night

One night she can't forget. One night he can't remember.

I can't believe I just slept with Jordan Hammond. My crush since junior high. The only man I have ever loved. The guy I compare every other guy to—who also happens to be my sister's ex-fiancé.

Funny story. Jordan doesn't remember that night we shared. But I do. Every last detail.

I used to be in love with Jordan Hammond. But not after that night.

About That Night is an enemies-to-lovers, small town, New Adult romance. **1-Click** your copy today. Releases January 17, 2023.

Want to read an excerpt from the book? You can on **Verve Romance**. It's free.

Wanderlost

Bennett was beautifully broken. But he was mine.
And I loved every jagged, damaged piece of him.

"If I could give this book 10 stars, I
absolutely would." – Carissa
"Absolutely beautifully written." - My Book Filled Life

Love wasn't worth the pain of disappointment and rejection that followed, so Harper Collingswood locked up her heart and swore she would never allow another man to break it. However, Harper couldn't have anticipated Bennett McIntyre crashing into her life. Literally. Some would call it fate. Some would claim serendipity. Others would say it was destiny. Whatever it was called, it was terrifying. Harper had barely survived one tragedy. Would she be able to survive Bennett as well?

"I rarely use this word, but this was
a beautiful book." – Saryas

Bennett McIntyre used to have dreams. He used to laugh and be the center of attention. Mr. Popular who had women clamoring to catch his eye and his attention. He was a rising star in baseball with a bright future ahead of him. But he wasn't that person anymore. Bennett also wasn't prepared to come face-to-face with the angel who had saved him on that horrific day six months ago. He wasn't at all prepared for Harper Collingswood.

One damaged woman who was afraid to love again.
One broken man who was lost to anger and darkness.
One perfect love.

"This book deserves the 5 stars times 100!" – Sara

Reader's Note: *Wanderlost* is a steamy, New Adult, friends to lovers, small town, sports romance, and the second book in The Montgomerys series of stand-alone novels. You do not have to read the other books in The Montgomerys or the Fallen Brook Series to read *Wanderlost*; however, *Wanderlost* is part of the Fallen Brook world of books, and characters from previous books will pop up in the story. Each stand-alone in The Montgomerys series focuses on one of Fallon Montgomery's half-siblings. *Wanderlost* is Harper's story and touches upon topics that may be triggering to some sensitive readers such as flashbacks to an active shooter situation in a school setting, depression, drinking, violence, and reference to drug use. The story also contains foul language. Any sexual intimacy between the characters is consensual. Recommended for mature readers.

Wanderlost is available now on Amazon or free with Kindle Unlimited.

That Girl

That Girl is the winner of the 2021 Chesapeake Romance Writers Rudy Award for Romantic Suspense and a Contemporary Romance Writers 2021 Stiletto Finalist!

I was that girl; the one from a broken home who lived on the poor side of town. He was that guy; NFL football quarterback and Mr. Popular. He told me he would never leave. He lied. Now he's back. But I'm not that girl anymore.

Aurora St. Claire is that girl. The one who excels at academics. The one from a broken home who lives on the bad side of town. The one with an alcoholic mother who couldn't care less if she existed. The one with an abusive older sister who would give her bruises instead of hugs. The one who keeps to the shadows, trying not to be seen. Sometimes the best families are the ones you create, not the ones you are born into. Aurora never knows what a true family is like until she has one suddenly thrust upon her at the age of eighteen. It takes a single revelation from a stranger to change her life forever. Then JD Hallstead comes barreling into her life. He is everything she never thought she wanted, but everything she craves. That is, until the day he destroys her and leaves her heart to burn to ashes in his wake. What is the adage? The flip side of love is hate. Well, her hate burns bright, and it has a name: Jackson Dillon Hallstead.

JD Hallstead is that guy. The one who is Mr. Popular and Quarterback King of Highland High. The one voted class president and most likely to succeed. The one who girls go crazy over and guys want to be. The one with a controlling, abusive father who will go to any lengths to keep his son in check. The one with the secrets. Aurora is the girl JD has secretly crushed on for years. It takes a friend's tragic death to bring Aurora and JD together. It takes JD's secrets to tear them apart. Aurora tells JD everybody leaves. He promises her he never will. He lied. Now, JD will do anything, fight anyone, give up everything, to get Aurora back. Aurora said JD broke her heart. Who better than him to put it back together?

But the thing about secrets is that they always come back to haunt you. The question is: How far will JD go to protect the woman he loves before those secrets destroy them all?

**That Girl is available now on Amazon
or free with Kindle Unlimited.**

The Fallen Brook Boxed Set

Want more Fallon, Trevor, Elizabeth, Ryder, and the rest of the Fallen Brook group? Find out how it all began.

Fall in love with Fallen Brook and find out why readers say:
"Everything about this series is addicting..."
"This series ripped my heart out. I don't think I've ever read one that affected me like this one did..."
"This is love like nothing that I have ever read. Original, complex, emotional and amazing...This story is a journey of the best kind."

The Fallen Brook Boxed Set is now available on Amazon and free with Kindle Unlimited. This 1200-page set includes All Our Next Times, Paper Stars Rewritten, Broken Butterfly, bonus chapters in Julien's POV, and a brand-new novella exclusive to the boxed set, *Fallen Brook Forever*. 1-Click to get it now on Amazon or read for free with Kindle Unlimited.

Also by the Author

Under Jennilynn Wyer (New Adult & College, Contemporary romance)

The Fallen Brook Series

#1 All Our Next Times

#2 Paper Stars Rewritten

#3 Broken Butterfly

The Fallen Brook Boxed Set with bonus novella, Fallen Brook Forever

The Montgomerys: Fallen Brook Stand-alone Novels

That Girl* [Aurora + JD]
Winner of the 2021 Chesapeake Romance Writers 2021 Rudy Award for Romantic Suspense
A Contemporary Romance Writers 2021 Stiletto Finalist

Wanderlost [Harper + Bennett]

About That Night [Jordan + Douglass]

Savage Kingdom Series: A dark, enemies to lovers, mafia RH romance

#1 Savage Princess
Audiobook now available at Amazon, Barnes and Noble, Chirp, Apple, Kobo, Google Play, Audible, Spotify, Overdrive, Audiobooks.com, and many other retailers

#2 Savage Kings

#3 Savage Kingdom

Forever M/M Romance Series (A Fallen Brook Spin-off)

#1 Forever His (Julian's POV) Pre-order now. Releasing April 4, 2023.
A Contemporary Romance Writers 2021 Stiletto Finalist

#2 Forever Yours (Elijah's POV)

#3 Forever Mine (Dual POV)

Beautiful Sin Series: A dark, enemies to lovers, reverse harem

#1 Beautiful Sin

#2 Beautiful Sinners

#3 Beautiful Chaos

Under J.L. Wyer (High School & Young Adult)

The Fallen Brook High School Young Adult Romance Series: a reimagining of the adult Fallen Brook Series for a YA audience

#1 Jayson

#2 Ryder

#3 Fallon

#4 Elizabeth

The Fallen Brook High School YA Romance Series Boxed Set (Books 1-4) with bonus alternate endings

YA Standalones

The Boyfriend List
A Contemporary Romance Writers 2022 Stiletto Finalist

Letter from the Author

(unedited)

Dear Reader,

Once again, thank you for coming on this crazy, wild journey with me. As a romantic fiction writer, we have to take some free rein with subject matters when crafting our stories. I had a lot of fun writing the Savage Kingdom Series and delving into my darker side. I've also enjoyed all the reader and blogger feedback. The love you have for Andie, our broken yet fiercely strong protagonist, and her men. I enjoyed reading all the social banter about Jax and Liam. Liam came in strong in book two and stole a few of Jax's ladies. And, like I had hoped, Rafe was able to redeem himself and win some of you over by the end. As one reader put it, "I didn't want him to choke on a cactus anymore."

If you haven't already heard, the Savage Kingdom Series is coming to audiobooks! The audiobook of Savage Princess is now live with Savage Kings and Savage Kingdom to follow. The books will be narrated by the very talented Keira Grace. The audiobooks will be wide and available in all markets including Amazon, Barnes and Noble, Chirp, Apple, Kobo, Google Play, Audible, Spotify, Overdrive, Audiobooks.com, and many other retailers.

My next RH series is Beautiful Sin. How did you like the sneak peek chapters? I'm looking forward to diving into a new world and exploring new characters. Of course, I have a few twists that I'll throw at you along the way.

If you haven't read my other books, check them out. I have a reputation for drinking the tears of my readers. My Fallen

Brook Series (All Our Next Times, Paper Stars Rewritten, and Broken Butterfly) is an angsty, twisty-turny, emotional roller coaster that involves a love quadrangle between childhood friends. You'll definitely want some tissues for Broken Butterfly. The Montgomerys Series of stand-alones takes place right after Broken Butterfly and each book focuses on one of the half-siblings of Fallon Montgomery. Fallon is the "Jax" of Fallen Brook and has been "licked" a lot. (You know who you are!) That Girl is Aurora + JD's story; Wanderlost is Harper + Bennett's; and About That Night is Jordan + Douglass's. Each story is packed with my signature WTF moments, strong women, and swoon-worthy book boyfriends.

Now for my thank yous. Thank you to my wonderful village of women who keep me laughing and listen to me rant when I need to. I love you all bunches.

Thank you to Ellie, my awesome copy editor at My Brother's Editor, for your support and love for my stories, and for the hard work you put in.

Thank you to my wonderful Beta Girls group: Rita, Jennifer, and Jillian.

Thank you to all the book bloggers who support me, and the supportive author community on Instagram. I couldn't do this crazy job as a romance author without your support!

Thank you, Nala, for our weekly author meetings where I can hash out ideas, get inspiration, and meet my goals. Your organizing skills are truly inspirational!

Thank you to my husband and family who support me one hundred percent every day. Love you so much!

And thank you, reader, for coming along this crazy journey with me and supporting independent authors like myself.

Jennilynn Wyer

About the Author

Jennilynn Wyer is a Rudy Award-winning author of Romantic Suspense and a three-time Contemporary Romance Writers Stiletto Finalist. She writes steamy, New Adult romances as well as dark reverse harem romances. She also pens YA romance under the pen name JL Wyer.

Jennilynn is a sassy Southern belle who lives a real-life friends-to-lovers trope with her blue-eyed British husband she met in college. When not writing, she's nestled in her favorite reading spot, e-reader in one hand and a cup of coffee in the other, enjoying the latest romance novel.

Connect with the Author

WEBSITE | EMAIL | FACEBOOK | INSTAGRAM | TIKTOK | TWITTER

GOODREADS | BOOKBUB | AMAZON | NEWSLETTER | VERVE ROMANCE

SUBSCRIBE TO MY NEWSLETTER
for news on upcoming releases, cover reveals, sneak peeks, author giveaways, and other fun stuff!

JOIN THE J-CREW: A JENNILYNN WYER ROMANCE READER GROUP
Join link https://www.facebook.com/groups/190212596147435

Printed in Great Britain
by Amazon

86688918R00156